Praise for the Knitting Mysteries

Dropped Dead Stitch

"Sefton skillfully handles a sensitive topic while weaving
in happier moments." —*Publishers Weekly*

"Sefton weaves yarn, fiber arts, and cooking into the mystery in ways that enhance it." —*Booklist*

"Heartwarming . . . Delightful characters."
—*Romantic Times* (4 stars)

"Very poignant and emotionally wringing."
—*Gumshoe Review*

Fleece Navidad

"Perfect for creating a warm, celebratory holiday atmosphere that readers will relish. [Do] drop in at the House of Lambspun and join its cozy knitting circle for excellent camaraderie and conversation." —*Mystery Scene*

"As feel-good a cozy as you can get . . . A perfect read either while waiting for Christmas to arrive or when snuggling down after the turkey dinner has been devoured."
—*Mystery Books News*

W9-CCM-190

"Visit Kelly Flynn and her friends for the holidays—it's never dull and will make you nostalgic for good friends and good times . . . You'll certainly enjoy these tasty recipes and the knitting projects." —*Gumshoe Review*

"A fun, quick read to curl up with when the stresses of the season get to be too much. Knitting and patterns and holiday recipes of the treats Kelly and her friends share complete the experience." —*The Mystery Reader*

"*Fleece Navidad* has it all: gift shopping, knitting Christmas gifts, baking—even a church pageant." —*Cozy Library*

"An enjoyable cozy mystery with a wonderful cast."
—MyShelf.com

"During the cold, dark winter months, this knitting mystery will provide a few hours of warmth." —*Romantic Times*

Dyer Consequences

"Make a glass of lemonade, find a porch swing and cozy up to this cozy." —*Colorado Springs Independent*

"They just keep getting better . . . Each visit with Kelly and her friends becomes more enjoyable than the one before."
—*Gumshoe Review*

"Sure to please series fans." —*Publishers Weekly*

A Killer Stitch

"Plenty to enjoy . . . Settle back in front of a cracking fire and enjoy the company of Kelly and co." —MyShelf.com

"Deft pacing and witty dialogue should have readers eager to spend more time with Kelly and her friends."
—*Romantic Times*

"As light and fluffy as one of Kelly's balls of yarn . . . Readers may enjoy reading this book almost as much as they'll delight in knitting the cable knit scarf." —*Library Journal*

A Deadly Yarn

"A terrific series with a heroine who grows more and more likable with each investigation." —*The Mystery Reader*

"The whodunit is well crafted . . . A delightful mystery."
—*The Best Reviews*

Needled to Death

"Nonknitters and fiber fanatics alike will enjoy the yarn shop setting." —*Romantic Times*

"Kelly is easy to like . . . A fun, quick read."
—*The Mystery Reader*

"[A] tightly stitched tale." —*The Best Reviews*

Knit One, Kill Two

"Cozy up with a great new author . . . Well-drawn characters and a wickedly clever plot—you'll love unraveling this mystery!" —Laura Childs, author of *The Teaberry Strangler*

"A clever, fast-paced plot, with a spunky sleuth and a cast of fun, engaging characters. *Knit One, Kill Two* delivers the goods." —Margaret Coel, author of *The Silent Spirit*

Dropped
Dead
Stitch

Maggie Sefton

BERKLEY PRIME CRIME, NEW YORK

THE BERKLEY PUBLISHING GROUP
Published by the Penguin Group
Penguin Group (USA) Inc.
375 Hudson Street, New York, New York 10014, USA
Penguin Group (Canada), 90 Eglinton Avenue East, Suite 700, Toronto, Ontario M4P 2Y3, Canada
(a division of Pearson Penguin Canada Inc.)
Penguin Books Ltd., 80 Strand, London WC2R 0RL, England
Penguin Group Ireland, 25 St. Stephen's Green, Dublin 2, Ireland (a division of Penguin Books Ltd.)
Penguin Group (Australia), 250 Camberwell Road, Camberwell, Victoria 3124, Australia
(a division of Pearson Australia Group Pty. Ltd.)
Penguin Books India Pvt. Ltd., 11 Community Centre, Panchsheel Park, New Delhi—110 017, India
Penguin Group (NZ), 67 Apollo Drive, Rosedale, North Shore 0632, New Zealand
(a division of Pearson New Zealand Ltd.)
Penguin Books (South Africa) (Pty.) Ltd., 24 Sturdee Avenue, Rosebank, Johannesburg 2196,
South Africa

Penguin Books Ltd., Registered Offices: 80 Strand, London WC2R 0RL, England

This is a work of fiction. Names, characters, places, and incidents either are the product of the author's imagination or are used fictitiously, and any resemblance to actual persons, living or dead, business establishments, events, or locales is entirely coincidental. The publisher does not have any control over and does not assume any responsibility for author or third-party websites or their content.

PUBLISHER'S NOTE: The recipes contained in this book are to be followed exactly as written. The publisher is not responsible for your specific health or allergy needs that may require medical supervision. The publisher is not responsible for any adverse reactions to the recipes contained in this book.

DROPPED DEAD STITCH

A Berkley Prime Crime Book / published by arrangement with the author

PRINTING HISTORY
Berkley Prime Crime hardcover edition / June 2009
Berkley Prime Crime mass-market edition / June 2010

Copyright © 2009 by Margaret Conlan Aunon.
Excerpt from *Skein of the Crime* by Maggie Sefton copyright © by Margaret Conlan Aunon.
Cover illustration by Chris O'Leary.
Cover logo by axb group.
Cover design by Rita Frangie.
Interior text design by Stacy Irwin.

ISBN: 978-0-425-23519-5

BERKLEY® PRIME CRIME
Berkley Prime Crime Books are published by The Berkley Publishing Group,
a division of Penguin Group (USA) Inc.,
375 Hudson Street, New York, New York 10014.
BERKLEY® PRIME CRIME and the PRIME CRIME logo are trademarks of Penguin Group (USA) Inc.

PRINTED IN THE UNITED STATES OF AMERICA

10 9 8 7 6 5 4 3 2 1

Acknowledgments

This was a special book to write in that it dealt with a very sensitive subject, and I wanted to make sure I handled it with sensitivity and respect.

Special thanks go to a dear friend of mine who is also a PhD psychologist, author, lecturer, and retired faculty member of Purdue University, Dr. Kathryn N. Black. Dr. Black is one of the most gifted teachers and counselors I've ever met. And that's saying a lot, since I've spent nearly thirty years living in academic communities. Dr. Black has counseled many patients over the years and was kind enough to share some of her insights with me.

I also want to thank Ginger Mohs, a former detective with the Fort Collins Police Department. Ginger provided quite an education into criminal behaviors, including crimes committed, patterns of behavior, police procedures, as well as charges and sentencing. Ginger's a great gal, and our "coffee consults" were as enjoyable as they were educational.

Cast of Characters

Kelly Flynn—financial accountant and part-time sleuth, refugee from East Coast corporate CPA firm

Steve Townsend—architect and builder in Fort Connor, Colorado, and Kelly's boyfriend

KELLY'S FRIENDS:
Jennifer Stroud—real estate agent, part-time waitress

Lisa Gerrard—physical therapist

Megan Smith—IT consultant, another corporate refugee

Marty Harrington—lawyer, Megan's boyfriend

Greg Carruthers—university instructor, Lisa's boyfriend

Pete Wainwright—owner of Pete's café in the back of Kelly's favorite knitting shop, House of Lambspun

LAMBSPUN FAMILY AND REGULARS:
Mimi Shafer—Lambspun shop owner and knitting expert, known to Kelly and her friends as "Mother Mimi"

Burt Parker—retired Fort Connor police detective, Lambspun spinner-in-residence

Hilda and Lizzie von Steuben—spinster sisters, retired school teachers, and exquisite knitters

CAST OF CHARACTERS

Curt Stackhouse—Colorado rancher, Kelly's mentor and advisor

Jayleen Swinson—Alpaca rancher and Colorado Cowgirl

Connie and Rosa—Lambspun shop personnel

Prologue

Early February

Kelly Flynn jerked awake. Was that her cell phone ringing? The jangling noise sounded through the darkened cottage bedroom again.

Who the heck would be calling in the middle of the night? Kelly fumbled beside the bed toward the nightstand, fingers searching for her phone.

"Wha . . . phone . . . ?" her boyfriend, Steve Townsend, mumbled beside her.

"Got it." Kelly flipped open the little phone as she turned on the lamp. Sleep still clouded her eyes, so she couldn't make out the name flashing on the phone's view screen.

"Kelly Flynn here. Who's calling?" she demanded. Glancing at the bedside clock she saw the time. Two twenty. Not hearing a response, Kelly barked into the phone again. "If this is a crank call, I'm hanging up right—"

A woman's voice came, breathy. "Kelly, don't hang up . . ."

Kelly strained to hear, not recognizing the small voice. "Who is this?"

"It's me . . . Jen."

"Probably just a crank call. Hang up on 'em," Steve said, propping himself on his elbow, squinting at the sudden light.

Kelly shook her head and waved him quiet as she strained to hear her friend's voice. "Jennifer, is that you? Are you all right?"

There was a pause, then Jennifer whispered, "Can you come over, Kelly? Please . . ."

Kelly sat up in bed and threw back the covers. "Sure I can. What's the matter? Are you sick? That flu is going around."

"No . . . I'm . . . I'm . . . hurt . . ."

"Jennifer needs to go to the doctor?" Steve said, sitting up now.

Crossing the floor quickly, Kelly grabbed her jeans from the closet and tried wiggling into them while she held the phone to her ear. "You hurt yourself? What happened?"

"Not me . . . he . . . he . . ." Tears flooded Jennifer's voice.

Kelly held absolutely still in the middle of the bedroom, jeans half zipped, sweatshirt halfway over her head. A shot of cold ran right up her spine. "Someone hurt you, Jen? Who was it?"

"*Son of a bitch*," Steve swore as he leaped out of bed.

Jennifer's wet voice came again. "A guy at the bar followed me home." An anguished choke. "Can you come over please?"

"I'll be right there," Kelly said, pushing her arm through the backwards sweatshirt. "Lock your door."

"We'll take my truck," Steve said as he strode nude across the small bedroom.

"Steve's coming, Jen—"

"*No!* I can't see anyone else . . . not yet. Just you. Please, Kelly . . . *please!*"

Kelly waved at Steve as he grabbed his discarded jeans from the chair. "Okay, Jen, whatever you say. I'll come alone."

"Call when you're at the door, so I'll know it's you."

"Don't worry. I will. I'm leaving now, okay? See you in a few minutes," she said as she flipped off her phone. "Jen says she can't see anyone else right now. Just me."

"No way! What if that guy is still around?" Steve protested.

"I'll park right in front of the condo building. It'll be okay," Kelly reassured him. "I'll call you as soon as I get there, I promise," Kelly said as she headed toward the front of the cottage, Steve right behind her.

3

"If I don't hear from you in twenty minutes, Kelly, I swear to God, I'm driving over there," Steve warned.

Kelly pulled on her ski jacket and grabbed her bag. "Twenty minutes. Promise."

Kelly's Rottweiler, Carl, raised his head from his doggie bed in the corner of the dining room and blinked at the conversation taking place in the middle of the night.

"And find out that bastard's name so I can beat him up."

"Go make some coffee and calm down." She waved at him as she headed out the front door.

"Yeah, right," Steve called as Kelly carefully made her way down the icy, snow-packed front walk. Normally, the thought of coffee would send the caffeine lobe of her brain into alert. But right now, Kelly couldn't feel anything except the cold inside her gut.

Kelly stared at her best friend's scratched, swollen face, the dark purplish bruises already forming on Jennifer's neck. Kelly's heart wrenched inside her. "Oh, Jen . . . I'm so sorry," she whispered.

Jennifer sat hunched on her living room sofa, wearing a dark sweat suit. She stared at her hands, clenched in her lap.

"You said he followed you home. Did he break in or something?"

Jennifer shook her head. "No . . . he knocked and said someone from the bar left something for me." She raised her head and closed her eyes. "I should never have believed him. When I opened the door, he pushed inside and grabbed me."

Kelly placed her hand on Jennifer's arm and squeezed. "Did you know him from the bar?"

"No, I hadn't seen him before tonight. I was there with friends, and when they left he came over and sat down beside me." A pained expression crossed her face. "He was one of those cowboy charmers . . . you know, full of sweet talk and lies. I started flirting with him for a while until I went home. I guess I didn't notice him following me."

Kelly noticed the bruising on Jennifer's wrists, and the anger that was simmering inside heated to a boil. She sprang from the sofa. "We've got to get you to the hospital right now, Jen. You need to be treated." She took out Jennifer's shamrock green winter coat from the closet. "Here, Jen," she said as she helped her friend from the sofa, then held the coat open.

Jennifer slipped into the coat and took the purse Kelly offered.

"I'd better give Steve another call on the way over so he'll know where we're going." Taking Jennifer's arm, she guided her toward the front door. "And when we're at the hospital, we're going to call the police. You're pressing charges against the bastard who assaulted you."

Jennifer drew back, pulling away from Kelly, her face pale white beneath the ugly red scratches. *"No! No!* I can't!" she cried.

"Yes, you can, Jennifer." Kelly reached for Jennifer's arm again. "I'll be right beside you the entire time."

Jennifer shook off Kelly's hand and backed up. "I can't press charges, Kelly. No one would believe me!"

Kelly shook her head, trying to dismiss her friend's fears. "Of course, they will, Jennifer—"

"Of course they *won't*!" Jennifer insisted. "I'm at the bar all the time, and I'm always leaving with guys. You know that. Face it, Kelly. Nobody would believe me if I said some guy raped me. They saw me drinking and joking around with him. They wouldn't believe me, Kelly!"

Kelly sought for an answer to Jennifer's claims, searched for a way to refute them. She believed Jen and so would all of Jennifer's closest friends. But those regular bar patrons, the "barflies" as Jen called them, they weren't real friends. And maybe they wouldn't believe her. Maybe Jennifer was right. "But, Jen . . ." she tried again.

Jennifer's face started to crumple, tears spilling out of her eyes and down her cheeks. "They wouldn't believe me, Kelly. They'd laugh . . . they'd laugh . . ." She choked back a sob.

Kelly felt her heart break, and she opened her arms to her wounded friend. Jennifer collapsed against Kelly's chest and wept, great wracking sobs shaking her body. Kelly held her friend as tears ran down her own face.

One

Early May, three months later

Kelly yanked open the door to House of Lambspun, the knitting shop directly across the driveway from her cottage. Both cottage and knitting shop were identical in design—beige stucco, red-tiled roof, Spanish colonial. But where the cottage was getting cramped with Steve and Kelly bumping into each other, the sprawling knitting shop was spacious and inviting. Rooms opened and flowed one into another, and all of them spilled over with yarns and fibers.

Springtime bright colors greeted Kelly as soon as she entered the foyer, beckoning her to touch. Fluffy balls of eyelash yarns—yellows, greens, reds—and glistening skeins of multihued ribbons, all waiting to be turned into scarves, warm weather tops, sleeveless vests, or whatever. Kelly fingered the soft fibers, stroking the ribbons as she passed by, getting her tactile "fix" for the day.

She spied her friend Megan in the adjoining room, seated at the long library table where knitters, spinners, and other fiber workers regularly gathered. A bright yellow, loose-knit sweater was forming on Megan's busy needles. "I'm glad to see someone else taking a break from the computer screen," Kelly said as she deposited her coffee mug and knitting bag on the table. "I swear, we're probably ruining our eyes staring at the computer all day."

Megan glanced up with a bright smile, fingers still working the yarn. Kelly couldn't understand how Megan and friends could knit without looking.

"Yeah, I know how you feel. I needed a break. My latest client insists that I join in his conference calls every week with his entire IT staff, and he had loads of charts filled with columns of numbers and figures." Megan brushed her jet-black hair away from her face. "Boy, I have to blow up those figures double-size to see them."

"Don't mention figures to an accountant. It makes us antsy," Kelly teased as she pulled out the summer vest she was knitting with varying shades of red yarn, crimson to deep rose. "I've already started those corporate accounts that Curt referred to me. He knew I was looking for some additional consulting." She pic-

tured Colorado Rancher Curt Stackhouse, her fatherly
mentor and advisor.

"Curt's always looking out for us. It's like having
another Dad." Megan's smile faded. "He was in here
yesterday with Jayleen. They were bringing the last of
those fleeces from his storage room into the shop. Curt
came over to me while Jayleen was up front with the
staff, and he asked how Jennifer was doing. I told him
she's doing much better now, thanks to that therapist
Lisa found. Curt looked real relieved to hear that and
said he would tell Jayleen. They've been so worried."

Kelly remembered how concerned everyone in the
Lambspun shop family had been after they heard about
Jennifer's assault. But like true family, all of Jennifer's
friends and everyone who cared for Lambspun's lively
free spirit closed in tightly around her in loving support.

"Thank goodness for Curt, otherwise Steve and
Greg would have found that guy and beaten him to a
pulp."

Megan looked up, astonished. "How could they find
him? Jennifer didn't know his full name."

"They went over to the bar one night and grilled the
bartender. He said he couldn't remember the guy's name
because he didn't come into the bar that often. But
Steve and Greg tried to track him down anyway. They
would have done it, too." She gave a wry smile. "Even
Pete asked to go along. He was out there behind the
café every day, pacing back and forth, he was so upset.
Steve told me that made him think twice. That and
Curt's conversation."

"When was that?"

"A couple of weeks after it happened. Curt invited both Steve and Greg over one night." Kelly concentrated on her knitting, sliding one finished stitch after another off the left needle and onto the right. "He reminded them both that if they found out who the guy was and went to 'teach him a lesson,' they'd wind up being charged with assault. Then *they* would go to jail rather than the scumbag. Of course, Curt had lawyer Marty there to bolster his argument."

Megan blinked. "My Marty? I don't remember his saying anything."

"Yes, *your* Marty. He made the legal case, and he probably didn't tell you because if you recall you were still bursting into tears anytime someone mentioned what happened." She gave Megan an encouraging smile. "So, that's probably why Marty didn't say anything."

Megan stared at her needles again. "I know, I know."

"Good thing Jennifer told you to knock it off, or you'd shrink your yarn."

Megan laughed at that.

"I swear it was all we could do to keep Mimi from finding out," Kelly said, picturing Mimi Shafer, the motherly shop owner. "She kept wondering why you were tearing up and leaving the table."

"I'm sorry, I couldn't help it," Megan said, fingers nimbly working the lemon yarn.

"Thank goodness Mimi believed Jennifer's story about getting caught in the middle of a bar fight. She was horrified enough to see her scratched, swollen face. If Mimi ever learned the truth, it would break her heart." Kelly's voice had dropped lower, so as not to be overheard.

Other customers had entered the room and were browsing through the yarns. Two of the four walls of the main knitting room were covered with bins brimming over with yarns of wool and mohair, alpaca and silk. The other walls were lined with bookshelves, crammed with books on every fiber topic imaginable—knitting, crocheting, weaving, spinning, dyeing fibers, and every type of garment. And then, there were the magazines. Shelves of them. Kelly was always amazed at the wealth of information that appeared monthly. *How could Mimi and her shop "elves" keep up with it all?*

"Great timing," Jennifer's voice sounded from the archway leading into the central yarn room. "Things have finally slowed down at the café, so I can take my break. Brother, were we slammed this morning." Jennifer pulled out a chair beside Kelly and settled in, knitting bag on her lap.

"Hey, you finished your sweater," Megan said. "Looks great."

Admiring the lime green sweater Jennifer was wearing, Kelly added, "I can't believe you're finished. You were still knitting on it day before yesterday."

Jennifer removed a pale pink yarn and knitting needles from her bag. "Well, Pete's catering job last night didn't take us as long as he thought. I was back home by nine, so I was able to finish off the sweater."

"That shade looks great with your hair," Kelly added,

glancing at Jennifer's auburn shoulder-length hair brushing her shoulders.

Jennifer started casting pink stitches onto her needles. "Thanks. I was tired of shamrock, and the lime green just called my name."

"Gotta get back to work, guys. Don't forget pizza at our place tonight," Megan said, gathering the half-finished sweater into her knitting bag. "Marty said he'll pick up one of those wicked French tortes on the way home."

"Those chocolate ones? I'm in," Jennifer said.

Kelly playfully complained. "Ever since we've been getting together at night, I've had to watch my weight. My workouts are taking longer and longer every morning."

"Don't even mention weight," Jennifer said with a sigh. "We'd better give the desserts to High-Speed Metabolism Megan."

"Any extra desserts, we'll bring over to your place tomorrow night, Kelly," Megan said as she skirted the table. "Are you doing Thai or Mexican tomorrow? I forgot."

"I'll check with Steve. He keeps track."

"Either one is fine by me. I'm omnivorous, unfortunately." Jennifer's knitting needles moved faster.

Megan gave a goodbye wave as she headed out. "See you tonight, guys."

Kelly and Jennifer worked in comfortable silence for a while, and Kelly felt that peaceful feeling start to settle in—the meditative state that she'd discovered was an unexpected benefit to the pastime of knitting.

Then Jennifer spoke softly. "I know what you guys are trying to do."

"Do what?" Kelly replied, coming back from the peaceful place.

"You know what I mean. These last several weeks, we've all been getting together several times a week for dinner."

Kelly smiled to herself. Jennifer was too sharp not to notice her friends' attempts to include her in their regular get-togethers. In the three months since the assault, Kelly had watched Jennifer make an astonishing behavioral turnaround. She hadn't returned to the Fort Connor bar scene. Nights were now occupied with helping her part-time employer, café owner Pete, with his private catering jobs and joining her friends in their scheduled evenings of dinner and DVDs.

"Hey, it's fun," Kelly said, concentrating on her stitches. "Except I've gotta learn to say 'no' to the desserts."

"Well, just for the record, I know you guys are trying to keep me from being all by myself alone and . . . and I think it's sweet."

Kelly grinned at her friend. "Duly noted . . . just for the record." They continued to work quietly for another few minutes. This time Kelly broke the silence. "How're you doing, Jen?"

"Okay," Jennifer answered, eyes still on her stitches.

Kelly paused for a second. "I mean . . . how are you *really* doing?"

Jennifer kept casting on stitches for a few more seconds. "I'm doing better, Kelly. Really."

Kelly released an audible sigh. "I'm so glad, Jen. You look better, too. More . . . I don't know . . . more relaxed, maybe."

Jennifer gave her a little smile. "Yeah. I'm getting there. Moving to a new apartment really helped. And talking with Dr. Norcross, of course. I've never talked with anyone like her before."

Kelly noticed the lime green sweater had a scalloped neckline, not the turtlenecks Jennifer had been wearing for the last three months. The purple bruises on her neck had finally faded. "It's a good thing Lisa was taking Dr. Norcross's class at the university, otherwise she might never have found her."

"Hey, just the two I want to see." Lisa's voice came from behind them as she suddenly strode into the room. Plopping her oversized knitting bag on the table, Lisa stood over Kelly and Jennifer, hands on hips. "Please tell me you both are free this weekend. Well, all day Friday through Sunday. Please, pretty please."

"It depends on what you have in mind," Jennifer said, without looking up. "If you're teaching another one of those physical therapist workshops in the mountains, count me out. Being around all those buff, skinny jocks all weekend gave me a complex. And I've got enough of those already."

"Don't tell me. You're teaching another workshop

and you need us to do the fiber classes, right?" Kelly glanced up at her friend.

Lisa swept her long blonde ponytail back into a fabric band. "You're half right. It's a workshop in the mountains, all right. But it's not for physical therapists. And I do need you both to teach the knit and crochet sessions. The two gals who promised to help just called and backed out on me."

Kelly ran through her mental daytimer, weighing her workload. Two more days till the weekend. "If I work ahead, I guess I could manage it. What about you, Jen? Would Pete be able to do without your waitressing skills for three days? You up for a spring weekend in the mountains?"

"Pete would be okay because Sarah could come in and work for me. But I need to check the real estate office and see if I'm scheduled for floor duty this weekend. If not, then I could swing it. No clients have surfaced recently."

"We're going to a ranch up Poudre Canyon, back in the forest," Lisa tempted.

"Whoa, that did it. I'm in," Kelly said. "I'm still fumbling with the crochet hook, so I'll let you and Jen teach that."

"It will be gorgeous up there," Jennifer agreed. "Yeah, I have to admit I could use some peaceful quiet time in the trees and mountains. Walking in my neighborhood just doesn't do it for me."

"Steve and Greg will probably stock up on pizza while we're gone," Lisa said with a grin.

"Naw, they won't," Kelly countered. "Friday night is chili night at Jayleen's, remember? I bet the whole crew will show up on Jayleen's doorstep. Curt's always over there on chili nights."

"Tell Jayleen to save us some," Lisa said.

"You can have my share. I've gotta cut back. My butt is getting so big, it's in another time zone," Jennifer said, starting to knit a row of pink stitches. "By the way, who's going to be at this workshop anyway? You never said."

Lisa's laughter at Jennifer's comment quickly faded, and she paused for a moment, her expression sobering. "It's a workshop for women who've experienced sexual violence. Dr. Norcross is running it. I'm helping as part of my internship in the program."

Jennifer's busy needles stopped their rhythmic movements. She stared at Lisa for a long moment. Kelly held her breath, her needles pausing as well, waiting for Jennifer's reaction.

"Uhhhh, I don't know, guys," she said, glancing back to her yarn, fingers moving slower. "I'm not sure I want to do that. Not with all those strangers."

"You don't have to be in the workshops, Jen," Lisa reassured her friend. "You can simply be there for the knit and crochet sessions. "But if you wanted to listen in, I'm sure Dr. Norcross wouldn't mind. You know her."

Jennifer kept knitting, slower than before, focusing on the stitches forming, one after another. Lisa said nothing else, simply waited for Jennifer to speak.

Kelly held her tongue as long as she could before speaking in a soft voice, "It might be good, Jen. With Dr. Norcross there, you know."

"Maybe . . . I don't know," Jennifer said with a sigh. "I'm not used to a group thing."

"Listen, you can just hang with me if you're not comfortable," Kelly suggested. "We can hike up there. It's going to be gorgeous with the spring flowers bursting through the last of the snow cover."

"You can go horseback riding, too," Lisa offered. "The ranch we're going to has stables as well as cabins and stuff. People can ride every day if they like."

"What do you say, Jen?" Kelly said, leaning toward her friend. "A spring weekend in Poudre Canyon. We'll have a campfire and keep away the bears."

"And the mountain lions," Lisa offered with a wicked grin.

"That's supposed to encourage me?" Jennifer shot them both a look.

"Hey, there will be so much chatter going on, those varmints will head for Cameron Pass," Kelly promised with a laugh.

Jennifer released a long sigh. "Okaaaay, you guys. I'll do it if I can hang out and do my own thing, okay?"

"Absolutely," Lisa agreed, nodding vigorously as she caught Kelly's gaze.

Kelly and Lisa exchanged a look of careful optimism between them. Fingers crossed.

Two

Kelly leaned on the open passenger window of Lisa's car and watched the craggy rock walls of Poudre Canyon pull away from the road, opening to a meadow where pale green spring grass dared to make its presence known. At this altitude, nighttime temperatures still dropped to freezing. Mountain grass had to be hardy to grow in the canyon.

"Are we there yet?" Jennifer asked from the backseat for the umpteenth time.

"Almost," Lisa replied as she steered around a curve. "In fact, we should be coming to the turnoff in a couple of miles."

The road steadily climbed. Kelly saw signs of spring everywhere. Even the scrubby bushes had tinges of green showing in between the brown. Boulders pushed their smooth round shoulders through the ground, where spiky grasses grew out of crevices in the rocks.

SUVs and cars sped by, kayaks strapped on top. Cars were pulled off to the side of the road—empty. No drivers, no passengers, kayaks stripped from rooftops. They were in the water already. Water thrill seekers out for the day, testing themselves against the fast-running current. Some wouldn't return.

"Gorgeous, simply gorgeous," Kelly repeated, watching the canyon slope upward. "This ranch really is high up. A little farther up the road, and we'll be at the Pass. I wonder if we'll be able to see any mountain peaks from the ranch. That would be great."

Many Rocky Mountain peaks kept their icy glacial collars throughout the summer, especially the north-facing ones. The sun's warmth never had a chance to melt them. Ranges like Never Summer were true to their names. Snow glistened on their mountaintops year-round.

"I'm starting to get that mountain property itch again."

"Uh-oh. Better watch out, Jennifer," Lisa warned playfully. "She'll want to see properties pretty soon."

"Well, we've gotten some new listings this month, now that the spring thaw has gotten rid of the ice on the roads. I'll check them and see if there are any you might like."

"Actually, why don't you look for land parcels this time, Jen," Kelly suggested.

"I *knew* you and Steve would want to build rather than buy," Lisa declared. "He's an architect, for Pete's sake. Greg and I are dying to build a mountain place one of these days. We've almost got enough saved to buy some land."

"Do you want me to look up here, Kelly?" Jennifer asked, knitting needles still working despite the car's movements. "Last time, you were in love with Bellevue Canyon."

"Yeah, and I have to admit I'm still partial to that location. For one thing, it's closer to Fort Connor." She checked her watch. "This canyon is gorgeous, with the river and all, but it's farther away. We've been driving for an hour now, and we still aren't there—"

"Yes, we are," Lisa announced as she turned onto a dirt road. A wooden log arch rose above the road, carved letters proclaiming the LAZY C RANCH.

"Well, finally," Kelly said as they bumped along the road. She glanced to the backseat. "Wow, that blanket is nearly finished. I don't see how you can knit in a car on a bumpy road. How do you do that?"

Jennifer shoved the afghan into her bag. "Actually, you just have to relax into the car's rhythm. But right now I'd better stop or the needle will wind up my nose."

"Hey, we're coming to a clearing. There's the ranch house," Lisa said. "Look, people are already unloading cars."

Kelly saw several cars parked in the clearing ahead. A log beam ranch house was to the right of the driveway and set back. The stable, barn, and corral were to the left bordering the driveway, and a long rectangular log building was set in the middle. Kelly noticed trees running along the back of the property, and the land appeared to slope downward almost as if there was a stream or a creek bed running behind those trees.

"Looks like you can pull in over there." Kelly pointed to a space remaining beside a midnight blue minivan.

A woman carrying a duffel bag and another one holding a knapsack walked through the barnyard. They both were dressed in jeans and sweatshirts and appeared to be in their thirties or forties. Lisa pulled her car into the space as a younger woman in tee shirt and shorts walked past, backpack over her shoulder. Like the others, she was headed toward a tall, slender, gray-haired woman standing at the other end of the barnyard, holding a clipboard.

"How many people are signed up for this retreat?" Kelly asked as she opened the car door.

Lisa grabbed her bag and stepped from the car. "Eight have signed up, but we'll have to wait and see. Some people get cold feet at the last moment."

"I can understand that," Jennifer said as she exited the car, knitting bag over her shoulder. Looking around, she added, "Well, it certainly is pretty here."

Kelly turned in a full circle, surveying the Lazy C Ranch. It wasn't as pretty as the canyon property she'd fallen in love with over a year ago, but the ranch had its own rugged beauty. Kelly couldn't wait to start exploring.

"I see some paths winding toward the trees," she said as she grabbed her backpack and knitting bag from Lisa's trunk. "What's the drill? Will we be able to hike? I'd love to take a look around."

"We have to check in with Dr. Norcross first." Lisa started across the barnyard, Kelly and Jennifer following. "She'll tell us which cabins are available, and we'll get the class schedule. I think Dr. Norcross plans her first session right around one o'clock. We ought to be able to take a short hike before that. Then we'll be doing a fiber class after the session."

Another woman crossed the barnyard ahead of them, also heading for the group gathered farther ahead. "I'm glad I'll get the chance to meet Dr. Norcross. I've heard so much about her." Kelly glanced toward the retreat leader, noticing that Dr. Norcross was attired in jeans and a denim shirt exactly like hers. "I do admire her taste in clothes," she added with a smile.

"You'll really like her, Kelly. She's the most gifted and insightful psychologist I've ever met," Lisa said as they walked.

"Wow, that's high praise coming from you, Lisa," Kelly said, noticing a tall, rangy man stride from the stables toward the group of women at the edge of the barnyard. "What do you say, Jen? Is that a fair description?" Kelly turned back for Jennifer's reaction.

Jennifer didn't respond. She'd stopped walking and stood staring wide-eyed, straight ahead, her face ashen.

Kelly quickly went to her friend's side. "Jen? What's the matter?"

Lisa turned around and hastened over. "Jen, are you okay?"

"Oh, my God . . . it's him . . ." she gasped.

Lisa looked over her shoulder. "Do you know that guy?" She jerked her thumb toward the man standing with the group of women. "Who is he?"

Kelly knew immediately who the guy was. She could tell from her friend's reaction. "That's the guy who assaulted you, isn't it, Jennifer?"

"*What!*" Lisa rasped, dropping her voice as another woman sped past them through the barnyard, heading toward the group.

Jennifer didn't answer. She simply stared ahead, then she nodded slowly.

"*Bastard!*" Kelly hissed as she glared at the man, all decked out in cowboy garb—boots and jeans, Stetson dipped over his eyes. He stood, smiling a smirking smile, talking with Dr. Norcross and the women. Kelly felt her blood start to heat up as anger raced through her. She wanted to walk up to the man and wipe that smirk off his face. But lacking Steve's knockout punch, Kelly held herself back and seethed within instead.

Dr. Norcross held up her hands then and addressed the group. Kelly, Lisa, and Jennifer stood on the very edge, behind the others. "Gather around, everyone. Before we begin, the owner of this lovely ranch, Cal Everett, wants to say a few words of welcome." She gestured to Everett beside her.

Kelly quickly turned to Jennifer. Jennifer was still staring ahead, but color had returned to her face. Kelly glanced to Lisa, and they both moved closer together, blocking Everett's view of their friend.

"Howdy and welcome, ladies, to the Lazy C Ranch," Everett drawled with a wide smile. "We host a lot of groups here at the ranch, and we like to make sure they have plenty to do when there's free time." Gesturing to the college-aged boy beside him, Everett continued. "Rico, here, is in charge of the stables and horses and will schedule regular afternoon trail rides. You ladies don't have to worry. All our horses are gentle and operate on cruise control. So all you have to do is sit back and enjoy the scenery." His grin spread as laughter rippled around the group.

Kelly glared at Everett, who clearly enjoyed being the center of attention while he did his routine. She had no doubt it was a routine.

"And over there on the ranch house porch are Donny and Marie." He waved to the young couple leaning on the log railing that wrapped around the porch. "Like Rico, Donny and Marie are college students who spend their summers working in this little piece of heaven up here in Poudre Canyon. They're in charge of meals and housekeeping and taking care of you folks. All meals are served in the ranch house dining room. Feel free to spread out on the deck if you like. You'll know when it's chowtime because you'll hear Marie ring the bell."

Marie chimed in on cue and rang a large cowbell, its jangle clear in the mountain quiet. Again, Everett's audience responded with predictable amusement. Meanwhile, Kelly felt her nails digging into her palms.

Glancing at the muscles clenching Lisa's jaw, she knew her friend was also trying to hold herself back from storming forward to confront Cal Everett.

"I've told Dr. Norcross to feel free to use the back deck for sessions if you'd like. There's a real pretty view overlooking the creek back there. So, relax and enjoy yourselves while you're here. I usually try to stay out of everyone's way, but you can find me if you need me. I'm sure Rico and Donny and Marie will take care of everything you need." He gave them another wide grin. "Any questions, before I give you back to your leader?"

One of the middle-aged women up front spoke up. "I've noticed trails around the ranch. How far can we hike?"

"You can hike as far as you can go, ma'am," Everett said. "Until you run into the river. The trails end at the Poudre, at the edge of the property."

The group started talking amongst themselves then, and Everett headed back toward the ranch house. Jennifer's quiet voice sounded behind Kelly. "I've gotta go . . . I can't stay here . . . not now," she said, turning away.

Kelly's protective instincts rose up full force. "That's okay, Jen. I'll take you into town." Glancing over her shoulder she said, "Lisa, lend me your car keys, will you? I'll drive Jen home, then come back up. With luck I should return before our fiber session starts this afternoon."

Lisa followed after them, her face registering her

concern. "Are you sure, Jen? Do you want to talk with Dr. Norcross first?"

Jennifer stopped and looked at her friends. "I'm sorry, guys . . . I just don't think I can be here . . ."

"It's okay, Jen. I'll take you back—"

"Jennifer, I'm so glad you were able to come with Lisa," Dr. Norcross said as she strode up to them. "Is this your friend Kelly? I haven't had the pleasure." She extended her hand as she walked into their midst. "I'm so glad all of you could come this weekend."

Kelly shook her hand, searching for something to say. When she couldn't, she simply blurted in her usual direct fashion. "Nice to meet you, Dr. Norcross. But I was just about to take Jennifer back home. Lisa can explain."

A worried expression crossed Dr. Norcross's kindly face. "Are you feeling all right, Jennifer? Did you become ill?"

Jennifer glanced to the side and shook her head. "No, it's . . . it's something else."

"Go ahead and tell her, Jen," Lisa prodded gently.

Dr. Norcross looked expectantly from Jennifer to Lisa and back again. "Is there something I should know?"

"Yeah, there is," Kelly blurted again, before stopping herself.

Jennifer exhaled a long breath. "That guy who owns this ranch. He's . . . he's the one who . . . attacked me in February."

Dr. Norcross's pale blue eyes widened, and she

gazed solemnly at Jennifer. She glanced over her shoulder toward the ranch house where Cal Everett had gone after his welcome speech. Then Dr. Norcross turned her warm gaze to Jennifer once again. "Why don't you and I take a walk together, Jennifer? Would that be okay?"

Jennifer looked up and nodded. "Yeah . . . okay."

Dr. Norcross placed her arm around Jennifer's shoulders and gave her a squeeze. "There's a pretty trail over here by the trees that leads down to the creek below," she said as she and Jennifer walked away. Glancing over her shoulder again, Dr. Norcross said, "Lisa, you and Kelly can check in. Your cabin room is the farthest on the right side of the building."

Kelly watched Jennifer and her therapist walk toward the trees, and she felt that knot in her stomach start to loosen a little. Thank heaven Dr. Norcross was here. Otherwise, Jen would be sitting at home alone with all those horrible memories resurfacing throughout the weekend. And Kelly and Lisa wouldn't be there to help her.

The little voice inside Kelly's head whispered, *You mean, rescue her? You can't rescue Jennifer. You know that.* Kelly remembered what Jayleen had once said: "People have to rescue themselves."

That unsettling little reminder worked its way through Kelly's brain. Okay, so she couldn't rescue Jennifer. Jen would have to do that herself. With the help of good therapists like Dr. Norcross and others. But meanwhile, Jennifer's friends could do their best to smooth the road for her. After all, that's what friends do. They could do that, at least.

"That was great timing, wasn't it?" Lisa said, heading across the barnyard once again. "Thank God Dr. Norcross appeared."

"Yeah, let's see how Jennifer feels after they've talked. If she still wants to go home, I'll drive her," Kelly said, following Lisa. "Meanwhile, let's take a look and see how rustic these rooms are."

"Well, I don't see an outhouse anywhere, so I think we may be okay. That building looks like it has a classroom between the cabin rooms. So, there must be bathrooms inside."

"Don't be so sure. That outhouse may be hiding in the trees."

Kelly perched on the split-log railing that ran around the cabin and classroom complex. Now that it was early May, the trees were almost fully leafed-out with pale green leaves. The leaves would darken later in the month with the sun's lengthening days, moving toward summer.

Next would come the spring runoff. Or, the May Melt-off, actually, when mountain snows all over Colorado's Rockies started to melt and flow toward the creeks and streams, swelling them as they rushed toward the rivers. That was Kelly's favorite time to visit the river. Watch it roar through the narrows and crash against the rocks, hurrying downstream where it widened, deceptively calm until it turned another bend. White water again.

This canyon was named for the mountain river that ran through it—the Cache La Poudre. Starting high at the top of the Continental Divide, the river trickled down the mountains in a small stream that grew as it flowed out of the canyon.

In the early summer after the spring runoff, the Poudre—as everyone called it—ran high and fast. It was a class five kayaking river, five out of six on the danger scale, calling adventure seekers from all over to come and test their abilities against its treacherous currents.

Most people in Fort Connor had learned or heard how dangerous the Poudre River could be, especially in the spring. Its swollen waters concealed the labyrinth of rocks and boulders below, hiding the tree branches and limbs that reached out and pulled many a kayaker to their death. Experience was no match for hidden hazards that snagged the unsuspecting.

Strength was no match for the river's swift currents, either. Many a person who thought they could swim across the fast-rushing waters was swept away. Life jackets helped but did not guarantee safety. If someone was pulled under the water long enough, death was inevitable. It didn't take long to drown.

"Excuse me, I'm looking for Lisa," a woman called as she approached, startling Kelly from her dramatic reverie.

"She's inside the room," Kelly said. Noticing the woman's short curly dark hair, Kelly added, "Are you

Greta? Lisa said you and she were taking classes with Dr. Norcross at the university."

"Yeah, I'm Greta Baldwin," she said, extending her hand. "You must be Kelly."

Kelly gave her hand a shake. "Kelly Flynn. You're helping this weekend, too? Lisa convinced Jennifer and me to help her with the knit and crochet sessions."

"I'm teaching self-defense for women," Greta volunteered. "I teach classes at several of the sport facilities and health centers in town."

"Now that sounds like something useful," Kelly said. "I wouldn't mind watching your class."

Greta smiled wide, her eyes alight. "Sure thing, Kelly. But from what I hear, you don't need much help protecting yourself. Lisa's told me about some of your adventures."

"Ah, my reputation precedes me."

"Hey, Greta, good to see you," Lisa said as she came from the cabin. "Are they gathering in the classroom already? Have you met everyone yet? I've introduced myself to all six so far. Anyone else show up?"

Greta shook her head. "No, so I guess we have two no-shows. That's about par for the course, according to Dr. Norcross."

"Speaking of that, has she returned yet?" Lisa said, surveying the grounds. "She went for a walk with our friend Jennifer."

"They haven't shown up," Kelly said. "I've been keeping watch. Wait a minute . . . I think that's them over there, coming from the trees."

"Whew! Perfect timing, too." Lisa glanced at her watch. "Five minutes before class is scheduled to start."

"If Jen wants to go back, do you think you'll be able to handle the yarn session?" Kelly asked as she rose from her perch, anxiously peering across the spring grass, trying to decipher Jennifer's expression. Her friend was still talking with Dr. Norcross.

"Don't worry. I'll be fine," Lisa said.

"Everything okay with your friend?" Greta asked, glancing toward Jennifer.

"Yeah, they had a little chat, that's all," Lisa replied.

Dr. Norcross gave Jennifer's arm a squeeze, then walked toward the classroom building in the middle of the complex. Jennifer turned, spotted Kelly and friends gathered on the porch, and headed their way.

"How's it going?" Kelly tried to hold back, but as usual she couldn't.

"Better," Jennifer said, giving a little nod. "Dr. Norcross and I talked a lot, and she told me I could choose to do several things. Whatever I decided would be perfectly okay. I had choices. But I needed to be comfortable with my choice."

Kelly held her breath, waiting to hear what Jennifer was about to say. *Choices.*

Jennifer looked out toward the trees beyond, her hands shoved into her jeans pockets. "She said I could go home now if I wanted to, and that would be fine. Or I could stay and help you guys teach the yarn sessions like we planned. Or, I could stay and do yarn sessions *and* sit in on the classes she's leading with the other six women. I wouldn't have to say anything if I didn't want to. No one has to speak if they don't want to." She paused. "Then she said I could also choose to stay and share my experience with the others. Maybe that would help someone else. It might help them move forward." Jennifer turned back to Kelly and Lisa. "I've decided to stay and share. Maybe my story will help someone else tell theirs."

Kelly gazed into her friend's eyes and fought back the tears that rose unexpectedly in hers. "I'm proud of you, Jen."

"Me, too," Lisa said and gave Jennifer a quick hug.

"Good for you, Jennifer," Greta added from behind them, her pale face solemn.

"And Doctor Norcross promised me I'd be safe here," Jennifer continued. "She called out Everett right there on his porch. Gave him hell, too. She told him she didn't want to see his face this weekend. And warned him he'd better stay in his house and away from me or any other retreat attendees. Everett turned white and ran inside the house."

"Way to go, Dr. Norcross!" Kelly cried in delight.

Greta glanced over her shoulder to where Dr. Norcross was gesturing from the doorway. "Hey, guys, I think the session is about to start. Why don't we walk in together," she said, beckoning Jennifer down the porch.

"See you at the yarn session afterwards." Jen gave a wave to Kelly as she walked away.

"I'm going in now," Lisa said. "Why don't you go on that hike, Kelly. You can explore for both of us."

Kelly stared after her friends for a few seconds, then headed toward the trees. They'd been beckoning her ever since she arrived.

Three

Lisa scattered an assortment of colorful yarns across pine picnic tables that were clustered together on the wooden deck. Kelly moved chairs around to create a rough imitation of the Lambspun knitting table. A more rustic setting, but also a more beautiful one, Kelly had to admit.

The deck that stretched out in back of the ranch house was definitely inviting. It urged Kelly to sit and look and listen. Gaze at the rocky walls of Poudre Canyon she could see through the trees beside the creek that flowed below. Listen to the music of the water rushing past. Perched on the edge, the deck jutted out over a rocky slope that angled down toward the creek bank.

It was a shame to waste this beautiful view on that bastard, she thought.

"Here they come," Lisa announced.

Kelly spotted the women wandering around the outside of the ranch house. They slowly trickled onto the deck, talking in subdued voices, commenting on the scenery. That is, until they saw the yarns scattered on every table. All donated by Mimi at Lambspun. Exclamations of "How pretty," "Feel this, it's so soft," "Look at these colors," and "Is this a yarn?" The women indulged themselves like all visitors to the knitting shop. Indeed, it had been Kelly's own experience when she first fell down the rabbit hole into that wonderland of fiber.

"Sit wherever you like," Lisa directed, motioning to the women who surrounded the picnic tables. "We've tried to re-create our long knitting table at Lambspun back in town. It's where everybody gathers. Knitters, spinners, weavers, and hookers."

A young woman with short brown hair and a name tag reading CASSIE gave her a shocked look.

"*Hookers* are what we call ourselves when we're crocheting, because we use the hook instead of needles." Lisa gestured, as if there was any confusion.

"Pick a yarn you like and we'll show you how to work with it. Most of these yarns will work well for knitting or crochet," Kelly announced as she watched the women pick over the yarns, making their selections. "We've got some real simple projects you can start on."

"Did all these yarns come from that shop in town?" a short brunette asked as she examined a ball of lime green chenille. Hair pulled back in a ponytail, she had a name tag that said EDIE.

"Yes, Mimi Shafer, the owner of Lambspun, donated the yarns and supplies for this retreat."

"Shrewd marketing move," said a slender, thirtyish blonde named Nancy, as she scrutinized a fluffy skein of indigo merino wool and mohair.

Kelly had to laugh. "You're right about that. Mimi is a shrewd business owner as well as a kindhearted contributor to local causes."

"What are we going to use on these yarns? We need needles and hooks," a girl with a state college tee shirt asked, holding aloft a ball of fluffy hot pink eyelash yarn. Her name tag said SUE.

Kelly held up a canvas bag. "Don't worry. We've got a bunch of needles and hooks of all sizes. We're covered."

"What kind of projects do you have?" a fortyish frosted blonde asked. DAWN was printed in block letters on her name tag. "I knitted a scarf once, but it was years ago."

"Oh, you'll get the hang of it again quickly," Kelly promised. "That yarn you've got right there would make a great scarf for winter if you use smaller needles. If you want something for summer, then pick one of those eyelash yarns—those little spiky fluff balls in the rainbow colors." She pointed to several. "You can make a real cute summer scarf with larger needles."

The women proceeded to move around the tables, examining yarns as Jennifer sidled up beside Kelly. "Wow, this is almost like an entirely different group."

"What do you mean?"

"At the session, nobody talked at all. Well, just one woman. But everyone else kept their mouths shut, including me. It was hard to get a read on them, everybody was so subdued and quiet. But now . . . just look at them." She gestured toward the women, chattering to each other, comparing yarns, comparing stories of scarves gone awry and sweaters that went on forever. Smiles were everywhere. "Fiber fever at work. You've gotta love it."

Kelly chuckled. "Well, Mimi certainly will. We're probably creating several new customers for her shop this weekend."

"And for those of you who've never done any knitting or crocheting, we've got a super easy project that will teach you both. A simple knitted washcloth with a crocheted edge. Believe me, it's easy," Lisa announced.

"How big is it?" a tall redhead with spiky hair asked. Her name tag said JANE.

Lisa held up her hands, indicating a square. "Regular washcloth size. Don't worry. You won't be knitting a towel," she teased.

Dr. Norcross slipped beside Kelly and Jennifer. "I'm amazed at the transformation with this group. They're animated now. More like the women I see in my office when they're alone with me. I may have to add these fiber sessions to every workshop I teach from now on."

"Jennifer says it's the power of fiber," Kelly said with a grin. "I think she's right. It happens all the time when we're around the table at Lambspun. People start talking with each other, and strangers become friends. It's really amazing to watch. Maybe because it's so relaxing and peaceful. Kind of Zenlike when you're all alone."

Dr. Norcross surveyed the women for a long moment. "We may be on to something. Let's see what happens when everyone settles and starts working on their projects. Maybe some of them will be relaxed enough they'll feel safe to share. We'll see."

"Okay, pick a yarn and find a seat around the table. Kelly and Jennifer and I will be coming around to help you start. Tell us what you want to make, and we'll get those needles and hooks distributed."

The women snatched up their selections, exchanging yarns with each other, then finally settled in their chairs. "Here, Jen, take some of these and start at that end of the table, and I'll start here. Lisa can work the middle," Kelly instructed, handing Jennifer several needles and hooks.

"Aye, aye, Captain," Jennifer said with what looked like her old smile and teasing tone. That gladdened Kelly's heart as she approached the eager fiber workers surrounding her.

"And I swear, no matter how much I knitted on that sweater, I never saw any progress," Jennifer said. "It was the sweater that wouldn't die. It stayed the same, no matter how much I knitted."

"That's impossible," Cassie said. "Your eyes were playing tricks on you. It had to get longer."

"Well, it finally did," Jennifer continued. "I got disgusted with it and shoved it into a bag at the back of my closet. When I took it out a year later, it had grown a foot in length."

"Yeah, riiiight," Edie said, knitting carefully on a washcloth. Several rows of soft lime green French chenille hung from her needles.

"That sounds like the knitter's version of 'fish stories,'" Nancy said.

"Ooooh, my yarn's knotted or twisted or something," Dawn complained, a loose eyelash scarf coming to life on her needles. She leaned next to Lisa, who was sitting beside her.

"Here, I'll show you how to fix it," Lisa said, examining the stitches.

Kelly worked the soft beige French chenille that she'd chosen. Those washcloths did look super easy. She decided to keep the light mood going. The entire group had been knitting and crocheting peacefully and quietly, with occasional calls for help. So far, the women had talked about their jobs and their families. That was all.

"I have to admit that story does sound fishy, Jennifer," Kelly teased, listening to the soft laughter. "Were you checking that sweater late at night after you'd come home from the bar?"

Kelly noticed that college-aged Sue and Cassie

quickly glanced up at her teasing comment. Kelly felt certain that Jennifer would pick up her lead and play along. Maybe they could relax this group even more.

"Nope, I was cold sober every time I checked on the knitting," Jennifer responded as Kelly had hoped, voice returning to that familiar lighthearted tone that was Jennifer's trademark. "Believe me, I never did any knitting when I'd come home from the bars."

"Which ones do you go to? In town, I mean?" Nancy asked.

"Oh, I liked several in Old Town, especially the dance clubs. That was in my salsa phase." Jennifer's fingers worked the pink wool, and rows of stitches gathered swiftly on her needles as the afghan grew. It was almost finished now. "But one of my favorites was The Empire Room on the north side of town. It's nice without being too snooty. So, I'd go over there several nights a week and meet guys."

"I've been there," Cassie added softly. "But I never went often. It always seemed that everyone . . . well, everyone knew everyone else. And I kind of felt . . ." She shrugged her shoulders. "I don't know, left out, I guess."

Jennifer nodded her head. "Yeah, you're right. It can be like that. I used to know a lot of people there, too. Then, they kind of all drifted away."

"What happened?" Sue asked, yellow chenille yarn dangling. She was making a washcloth.

"Oh, most of them either got married, moved away, or got sober," Jennifer said in the line Kelly had heard her use before. She'd always detected a hint of wistfulness in the observation.

Several of the women chuckled and added similar experiences.

"How's your friend Diane doing? I haven't heard you mention her for a while," Kelly asked, deciding to keep this train of thought going in case Jennifer was heading somewhere.

"Diane's doing well and working for a landscape firm," Jennifer said, needles picking up speed. "She's one of my old bar buddies, and we used to hit practically every bar in town. Unfortunately, Diane started drinking way too much, and that got her into major trouble. She did a lot of thinking afterwards and went sober last year with the help of AA. I've gotta give her credit. She's really rebuilt her life." Jennifer paused for a moment, then added softly, "Diane's never been back to the bars. I'm proud of her. In fact, I'm going to try and follow her example."

"You mean getting sober or staying away from the bars?" Edie asked, glancing up from her crochet hook. The lime green washcloth coming into shape.

"I'm trying to do both, actually," Jennifer admitted. "I've stayed away from the bars for three months now, and I've changed my drinking habits, too."

"What do you mean?" Sue asked.

"I used to be the Margarita Queen," Jennifer said with a wry smile. "I always thought it helped my salsa style. But, I cut them out. I only drink a little wine now, that's all."

"Man, I don't think I could give up my margaritas," Jane said, more rows forming on her pink chenille washcloth.

"Do you think you were getting . . . you know, drinking too much like your friend Diane?"

Jennifer knitted quietly for a few seconds. "You know, I never used to think so. I was so sure I could handle the drinks. I mean, I'd never passed out or gotten falling down drunk like other people, so I thought I was doing okay." She paused, then added, "But I've changed my mind. I think it dulls my instinct."

Dawn eyed Jennifer carefully, as did the others. "What happened to change your mind?"

"A guy followed me home one night. He and I had been sitting and talking at the bar, and I had way more than usual," Jennifer said softly, concentrating on the pink stitches. "He showed up at my door later and said I'd left something at the bar. Then he forced his way into my apartment." She shook her head sadly. "I wish I'd never opened that door."

Kelly noticed that everyone around the table had stopped working on their projects, yarns and needles dropped in their laps. They stared at Jennifer. Only Kelly, Lisa, and Jen kept working their fibers. Everyone else stared. Kelly glanced at Dr. Norcross, who was watching the women carefully.

"What happened?" Cassie asked, her huge brown eyes staring wide.

"He raped me," Jennifer said, her voice dropping, still not looking up.

"*Son of a bitch!*" Jane spat, then launched into a string of curses that Kelly hadn't heard since her father was alive.

"Don't blame yourself, Jennifer. He probably would have broken down your door to get in," Greta said in an angry voice.

"You pressed charges, didn't you?" Dawn asked, peering at Jennifer.

Jennifer shook her head.

Dawn looked shocked. "But you have to! You can't let him get away with it! Police found the guy that broke into my apartment, and I made sure he went to jail. He's in Canon City right now."

"Maybe Jennifer doesn't want to go to court," Sue suggested. "Not everyone can face things that way."

"Don't you want to make him pay for what he did to you?" Edie demanded.

Jennifer didn't answer, just kept knitting quietly, while the various comments bubbled around her. Kelly kept her mouth shut, as did Lisa, watching everything, just like Dr. Norcross. Wondering what Jennifer would say.

"Yeah, I really would like to make him pay for what he did," she finally responded. "But I'm afraid that would never happen. I'd been going to the bars for years, and I usually took some guy home at night. So, maybe he'd never be convicted. Maybe no one would believe me. Everybody at the bar could testify that they saw me drinking with him earlier that night. Face it, folks. We've all heard the stories about what happens when those cases go to trial. Even girls who've never been to a bar in their lives are splattered with mud." She shook her head. "It would be really ugly."

Kelly was amazed at the strength she heard in Jennifer's voice and was proud of her friend's honesty, even though it saddened her that Jennifer thought no one would believe her. Her friends did.

Meanwhile, Dawn and Jane expressed their anger and frustration at the injustice of the situation. Sue and Cassie, Edie and Nancy sat knitting or crocheting and adding occasional comments.

"I still think you should confront him," Dawn declared. "Accuse him to his face. Hold him accountable. What do you think, Dr. Norcross?"

Dr. Norcross looked up from the afghan she was crocheting. "Everyone is different, Dawn. And each one of you is on your own path." She paused. "Besides, Jennifer *has* confronted the situation this weekend, haven't you, Jennifer?"

Jennifer glanced up, her face solemn. Everyone stared raptly, waiting for her to speak.

When she didn't, Dr. Norcross spoke. "Would you like to tell them, Jennifer?"

"Okay," Jennifer said, returning to her afghan, more rows appearing. "The guy who attacked me is the owner of this ranch, Cal Everett. I didn't know his name until he introduced himself to us earlier."

A collective gasp sounded all around the deck. Then the women exploded with angry accusations.

Jane let fly with another stream of curses and

pushed back her chair. "That pig! I'm gonna go punch him out."

"Settle down, Jane," Dr. Norcross said, holding up her hand. "This is Jennifer's situation, not yours. And she's handling it. Jennifer and I took a walk before the session, and Everett happened to cross our path. Jennifer stood right there and stared him down. Meanwhile, I told him I didn't want to see him anywhere near any of you this entire weekend. So, I don't think Cal Everett will show his face except at night, and we'll be around the campfire or in our cabins."

"What'd the scumbag say?" Dawn asked, picking up her knitting needles again.

"He didn't say a word," Jennifer said. "But he looked scared and went white as a sheet, then ran inside his house. It felt good to watch that."

"Good for you, Dr. Norcross!" Edie said with a small smile.

"I still think we should all go and confront him. Scare the snot out of the punk."

Several comments greeted Jane's inventive suggestion. Kelly decided this was as good a place as any to add a comment, even though it wasn't her discussion.

"I know how you feel, Jane," she said. "Some of Jennifer's friends and I wanted to round up a posse and go get him, but one of our lawyer friends reminded us that wouldn't be a good idea. We'd wind up getting charged with assault, not Everett."

"I still think he deserves punishment," Edie said, scowling.

"Punishment comes in many forms," Dr. Norcross said. "I don't advise letting thoughts of vengeance occupy your mind. Vengeance has a way of backfiring."

That comment sparked another animated conversation which lasted several minutes. Then peaceful silence fell upon the group for a while until another soft voice spoke up.

"I know what Jennifer means . . . about the bars and all," Sue said. "The same thing happened to me one night."

Kelly watched the women drop the yarns to their laps once again as they listened intently to the next confession.

Four

"Okay, come at me from behind again," Greta said from the front of the classroom.

Kelly stood beside Jennifer and watched Greta as she moved through the routine.

Jane had volunteered to be Greta's helper, and her job was to "attack" Greta from the back and from the front. Jane was nearly a foot taller than Greta and packed a lot more muscle than the smaller teacher. Nonetheless, Kelly was fascinated to see Greta toss the unsuspecting Jane over her shoulder when Jane tried to grab Greta from behind. *Blam*. Jane was flat on the practice mat.

The result was the same when Jane tried to come straight at Greta—flying at her face. Greta moved her body to use the force of Jane's attacking movement against her. Once again, Jane was on the floor.

"Boy, she's good," Jennifer observed.

"Yeah, she is. No wonder she teaches so many classes," Kelly said.

Lisa joined them at the back of the classroom. "Greta certainly makes it look easy."

"It doesn't look easy to me," Jennifer said, watching Greta's movements.

"Have you ever tried any martial arts?" Kelly asked Lisa.

"Once, years ago, but I didn't stick with it. If I ever want to learn again, I'll definitely join one of Greta's classes. She's good."

"Yeah, and tough for someone that small. She doesn't look like she's much over five feet tall."

Kelly was intently watching Greta's movements when the familiar jangle of her cell phone sounded. She quickly backed away from the others. "See you guys at lunch," she said as she headed toward the classroom doorway and flipped open her phone. Her friend Jayleen's voice greeted her as she stepped outside onto the lodge porch.

"Hey, Kelly, I hope I'm not interrupting you or anything, but I was wondering how Jennifer was doing and all. Megan told me that you and Lisa were taking her to some psychologist workshop up in Poudre Canyon."

Kelly could hear the concern in the alpaca rancher's voice. Jayleen was like an older sister to Kelly and her friends. She had been down many of life's troublesome paths and had the wounds to show for it. So, she was always looking out for them.

"That's right. Jennifer's therapist is leading a retreat for women who've been sexually assaulted like Jen. Lisa asked us to come up and teach the fiber classes. Lisa's helping organize it because Dr. Norcross is her professor at the university."

"Good for Lisa. I've talked to Jennifer about joining some of those support groups, but she always shied away. I swear by them. I wouldn't be sober today without their help."

Kelly stepped off the lodge porch and strolled through the barnyard toward the creek. It was almost lunchtime, so she might as well talk to Jayleen and enjoy the rushing waters at the same time.

"You'll be pleased to hear that Jennifer actually started attending the workshop sessions, and she played a big role yesterday in helping the others start to share their stories. Nobody was talking until we started the yarn sessions, and once everyone started working on their projects, then they began opening up. But it wouldn't have happened if Jennifer hadn't started the ball rolling."

"Well, I'll be damned. Good for her." Jayleen's throaty chuckle sounded. "You tell her I'm proud of her."

"I am, too, Jayleen," Kelly said, noticing Donny and Marie setting up the tables on the deck behind the ranch house. They walked across the barnyard, arms laden with plates and cups, soft drinks, and a coffee urn.

"And there was an unanticipated benefit in coming to the retreat, too. Have you ever met a ranch owner by the name of Cal Everett?"

"Nope, can't say that I have. The name doesn't ring a bell."

"He opens his ranch to retreat groups, and we're at his ranch in Poudre Canyon right now. Turns out, he's the guy who assaulted Jennifer."

"*WHAT!*" Jayleen shouted on the other end of the phone.

"Yeah, Jennifer never knew his full name, but she took one look at him and—"

Kelly didn't finish her sentence because Jayleen exploded in a string of angry curses that rivaled Jane's earlier diatribe. Kelly waited until her friend's salty stream had finished.

"Yeah, you can imagine our shock."

"Damnation, girl! How'd Jennifer take it?"

"Actually, it helped Jennifer open up, I think. She and Dr. Norcross took a walk before the session and Jen got to look Everett in the eye and not back down. Then Dr. Norcross gave him hell and told him to stay away from everyone."

"I would've paid to see that, I swear I would. Wait'll I tell Curt. He'll be glad to know where we can find that no-good so-and-so."

"Now, Jayleen, remember what Curt told Steve and Greg. No matter how much they want to put some hurt on Cal Everett, we can't do it. He'd just charge us—"

"I know, I know, I know."

Kelly spotted Everett emerging from the ranch house, looking both ways around the barnyard, then yanking his Stetson down over his eyes and heading toward the emerald green truck parked next to the barn.

"Listen, Jayleen, I've gotta hang up now. But tell Burt and the guys that I'm getting Everett's truck license so Burt can ask the cops to run a check on him. See if there are any outstanding speeding tickets or something they can get him for."

"Tell Jennifer we're proud of her, and I'll make another pot of chili for her this week."

"Will do. See you after the weekend," Kelly said before clicking off. Shoving the phone into her jeans pocket, Kelly set off on a different path across the barnyard.

Whether it was Greta's proactive defensive techniques or the conversation with Jayleen or her own desire for confrontation—whatever it was—Kelly decided to intercept Cal Everett at his truck. Confront the bastard and see if she could spook him. Once Dr. Norcross had confronted Everett, he'd definitely kept a low profile. No one saw him around the ranch all day yesterday. Only the glow of his cigarette and the constant hacking smoker's cough floating on the night breeze gave a clue as to his presence on the deck yesterday evening.

Kelly called out as Everett neared his truck, "Everett! I want a word with you."

Cal Everett spun about, and to Kelly's immense

gratification, actually looked apprehensive as she strode up to him. She was almost as tall as he was, and Kelly pulled herself to her full height as she put her hands on her hips and glared at him.

"Yeah, what is it?" Everett said warily, glancing about the barnyard.

"I want to put you on notice that if you ever get anywhere near my friend Jennifer again, you'll regret it. First, you'll have to get past me. And the rest of her friends back in Fort Connor will be watching your every move, Everett. One of them is a retired cop, so you can be sure your license plate will be checked out. You'd better stay up here in the canyon and keep out of Fort Connor, if you know what's good for you."

Everett's shifty blue gaze darted around. "Listen, I don't want any trouble, you hear."

Kelly advanced closer, her finger pointed close to his chest. "You stay away from Jennifer, or her friends will beat the snot out of you," she warned, borrowing Jane's colorful phrase.

Everett's gaze hardened. "I don't take to threats," he snarled.

"Then stay away from Jennifer." Kelly leaned closer and jabbed her finger into his chest before turning away.

Kelly was startled to see Donny and Marie right behind her, staring wide-eyed at the confrontation. Their expressions clearly revealed surprise at what they overheard. Kelly sped past both of the college student helpers as Cal Everett's huge truck engine rumbled to life.

* * *

"**Hey,** look at that," Jane said, holding up the completed washcloth. "It doesn't look half bad."

"It looks better than that, Jane," Lisa said. "You've done a great job. Anybody else finished a washcloth?"

"Working on it," Sue said. "Maybe I'll finish it this afternoon rather than go riding. Can we stay here on the deck?"

"Sure, I think we can stay until the kids set up for dinner." Lisa picked up Jennifer's pale pink afghan and draped it over the deck railing for all to see. "See how much Jennifer got done just sitting out here. Projects go pretty quickly with the larger needles."

Kelly glanced at her watch. "Actually, Donny and Marie will be setting up for dinner pretty soon. Would you believe it's nearly four thirty?"

"Isn't it amazing how time flies by when you're doing this fiber work. Does everyone notice, or is it just us?" Dr. Norcross asked as she stood up.

Dawn pushed back her chair. "Well, I certainly had forgotten how satisfying and relaxing this was." She held up a pink and yellow eyelash scarf. "I'm going to keep this going. When did you say the shop gathers around the table?"

"Well, you can always find people around the table, no matter when you come," Lisa said, gathering up the extra yarns and shoving them into a tote bag. "But there's an evening session on Tuesday nights as well as morning and afternoon sessions. Just bring your work, and you'll always find someone there." Kelly and Jennifer joined her cleanup, collecting stray needles and hooks and scissors.

Donny and Marie appeared on the deck then, bright smiles in place. "Hey, folks, we're going to set up for dinner now."

The rest of the women took their yarn projects and began to leave, as the two helpers started rearranging tables.

"What's for dinner?" Lisa asked as she followed behind the others leaving the deck.

"Spaghetti and meatballs," Marie sang out cheerfully. "I'll be ringing the bell in a half hour, so bring an appetite."

"That's never been a problem," Jennifer said.

"Pasta, again?" Edie complained. "I'd better take another hike after dinner."

"Not a bad idea," Kelly said as the group crossed the barnyard.

The sound of roaring engines caught her attention as Cal Everett's emerald green truck came speeding up the ranch driveway. Kelly spotted a dark blue pickup swerve into the driveway, too, following right behind. Kelly and the others ran to the lodge porch as the two trucks roared into the barnyard.

Everett stepped down from his truck as the blue pickup barrelled up behind him and jerked to a stop. A tall man wearing a flannel shirt and baseball cap leaped from his truck and charged toward Everett.

"You can't run away, Cal," he yelled. "That payment

is past due, and you know it. I want my money, and I want it now!"

"Hold your horses, Bill. You'll get your money in a couple of weeks, like usual. You know I'm good for it," Everett said, ambling up to his irate visitor.

"Dammit, Cal. You've been late with every payment since January. I've had it. I'm going to give you till tomorrow to come up with that money, or I'm gonna put a lien on those river acres."

"The hell you will!" Everett challenged, getting right in Bill's face. "I'm paying that note off. You got no claim on that land!"

Kelly stood on the lodge porch with the other women, transfixed like everyone else by the heated argument taking place in the barnyard. The men were toe-to-toe, in each other's faces.

"You backed up the note with that land. I never would have loaned you the money otherwise, and you know it. If you want to save the land, then pay the note in full. You've jerked me around for the last time."

"I can't come up with the money that fast, Bill," Everett protested, backing off a bit.

"Then I'm going to put a lien on it, I swear to God, I will."

Everett exploded in a string of curses, then stalked off.

"Don't think you can walk away from this, Cal! I'm coming back, and we're gonna have this out once and for all!" Bill threatened before heading to his truck. He roared off in a cloud of dust.

Kelly watched Bill's blue truck disappear down the driveway. *What was up with Everett and Rancher Bill?*

Kelly rested her chin on her knees, watching the campfire flicker in the dark. She snuggled into her jacket. Springtime in the Rockies was still cool during the days and downright cold at night.

The fire snapped, sending sparks and embers floating above. She was reminded of the camping trips she and Steve had taken last summer and fall. Curled up in sleeping bags—sometimes inside their tent, snug and safe, and sometimes outside gazing up at the stars. Carl on a leash beside them.

The murmur of women's voices around the campfire rose and fell as private conversations and joint sharing that had begun this weekend continued in the dark. She looked over at Jennifer, who was staring almost mesmerized into the fire, while Dawn and Edie talked beside her. Lisa was speaking softly with Nancy, and Dr. Norcross and Greta were deep in conversation. Jane and Sue and Cassie were still roasting marshmallows on sticks. Kelly had had her fill of the sticky treat earlier.

Glancing up at the canopy of black above her head, Kelly found the familiar stars her father had first shown her as a child. The constellation of Orion. Sirius, the Dog Star. The Big Dipper and Little Dipper.

The low hoot of a nearby owl announced the night predators were out, whether taking flight or stalking through the grass. The hunt was on.

Detecting some movement on the deck behind the ranch house, Kelly thought she glimpsed Cal Everett pacing about the deck as he had been most of the night. The glow of his cigarette and that frequent smoker's cough announced his presence. His voice carried on the breeze as he argued loudly with someone on the phone. Kelly figured he was trying to find ways to come up with the cash he owed his irate creditor. The man named Bill sounded like he had run out of patience long ago.

Lisa stood up and stretched. "I think I'm turning in, guys," she said. "How about it, Jen? Want to go back to the cabin?"

Jennifer pulled herself off the ground and shoved her hands in her jacket pockets. "I'll be there in a few minutes. I feel like walking for a little while. Don't stay up."

Kelly rose and stretched. Sleep sounded like a good idea. It was funny how you got sleepy earlier higher up in the mountains. "You want some company, Jen?"

"No," she said, shaking her head. "I actually need to be alone for a little while. You guys go on back."

"Okay, be careful," Kelly warned as she and Lisa headed toward the lodge. "Don't get too close to the trees. The varmints are out."

Jennifer didn't answer.

Five

"**Boy,** am I hungry this morning," Lisa said as she swept up her blonde ponytail into a scrunchy band behind her head. "I hope there are pancakes."

"Let's hope *not*," Jennifer said, tying her sneakers. "Hot breads are my downfall."

"You know, if I was smart, I'd take a run before breakfast, then I could have those pancakes with a clear conscience." Kelly said as she stood in the cabin doorway waiting for her friends.

Another gorgeous mountain spring morning beckoned. The early green leaves were almost translucent they were so pale—fragile and soft. Summer's deep green had yet to come. But it was on its way. By the end of May, summer would be upon them all. Meanwhile in the mountains and in town, there was still a chance of mid-May snows. That's why most gardeners waited to plant delicate annual flowers until after Mother's Day.

Lisa and Jennifer joined Kelly, and they all headed across the barnyard, waving to some of the other women who'd become friends this weekend. Today, Sunday, all of them would return to their normal lives and routines.

"Ummm, I smell bacon," Lisa said as she waved to Sue and Jane.

Kelly sniffed the delicious aroma, and her stomach rumbled. *What is it about mountain air that makes you hungrier?* She never could figure that out. She really would have to take a run this morning.

"When does the retreat wrap up today?" she asked Lisa, acknowledging Cassie's wave as they approached the deck.

"There will be a session this morning, then Dr. Norcross hopes there'll be time for a trail ride after that, right before we leave. I think everyone would enjoy it."

The enticing aromas of breakfast grew stronger as Kelly and her friends joined the others on the deck. Like the other meals, buffet servers were set up inside the ranch house dining room through the glass patio doors. Kelly noticed that Jane, Dawn, Sue, and Nancy had already filled their plates and were settling at tables on the deck. Greta and Edie were seated at another table, hunched over bowls of oatmeal.

"Yep, pancakes," Jennifer said, eying the plates.

"And my usual downfall—scrambled eggs, sausage, and bacon. Now, if I could just restrict myself to one, I'd be okay."

Kelly didn't plan to restrict herself at all, and eagerly joined the buffet line. Breakfast had always been her favorite meal for some reason. Maybe because she and her dad always had special breakfasts every weekend. Lots of memories were associated with breakfast.

Donny and Marie scurried back and forth, bringing pans of biscuits and bowls of gravy and platters of fruit.

"Oh, no, not gravy," Jennifer complained. "I'm doomed. Hand me a biscuit, will you, Kelly?"

"Here, take two, they're small." Kelly used tongs to snag two hot biscuits and dropped them onto Jennifer's plate.

"They won't be as good as Megan's," Lisa said.

Jennifer ladled gravy over the steaming breads. "They'll do until Megan bakes again."

Dr. Norcross joined the line. "Well, I have to admit I'll miss these breakfasts," the slender professor announced.

"That's easy for you to say, Professor," Cassie countered, scooping up fresh fruit into a bowl. "You're as skinny as a rail. I've got to get back to my bran flakes, dull as they are."

"That's too virtuous for me," Jennifer said, snagging some bacon.

"Is Everett in his office this morning?" Dr. Norcross asked Donny as he refilled the juice pitchers. "I wanted to check to see if we could schedule a trail ride before leaving."

"You know, I haven't seen him, ma'am," Donny said, pausing. "That's kinda unusual, too. He usually takes his breakfast early."

"Maybe he's sleeping in this morning," Dawn said drily. "Sounded like he was on the phone late last night. You could hear him all the way out at the campfire."

Donny shrugged and returned to the kitchen, clearly not about to speculate on his boss's late night activities.

Kelly grabbed a glass of grapefruit juice and followed Lisa and Jennifer onto the deck. Noticing several knitted and crocheted afghans draped over the deck railing, she said, "Lisa, don't forget the blankets and stuff you brought. We left some things on the deck yesterday afternoon when we finished up quickly."

"Forgive me if I don't talk," Jennifer said as she settled at the table. "My face will be in my plate for a few minutes."

Kelly laughed as she pulled out a chair. It was good to hear Jennifer's joking comments. It was the first lighthearted comment Jennifer had made since arriving at Cal Everett's Lazy C Ranch. If it took biscuits and gravy to help Jennifer regain herself, then bring on the gravy.

Swallowing a yummy mouthful of eggs and bacon, Kelly buttered her pancakes and took a bite. "Anybody up for a run this morning?" she asked around the deck. "I don't know about you folks, but pancakes twice in two days are deadly for me."

"Oh, yeah."

"Me, too."

"Hey, it's the weekend."

The good-natured comments flowed around the deck as Kelly indulged herself in her favorite "comfort" foods. She was considering going back for the wicked biscuits and gravy, when Lisa spoke.

"Jen, I don't see your afghan on the railing with the others that I brought. Did you take it inside already?"

Jennifer glanced over her shoulder. "Not yet. I wonder if it blew off last night."

"Well, it won't go far," Cassie observed as she rose from the table, empty plate in hand. "I'm going back for seconds. Can I get some juice for someone?"

"Yeah, some OJ would be nice." Jane raised her hand.

"Cassie, would you take a look over the side of the deck, please, and see if my afghan fell down there?"

"Sure," Cassie said, strolling to the railing. "It probably just blew—" Cassie's sentence was cut short with a gasp. *"Oh, my God!"*

Kelly stared at Cassie, who was pointing toward the ground below the deck. *What on earth was there?* Maybe a mountain lion's leftover, half-eaten carcass. She rose to see what had concerned Cassie, as did Dr. Norcross.

"He's not moving. Is . . . is he *dead*?"

Kelly raced to the railing and peered over. Cal Everett lay sprawled on the rocky slope below, Jennifer's pale pink afghan draped across his chest.

Dr. Norcross took in a sharp breath beside Kelly. "Oh, my God. We have to call an ambulance."

All the women ran to the railing then and leaned over, staring below. Their shocked exclamations broke the quiet.

"Oh, my God!"

"Damn."

"How awful!"

"Do you think he's still alive?"

"Not likely. Look at him. His eyes are fixed and staring."

"Oh, gross!"

"He had to be drunk."

Dawn shook her head as she continued to stare down the slope. "A yarn-covered corpse."

Cassie shuddered as she turned away. "I can't look anymore."

Kelly slipped her cell phone from her pocket. She'd make the call, even though she could tell it was too late for an ambulance. Cal Everett's death-gray face told her so.

Six

Kelly watched Lieutenant Peterson talking to Dr. Norcross, notepad in hand. She remembered Peterson's careful procedures when he'd investigated another murder in one of the nearby canyons a couple of years ago. Kelly and Jennifer had found the body of an alpaca rancher friend in her beautiful mountain home—murdered. Kelly wondered what the county police detective would say when he saw her. She had involved herself in some of his other investigations since then.

Kelly and her friends stood in the barnyard as Peterson and two uniformed officers interviewed the workshop attendees and ranch staff. One uniformed county policeman was listening to Donny and busily writing in his notepad. Several feet away, another policeman interviewed Marie, who was wiping her nose with tissues. All the women in the workshop had been interviewed by the officers and now stood in quiet clusters talking and watching the police go about their work.

"What an awful way to end a great weekend," Lisa said as she observed the proceedings. "I'll bet he was so drunk he took a header off the deck. I saw him carry a full bottle of liquor to the deck last night while I was searching the slope for more brush to add to the fire."

Kelly pondered. "Well, that would explain why his voice kept getting louder and louder. He was yelling at someone on the phone several times last night."

Kelly glanced at Jennifer, who was strangely quiet. She'd barely said a word since Everett's body was discovered almost two hours ago. "Are you okay, Jen? You still look stunned."

Jennifer kept staring ahead at the police, then answered in a quiet voice. "Yeah. Kind of."

Kelly figured her friend was still trying to process everything that had happened this weekend. First, Jennifer was confronted with the man who sexually assaulted her. Then, she shared her story with a group of total strangers. That was out of character for a private person like Jennifer.

And now she saw the man who assaulted her lying dead on a rocky hillside, his body spread out in a contorted heap with her beautiful knitted afghan across it.

Lisa slipped her arm around Jennifer's shoulders. "I don't know if this brings closure of sorts, Jen. But it does bring some sort of justice. He was a horrible man who met a horrible end. It must be Karma."

"Maybe," Jennifer muttered.

Jane and Sue wandered over to Kelly's cluster. "Well, I guess we can kiss that morning trail ride good-bye," Jane said drily. "Looks like everybody will be packing it in after this."

"I imagine Dr. Norcross will talk to all of us after those detectives are finished," Lisa said.

"How long do you think they'll keep us here?" Sue asked, looking anxious. "I've got to get back to my job. I work the afternoon shift at Family Times restaurant."

"Surely we'll be finished in an hour or so, don't you think, Kelly?" Lisa asked.

Kelly shook her head. "I don't know. Two years ago when Vickie Claymore was killed in Bellevue Canyon, Lieutenant Peterson was in charge of the investigation since it took place in the county. He's really thorough. I expect him to come back and interview some of us after he's talked with his officers."

"Oh, brother," Sue said, clearly unhappy.

Peterson approached his two officers, and they stood apart from everyone else and conferred. Both officers appeared to be reading items from their notepads while Peterson scribbled in his.

Dr. Norcross approached Kelly's cluster. Her pleasant expression was gone, replaced by worry. "This is quite involved. Detective Peterson was really focused in his questions. I must admit I felt 'grilled.' Has he spoken with any of you yet?"

"Not yet," Lisa replied. "But Kelly here has met him before, and she says he's not finished questioning people."

"Oh, dear. I hope it was nothing as traumatic as this event," Dr. Norcross said, looking at Kelly.

Kelly gave her a wan smile. "I'm afraid it was even more so. Both Jennifer and I were in Bellevue Canyon two years ago with a group of visiting knitters, and we walked in and found a weaver friend dead. Her throat cut."

"Whoa, that's ugly," Jane said.

Sue flinched. "Oooo, how gross."

"Yeah, it was," Kelly continued. "Detective Peterson was investigating then, too, and I was really impressed with his thoroughness."

Dr. Norcross glanced at Jennifer. "What's your impression of Detective Peterson, Jennifer?"

"Thorough, just like Kelly said. And he's actually kind of nice. At least he was when he talked to me. Kind of fatherly-like."

Jane snorted. "Never met a cop like that."

"Kelly's had more experience with police detectives than most people," Lisa added with a wry smile. "She's poked her nose into several investigations. We call it sleuthing. And it gets her into trouble sometimes, too."

"I can imagine," Dr. Norcross said, looking at Kelly with a smile.

"This investigation should be short and sweet. It's obvious Everett drank himself into a stupor and fell off his own deck. Finito. The end. Serves him right, I say.

Justice at last." Jane gave a terse nod, features hardened. "I'm just glad I told the bastard off last night when I had the chance."

"What do you mean, Jane?" Dr. Norcross's worry lines reappeared.

"I spotted him on the ranch house porch and told him he was a piece of—"

Kelly had to look away to hide her amused reaction as Jane filled in the rest of the sentence with expletives. Succinct and to the point, that was Jane.

"Ahhhh, did he say anything?" Dr. Norcross asked.

Jane shook her head. "Naw. He just scowled at me and ducked back inside. I figure he knew he was persona non grata around here this weekend."

Kelly noticed Detective Peterson heading their way. She waited until he was closer before greeting him. "Hi, there, Lieutenant Peterson."

Peterson gave her a little smile. "Ms. Flynn. I never expected to see you and Ms. Stroud under these circumstances again." He glanced from Kelly to Jennifer. "This is twice you've shown up at canyon death scenes."

"Just bad luck, I guess," Kelly said.

"I've already interviewed Dr. Norcross about the reason why all of you were gathered here this weekend," Peterson said as he flipped through his trusty notepad. "Why don't I interview you next, Ms. Flynn, and you can provide the local color."

Kelly tried not to smile at the detective's wry comment. "Sure, thing, Detective. By the way, some of the folks here have jobs back in Fort Connor they have to report to this afternoon. Any idea when you will be finished with the investigation?"

Peterson glanced back at the apprehensive faces staring at him. "We'll probably be finished in about an hour." Gesturing to the side, he added, "Why don't we take a little stroll, Ms. Flynn."

Kelly fell into step beside Detective Peterson and waited for him to begin his questions. She noticed the emergency medical crew loading Cal Everett's white-shrouded body into the back of an ambulance.

"Dr. Norcross told me that you and Ms. Stroud were accompanying her graduate student Lisa Gerrard here to help teach knitting and crochet to the workshop attendees, correct?"

"Yes, sir. Lisa has asked us to join her for other mountain retreats where we help with the fiber sessions. They're kind of a relaxing break from the workshop classes."

"Had you ever met the ranch owner, Cal Everett, before this weekend?"

"No, sir," Kelly replied. Suddenly concerned that Peterson might ask Jennifer the same question, Kelly added, "He was a stranger to most of us, I think. According to Lisa, Dr. Norcross makes all the arrangements."

It was a deliberate "fudging" of the facts, Kelly knew, but she was hoping to keep Peterson from stumbling onto Jennifer's past relationship with Everett. There was no need to put Jennifer through any more emotional pain than she'd been through already. Kelly recognized that she was in full-fledged "rescue mode" but didn't care. To Kelly's way of thinking, her friend's well-being took priority.

"Dr. Norcross said Everett was outside on the deck last night the entire time you folks sat around a campfire. Do you recall seeing Everett with anyone else on the deck? A visitor, perhaps? Someone from the workshop maybe?"

"No, sir. He seemed to be talking on the phone most of the time. He did have a visitor in the afternoon, though. And there was a real heated exchange between the two of them. Apparently Everett was late with his loan payments, and the guy came to collect."

"Yes, we've had several reports of that encounter. Someone named 'Bill' apparently."

"Everett's voice kept getting louder and louder last night. Sometimes I heard the word *money* floating out on the breeze. Sounded like he was trying to raise cash in a hurry."

Peterson caught Kelly's eye and smiled. "Putting things together again, Ms. Flynn?"

"Can't help myself, Lieutenant," Kelly admitted with a grin. "And for what it's worth, I think Everett got so drunk that he tripped and fell off his own deck."

"Well, that's certainly one theory."

"Lisa said she saw him bringing out a bottle of liquor to the deck last night. Any signs that he was drinking?" Kelly pressed.

"We're interviewing the ranch staff about that very subject," Peterson said as he flipped his notepad closed and turned to approach the others. "This was the first time any of you had been to this ranch or met Cal Everett?" he asked them.

"Yes, Detective," Dr. Norcross replied as heads nodded behind her.

"You were all seated around the campfire last night. Was Everett alone on the deck the entire time? Did any of you see someone with him? A visitor, perhaps?" he asked as he drew nearer the women, Kelly following behind.

Dr. Norcross and the others all answered.

"He was alone."

"I didn't see anyone."

"All by himself."

Kelly couldn't help adding, "He was on the phone a lot."

"Dr. Norcross, do you recall who was the last person sitting beside the campfire last night?" the detective asked.

Dr. Norcross pondered that question for a moment. "I believe I was, Detective. Greta Baldwin, the other graduate student, and I were the last ones to leave the fire. In fact, it was about nine o'clock when we doused the fire and returned to our cabins."

"Did you see anyone else out and about when you retired for the evening?" Peterson asked, jotting in his notepad again.

"No, sir, I didn't see anyone. You can ask Greta. She's the short brunette with the green sweatshirt standing next to the tall blonde woman, Dawn." Dr. Norcross pointed across the barnyard.

"Thank you, Dr. Norcross. You've been very helpful. And the rest of you as well." Peterson nodded to everyone in the circle around him. "I think you folks will be able to leave pretty soon. One of the officers will let you know, okay?"

"Thanks, Detective Peterson," Kelly called as he walked toward the next cluster of women standing in the barnyard.

"Well, that was painless," Jane said, watching Peterson approach Dawn and Greta. "You must have answered all his questions, Kelly."

"Well, I didn't answer so much as give him my opinions," she confessed.

"Why are we not surprised?" Lisa observed. "What'd you tell him?"

"I said I thought Everett got drunk and fell off the deck. I'm sure I wasn't the first one to say it."

"For sure. I told him the same thing." Jane gave an emphatic nod.

"Well, I did mention Everett's drinking," Dr. Norcross agreed. "I spoke with him before leaving the campfire last night, and he smelled of liquor then. He also had a full glass in his hand, I might add."

"I told the blonde officer that I saw him taking a full bottle out to the deck last night," Lisa added. "I'm sure we're not the only ones who noticed."

"You know, I passed by Donny when the officer was questioning him, and I swear I heard Donny say he found an empty whiskey bottle on the deck this morning," Sue added.

"Told you. He probably sat on the edge of the railing and *whoosh* . . ." Jane made a swan dive motion with her hands.

"Well, ladies, I think we should all start gathering our things so we'll be ready to leave when the police tell us," Dr. Norcross advised.

"Good idea," Lisa said. "Kelly, why don't you and Jen start while I help Dr. Norcross tell the others?"

"Okay, we'll meet out here in the barnyard," Kelly said as she and Jennifer set off toward the lodge.

As they walked in silence together, a stray memory surfaced in Kelly's mind. "By the way, Jen. Did you notice anyone near the deck last night when you were taking your walk? I figured you'd say something if you did."

Jennifer stared at the ground as she walked. "No, I didn't see anyone."

"How long were you out?"

"About an hour . . . I guess," Jennifer mumbled, then hastened ahead of Kelly toward the cabin.

Kelly stared after her friend, glad that they would be leaving soon. Jennifer needed to return home.

Seven

Kelly grabbed her coffee mug and followed Steve to the cottage front door. "Will you be able to join us in Old Town for dinner tonight, or will those meetings run long?"

Steve slipped on his leather jacket. "I'll try. But when you start talking about money, everything takes longer." He hastened through the door and down the steps.

"Tell me about it," Kelly said as she followed after him. "I'll go ahead and order pizza, so show up when you can." She gave him a quick kiss as he paused in front of his big red monster truck.

Steve reached out and grabbed Kelly around the

waist, bringing her next to him. "Hey, I need a better kiss than that. These bankers aren't too friendly right now."

Kelly slid her arms around Steve's neck and gave him a better kiss. Much better. "Good luck," she whispered after their lips parted. "I've got my fingers crossed."

"Keep them crossed," he said as he released her. "It's getting really bad out there. Buyers have gone to ground." He climbed into the truck and slammed the door.

"It'll get better," Kelly said, more hopefully than she felt.

The normally robust Fort Conner housing market was continuing its downward turn. Not a good time to be a builder or developer. New home construction had slowed almost to a standstill. There was still too much inventory on the market, and prices were spiraling lower.

Kelly was grateful Steve had branched out into some "mixed-use" development in the Old Town section of Fort Connor. Mixing retail with rooftops, so to speak. Last year, he'd renovated and remodeled a century-old warehouse and turned it into retail shops below with spacious lofts above. With views of the Cache La Poudre River meandering nearby, his Baker Street lofts had sold quickly in last year's better market. It was also the project closest to Steve's heart. He'd been imagining what could be done with that old warehouse ever since he was a college student.

Steve gave her a wave, and the truck engine rumbled into life as he drove off. Kelly continued across the gravel driveway to Pete's café, located at the rear of the knitting shop. Caffeine beckoned.

"Hey, Julie," she said as she entered the back door. "Fill 'er up, would you, please?"

"Sure thing, Kelly," the college-aged waitress said as she poured a dark stream into Kelly's mug. "Have a seat in my section. Jennifer is slammed. Burt's over here already."

Kelly spotted the gray-haired retired police detective seated near the bay windows, the remnants of a cinnamon roll on a plate before him. "Hey, Burt," she said as she approached. "Got any plans for that last bite of cinnamon roll? We ran out of breakfast stuff this morning, so Steve and I have been running on coffee."

Burt looked up, his lined face spreading with a warm smile. "You kids have got to slow down long enough to go to the grocery store."

"Yeah, I know. It's on my to-do list today." She swiped the morsel of pastry and popped it into her mouth. *Yum.* Brown sugar and cinnamon and butter and lemon cream cheese frosting all came together into a deadly mix of high taste and high calories. *Was there any other kind?*

"I was hoping you'd come by this morning, Kelly. Lisa called Mimi last night and told her what happened at the canyon retreat this weekend. I'm counting on you to provide the details. It sounds like something out of a movie."

Kelly nodded, then took a deep drink of coffee. "It was intense, I'll say that. I mean, we'd barely arrived

Friday when this guy, Cal Everett, saunters out of the barn to talk to everyone. We were all standing around in the barnyard. Jennifer took one look and froze."

"I can imagine. Did she tell you it was him?"

"Yeah, it kind of slipped out, I think. Anyway, Everett didn't see Jen because she ducked down behind Lisa and me. She wanted to head home right that minute. I was going to drive her, but Jen's therapist, Dr. Norcross, started talking to her. They went for a walk while Lisa and I set up the cabin. When they came back after an hour, Jennifer seemed better. Apparently Dr. Norcross told her it was all right to go home if she wanted. Or, she could stay and listen to the workshop sessions. Or . . . she could stay and share with the others in the sessions." Kelly caught Burt's gaze over the coffee cup. "Jennifer chose to stay and share, in case it could help someone else. I was so proud of her, Burt."

Burt sipped his coffee. "That took a lot of guts."

"Yeah, it did." Kelly toyed with the cup rim. "And tell Mimi that Jennifer used the fiber sessions to start talking."

Burt grinned. "You're kidding?"

"Nope. It was a stroke of genius, too. According to Jen and Dr. Norcross, the women weren't opening up in the workshops and talking. But once they got out to the deck where we had yarns spread all over, they loosened up. You know, touching all that soft yarn, they couldn't wait to start knitting and crocheting. After a few minutes, you could see them relax. That's when

Jennifer started sharing. And sure enough, once she did, others opened up as well. We must have spent three hours outside on the deck that Friday afternoon."

His face clouded. "Did that Everett try to say anything to Jennifer during the weekend?"

"No way. He barely showed his face after Dr. Nor-cross chewed him out. She confronted Everett after she and Jen talked outside. Dr. Norcross told him she was aware of what happened with Jennifer and warned Everett she didn't want him anywhere near the women at the workshop. His ranch helpers could handle it. After that, we barely saw him except late at night on the deck where he was drinking and talking on the phone."

Burt stared out the window, a small frown puckering his face. "He must have been drinking a whole heckuva lot to fall off his own deck. I wonder how he managed that."

Kelly shrugged, then drained her coffee. "I dunno, but I remember hearing his voice getting louder and louder late Saturday night when he was out there. Lisa saw him taking a full bottle of liquor to the deck, and apparently the ranch staff found an empty bottle there the next morning. So he must have been totally wasted. The slope beneath the deck is pretty steep and rocky."

"Did Peterson head up the investigation? I figured he would, since it's the county."

Kelly nodded. "He and his men questioned every-one. He even took me aside for the 'local color,' as he called it."

Burt chuckled. "Well, you and he have some history. This is the second time you've found a dead body in the canyon."

"Detective Peterson pointed that out," Kelly said with a smile. "And I kind of did my best to steer him away from questioning Jennifer."

Burt's smile disappeared. His Skeptical Cop expression appeared. "Oh? And how did you manage that, may I ask?"

"Well, I kind of glossed over an answer or two."

Burt's eyebrows shot up. "Can you give me an example of this glossing over?"

"Peterson asked me if I had ever met Everett before, and I was able to say 'no' truthfully. But I wanted to keep him from asking that same question of Jennifer, because then she'd have to admit her . . . well, her earlier encounter. Soooo, I told Peterson that I thought Everett was probably a stranger to everyone at the retreat because Dr. Norcross made all the arrangements." She sneaked a peek at Burt. He was giving her one of those looks he used whenever she "pushed the edges." Something Kelly was inordinately fond of doing.

"Kelly . . ." he chided softly.

"Hey, I said 'probably,' so it wasn't completely false." She held up her hands in a surrender gesture. "But it worked. Peterson asked all of them at the same time if they'd ever met Everett or been to the ranch before this weekend, so it was easier for Jennifer to kind of fade into the background."

Burt didn't scold again, simply shook his head. "I have to admit, I'm not feeling sorry for Everett at all. Sounds like the bastard got what he deserved."

"Yeah, I feel the same way. I know it's not good to speak ill of the dead, but with this scumbag, I say good riddance."

Burt glanced toward the other part of the café, where Jennifer was busy with her customers. "Jennifer seems a little quieter than usual today. That's not surprising, considering what she went through over the weekend."

Kelly watched Jennifer smile and talk with her customers. Outwardly, she appeared her usual self. Only close friends recognized she was more subdued. "Yeah, she was quiet all the way home when we drove back yesterday. And she immediately went to help Pete with some catering job that afternoon. I haven't had a chance to talk with her since we left the ranch."

"I imagine it will take some time. She's still seeing that therapist, right?" Burt asked before upending his cup.

"Yeah. I figure Jen will be talking with her again this week." Kelly drained her coffee. "She'll be okay." Kelly wished she felt as positive as her words.

Burt leaned back in his chair and folded his arms. "I'm just glad she's found someone who can help her. I know what a difference a good counselor can make. People go through rough times in life. Everyone needs a little help sometimes." He gave a crooked smile. "I pulled Jennifer aside back in February right after the assault and gave her a check. I told her I wanted her to schedule as many sessions with that psychologist as she needed, and I wasn't taking 'no' for an answer."

"That was sweet of you, Burt," Kelly said, not admitting she had made Jennifer the very same offer.

"Well, she burst into tears, Kelly," Burt said, shaking his head. "She told me that Dr. Norcross had gotten calls from Curt Stackhouse, Steve, Pete, Lisa, Greg, Megan, and Marty. All saying they would pay her bills anonymously. She was overwhelmed."

Kelly stared into Burt's kind eyes. She had never discussed her own actions with her friends. All of Jennifer's friends had quietly come to her aid at the same time. "Whoa. That's amazing. I did the same thing right after she made her first appointment. I guess all of us did."

"I told Jennifer that was testimony as to how much her friends valued her." Burt smiled. "Of course, that made her cry again, so I didn't say anything else. I just gave her a big hug."

"Sometimes hugs are the best thing you can give someone."

Suddenly a flash of movement behind Burt's shoulder caught Kelly's attention. She peered through the window and glimpsed a familiar face. *Pete*. Pacing outside on the patio along the edge of the fence, away from the café tables, back and forth, exactly like he had done the first two months after Jennifer was assaulted.

"Oh my gosh, Pete's pacing again. He'd finally stopped earlier this month. What happened?"

"I'm afraid it's my fault," Burt admitted. "I drew Pete aside early this morning before Jennifer came in and told him what we'd heard from Lisa. You know, I thought it might help him stop worrying about Jennifer. After all, the man responsible for hurting her is dead." He shook his head ruefully. "Unfortunately, I was dead wrong. This is the second time this morning Pete's been out there, walking back and forth. I wish I hadn't said a thing."

Kelly stared through the window at her friend, the kindhearted, gentle café owner. Pacing back and forth, worrying about Jennifer again. The fact that Pete was in love with Jennifer made it even worse. Everyone knew it, but no one said anything. Jennifer always acted totally oblivious to Pete's adoring looks.

Kelly knew her friend well. Jennifer was far too wise in the ways of male–female relationships to be unaware of Pete's feelings. A few months ago Kelly was all primed to have a "conversation" with Jennifer. But the traumatic events of February had changed everything.

"Don't feel bad, Burt. Pete was bound to hear it from either Lisa or me. You probably did him a favor by telling him early this morning before Jen came in to work." She checked her watch. "I'll go out to talk with him before I tackle my client accounts." Flagging down the waitress, Kelly held out her mug. Julie retrieved it quickly. The café staff was well-attuned to Kelly's caffeine addiction and were faithful suppliers. "Put it on my tab, Julie," she said as she pushed back her chair.

"Tell Pete I'm sorry," Burt said with a sheepish grin as he rose. "I'd tell him myself, but Mimi and I have some shopping to do."

"Stocking up on wools and such?" Kelly asked as she accepted the mug with a nod to Julie.

"Actually, this shopping trip has nothing to do with the shop," he said mysteriously. "See you later, Kelly." He gave a wave before rounding the corner of the café.

Kelly swung her knitting bag over her shoulder, took a deep drink of coffee, and headed for the door, intrigued by Burt's answer.

She heard something different in his voice and wondered what Mimi and Burt were up to. They'd been seeing each other for over a year now. Both had lost their spouses years ago. Mimi was divorced, and Burt's wife died of a heart attack. Both in their late fifties, Mimi and Burt seemed the perfect couple to Kelly and her friends. A wonderful example of love arriving later in life.

Taking another deep drink of coffee, Kelly headed for the café's back door and her anxious friend pacing outside. Sometimes, lovers had a harder time finding each other.

"Ooooh, pesto pizza," Lisa exclaimed. "Put that one in front of me."

"And me," Kelly added as she sipped her favorite Colorado microbrew. The colorful label had a mountain bike leaning against a tree.

"Steve's not here yet, so we can eat his share, can't we, Kelly?" Greg asked, lifting a slice from a tray the waitress set in the middle of the table at the outdoor café.

Kelly glanced around Old Town Plaza, searching for a glimpse of Steve. At six o'clock on a May evening, the sun was still high, moving toward the Summer Solstice, the longest day of the year. "He wasn't sure how long those meetings would take, so go ahead. We'll order another pizza when he comes."

"Is this the meeting with the bankers?" Marty asked before biting into a pepperoni-filled slice.

Kelly nodded as she savored the delicate pesto topping. *Too good.* Taking another sip of ale, she said, "Yeah, this is the 'let's get serious' meeting, where the money guys tell Steve if they're willing to extend the loan on his Wellesley development."

Greg shook his head. "I can't believe all those houses haven't sold yet. That's a nice little subdivision. Great starter homes."

"It's the same for every developer," Marty said, sipping his beer. Collar loosened, tie in his pocket, white shirtsleeves rolled up, Marty didn't resemble the razor-sharp trial lawyer he was during the day. "I've got clients who're having to restructure their company because they can't handle the debt they're carrying on their properties. It's getting bad."

Kelly studied the beer label with a worried frown. "Jennifer says the buyers who are out there are biding their time, waiting for prices of resale houses to drop even more. And sellers are slashing their prices in response. So, builders have had to do the same with new homes. It's really scary out there. I've never seen Steve so worried. And Jennifer is scrambling for clients."

"Speaking of Jennifer, let's hope this weekend will be a turning point for her," Lisa said, leaning her arms on the metal table.

Greg held out his bottle. "To Jennifer. A fresh start. God knows she deserves it."

Kelly clinked her bottle with her friends around the table as they all toasted a new beginning for Jennifer. The past was buried, or soon would be.

Megan ran her hand through her raven black hair as she sank back into the wrought iron chair. "Well, I have to be honest. I'm glad that guy's dead. I know it sounds awful, but maybe knowing that the guy isn't going to suddenly show up again will help Jen recover."

"Sounds like he already did last weekend," Marty said, reaching for a piece of pesto pizza. "Man, Jennifer must have totally freaked."

"Just about," Kelly said after taking another bite of pizza. "She didn't know the guy's real name until then."

"To Karma," Lisa said, holding up her nearly empty bottle. "He got what he deserved in my book."

"I still wish Steve and I could have beaten him up first," Greg added.

"What are we toasting?" Steve's voice came from behind Kelly as she and her friends clinked bottles once more.

"Karma."

"A bad end to bad guys."

"Burying the past."

"New beginnings."

"Gotcha," Steve said as he pulled out the waiting chair beside Kelly, a bottle of his favorite ale already in hand. "To Jennifer and a fresh start. Bless her heart." He upended his bottle.

Kelly handed him a slice of pepperoni pizza. "On a scale of one to ten, how was it? The meeting, I mean?"

Steve sank back in his chair and took another deep pull of his beer before answering. "On a scale of one to ten? About a two." He devoured the pizza slice.

"Ouch," Kelly said with a grimace. She reached out and placed her hand on his arm. "You mean they won't extend the loan?"

"Nope. But they did agree to restructure it, so the payments are reduced." Steve dangled the bottle by the neck over the edge of the chair.

"Hey, that sounds good," Lisa offered.

"For a price," Steve said, his face clouding. "I had to put up the Baker Street lofts as collateral."

Kelly drew back. "Oh, no, Steve . . . not Baker Street."

Steve's pet project. The one development closest to his heart. He'd just paid off the construction loan last year when all the units were sold. Now, there would be a lien against the property, and if the housing market didn't improve . . . Kelly didn't want to think about that scenario.

"Damn, Steve, I'm sorry," Greg said, clearly concerned.

"That one's your baby," Megan commiserated.

"It's only a lien, Steve. You can get it removed as soon as this cycle is over," Marty offered.

"Yeah, remember what Jennifer always says. Markets go up, and markets go down. It's a cycle," Kelly added, wanting to find something encouraging to say. "This is just a phase. The down part of the cycle. It'll start back up."

Steve gave her a crooked smile. "Let's hope it's soon, guys. Real soon. I've slashed prices on those Wellesley sites down to the bone. Profit margin is a memory. Hell, I'm thinking of renting them out just to help cover the loan payments."

Greg looked up. "Really? For how much?"

Steve shrugged. "Ohhhh, probably twelve hundred dollars a month. Definitely below market." He drained his beer.

Greg and Lisa exchanged glances. "You're kidding," they chimed together.

"The condo management just raised everyone's rent," Lisa said. "We'd be paying nearly twelve hundred for our three-bedroom condo near Old Town."

"How big are those Wellesley homes? Three bedrooms or four?" Greg probed.

"Both," Steve said, swinging the empty beer bottle by its neck. "Three bedrooms run around sixteen hundred square feet. Are you guys serious?"

Greg and Lisa grinned and spoke together again. "Absolutely."

Steve sank his chin in his hand and looked at his friends. "Guys, there are some strings attached. You'd have to be willing to let real estate agents schedule showings, so people would be coming through. We're still trying to sell those houses. That would be a bother for sure."

Greg shrugged. "That's okay. If Lisa and I are enjoying ourselves in the bedroom, we'll simply put a DO NOT DISTURB sign on the door."

Lisa swatted him. "Believe me, I can put up with some visitors in order to have a real house at last. It's taking us forever to save up a down payment."

"Yeah, and when we do, you'll be building it," Greg said, saluting Steve before he upended his beer.

"Well, you'll have time to save, guys. This downturn isn't over yet, I'm afraid."

Marty grinned from behind another piece of pizza. "Hey, Harry About-to-Be-Homeowner. When are you gonna invite us over for barbeque? Do you guys have a grill?"

Lisa's eyes lit up. "Whoa! That's right. We'll have a yard at last. Wow! No more grilling on the balcony."

"And all the yards are landscaped, too," Kelly added, bragging. "Steve's had grass and trees and bushes put in. And fences, too."

"Man, that is a deal," Megan said, taking a bite of pesto pizza.

"Yeah, it is." Greg nodded, toying with his empty bottle. "Whoa, grass means a lawnmower. Are those sales still on?"

Steve waved his hand. "Save your money. Since we're still trying to sell these houses, my yard crew will keep mowing."

"Wow! You guys are making out like bandits," Marty said, signalling the waiter. "Makes me wanta take a look over there. When can you have us over, Greg?"

Kelly joined in the laughter that flowed around the outside table while the waiter brought another round. Friends helping each other. That felt good. She ran her hand over Steve's arm and leaned closer. "Do you think you should ask for references?"

Eight

Kelly shouldered her way through the Lambspun front door, balancing her laptop computer, briefcase, and full coffee mug. It was a beautiful spring morning, and she didn't feel like working inside the cottage. Outside beckoned. Lambspun had a secluded side patio which would be the perfect place to settle into and work. But first, there was always time to indulge an attack of fiber fever. She could catch up on accounts while surrounded by spring yarns.

She paused in the central yarn room and indulged herself. *Touch, touch.* A bin of bamboo and silk beckoned first, shades of green from chartreuse to lime to shamrock. Next, a bin of hand-dyed merino wool and silk, all shades from Veracruz Vermilion to Santa Fe

Sunset. Soft and softer. Then, the crisp feel of silk ribbons enticed her fingers, all tied in bundles of blues and greens.

Kelly left the bins and plopped her laptop, mug, and briefcase onto the library knitting table.

"Well, good morning, Kelly," Mimi sang out as she walked through the room. "It's good to see you in the shop early."

"It's so pretty, I thought I might start working in here then move outside to that side patio under the arbor. It's one of those luscious spring days. The birds are singing, and I can't stay inside."

Mimi turned to her with a bright smile. "You work wherever you like, Kelly. In fact, I may bring one of my knitting classes outside if there's room at some of Pete's patio tables."

"I haven't looked yet. Is Pete still pacing on the patio?"

Mimi's smile disappeared. "Yes, I'm afraid he is. Poor dear. He says the pacing helps calm him down. Every time he starts worrying about Jennifer, he just can't stop. So, he goes outside." Mimi shook her head, looking for all the world like a Mother Hen worrying about one of her chicks.

Kelly nodded. "I told him that the retreat really had been good for Jennifer. She made some great strides there. But of course, he doesn't believe me, because he wasn't there to see it. Cal Everett's death overshadows everything. You can tell how Pete is thinking."

"I worry about him, though. He confessed to me last

year that he's got borderline high blood pressure, and all this worrying is not doing him any good," Mimi said as she rearranged fluff balls in a nearby yarn bin.

"Well, things should settle down soon," Kelly said, wishing she was as confident as she sounded. Jennifer was still deep into quiet. Kelly decided she had to find a few minutes today to talk with her friend.

Burt appeared around the corner then. "Mimi, that supplier from North Carolina is on the line. Do you want to take her call now or later?"

"Right now. I've been trying to get her for weeks." Mimi sped from the room.

"Busy, busy," Kelly teased as she settled into a chair and opened her laptop. Remembering something, she asked, "Hey, how was your shopping trip yesterday? What did you guys buy?"

Burt's curious little smile returned. "You'll have to go up front and ask Mimi. She'll show you. But right now, I thought I'd let you in on what I heard this morning." He pulled out the chair beside Kelly.

"What's up?"

"I called my buddy, Vern, with the county police and asked how Peterson's investigation into Cal Everett's death was going. I was curious if the cause of death was determined to be accidental due to Everett breaking his neck when he fell off the deck."

Kelly felt a little buzz somewhere inside. Her warning buzzer. "What'd Vern say? It was accidental, right?"

Burt nodded. "Yep, that's the official cause of death,

but he said that Peterson is extending the investigation at the request of the medical examiner."

"Why?"

"Apparently the medical examiner wants to look more carefully at how Everett fell. He told Peterson that in his opinion, Everett fell over the deck, straight down, headfirst. The examiner thought that was a little strange. He said if Everett was sitting on his deck railing, drinking, and fell over, he'd probably fall sideways. If he was so drunk he tried to kill himself, he probably would have climbed over the railing and jumped, falling face-first onto the slope below."

Kelly screwed up her face. "What? That sounds like a whole lot of conjecture to me, Burt. What do you think?"

Burt shrugged. "I don't know, Kelly. I confess I thought it was a lot of speculating, too. I mean, people's bodies turn and twist when they fall. But my friend said the examiner's real concern was that maybe Cal Everett was standing at the railing looking out and someone pushed him from behind. He thinks that would explain why Everett flipped over the railing and fell headfirst."

A cold chill ran up Kelly's spine. Was that possible? Did someone "help" Cal Everett over the railing? *Who would do that?*

Remembered images from the weekend retreat swirled through her head now. Jennifer confessing to the women on the deck that Friday afternoon, and Dr. Norcross revealing Cal's identity. The explosive angry outbursts that followed. Jane's angry threats to "beat the snot out of him." Dawn's repeated desire for Everett "to be held accountable." Edie saying he should "pay for what he'd done."

Faces came into focus along with angry voices and threats. Dr. Norcross telling how she'd confronted Everett earlier that day. Jane saying how she'd "called" him out.

Then another face appeared. The angry neighboring rancher named Bill, accusing Cal Everett of defaulting on his loan as he stormed away. Bill's departing threatening words: "I'm coming back, and we'll settle this once and for all!"

Was that who Cal was yelling at over the phone? Did Bill make a quiet late night visit to Everett's ranch? Did he lose patience with Cal's cheating ways and shove him in anger? Or, did Bill wait until Everett's back was turned to push him over the railing?

That scenario vibrated in Kelly's head, albeit because she'd witnessed the angry exchange between the two men earlier that day. Still . . . Rancher Bill seemed to have built up a considerable load of resentment against Cal Everett. Was it enough to push Bill over the edge . . . and Everett over the rail?

If, indeed, this was not an accidental death, then Rancher Bill looked to be the prime suspect to Kelly. After all, he had a reason to be angry at Everett, and he'd already threatened him. It had to be Rancher Bill, she decided. After all, who else had reason to kill Cal Everett? There was no one else there who had reason to—

Kelly's racing thoughts—and their conclusions—came to a screeching halt. Another face appeared before her eyes. A familiar face. Jennifer had reason to hate Cal Everett. More reason than Rancher Bill. And Jennifer took a walk alone that night before coming to bed. No one was with her.

A cold feeling settled in Kelly's gut. *No. Impossible.* Jennifer couldn't kill anyone. She knew her. But . . . this entire weekend was one huge emotional roller coaster for Jen. What if she momentarily lost her balance? What if she saw Cal Everett standing on the deck, drunk and oblivious? What if she walked up behind him and . . . pushed Everett? Just pushed him over the railing. Thinking he'd fall and hurt himself. Jennifer had acted stunned ever since Everett's body was discovered. Had she done anything? Was . . .

Kelly snapped out of the twisted scene scripting before her eyes like some bad soap opera. *That was impossible.* Jennifer couldn't hurt anyone. Even Cal Everett.

"Kelly? Are you okay? You kind of drifted away for a moment," Burt said.

"Sorry, Burt . . . I . . . I was lost in thought, I guess."

"Do you remember seeing Everett have an argument with some visitor named Bill? Apparently this Bill held a loan on Everett's property and Everett had been missing payments. According to Peterson, several women at the retreat witnessed this Bill threatening Cal Everett. Saying something like 'I'll be back and—' "

" 'We'll settle this once and for all,' " Kelly supplied.

"Then you witnessed it, too. How mad was this guy Bill?"

"He was really hot. Sounded like Everett had been jerking him around for months by not paying the loan, and the guy was threatening to put a lien on Everett's property."

Burt's eyebrows shot up. "Hmmmm, that's interesting. Money makes people do crazy things." He looked to the side. "How many people saw this argument?"

"Almost everyone at the retreat. We'd just left a fiber session on the deck and were going to our cabins before dinner. Cal Everett's truck roared up into the barnyard, spitting gravel, and this guy was right behind. We all stood there watching. It really got our attention, for sure."

"Well, I'm sure Peterson's gotten plenty of reports about this guy and is probably following up on them right now. So, I'll tell my friend to keep me posted." He rose from his chair. Giving Kelly a smile, he said, "I could tell your antennae were buzzing a few minutes ago, am I right, Sherlock?"

Kelly had to grin. "Yeah, you're right. I started sorting through faces at the retreat, wondering who might be responsible. Some of those women got almost as hot as Rancher Bill after hearing Jennifer's story."

Burt nodded. "Interesting. Well, it still sounds like this Bill guy is the most likely to have a serious grudge against Everett."

"That's what I think. Make sure you keep me in

the loop, Burt," Kelly said as she opened her laptop computer.

"Will do. I've gotta go finish those errands," he said as he walked away, then added, "Don't forget to check with Mimi up front."

"Check on what?" Kelly called over her shoulder, but Burt was gone. She clicked on her document icon and watched the list of client folders come into view, then paused before opening one.

Maybe she'd better go up front and see what Mimi and Burt bought the other day. After all, Burt kept hinting at something. If it was not for the shop, what could it be?

Kelly grabbed her ever-present mug and headed for the front room, where the customers and cash registers came together. Trailing her fingers through the yarn bins on the way to the front, she spotted Rosa, one of the shop clerks. Rosa was winding a skein of yarn into an easier-to-use ball for a customer. Kelly walked down the two steps into what used to be the family room of Uncle Jim and Aunt Helen's farmhouse. That was years ago, when the pastures held sheep instead of golfers.

Lots of childhood memories were captured in this room. Uncle Jim always put up a tall Christmas tree in front of the double bay windows. Kelly remembered sitting on the ledge of the Spanish tile fireplace in the corner, opening presents, laughing with her father and Helen and Jim. Kelly's father, Jack Flynn, had grown up in Fort Connor along with his sister, Helen. Their parents had owned and worked a sugar beet farm, back in the days when sugar beets were a commercial mainstay for northern Colorado farmers. Unfortunately, their farm wasn't very big and couldn't survive when the sugar beet business began to slide. Jack Flynn had gone to the local state university and majored in business, striving to provide a successful life for himself and his daughter. Kelly's mother, Alicia, had left them when Kelly was still a baby.

The past slipped away as Kelly deliberately focused on the family room as it looked now, an integral part of the knitting shop. Two bags of dyed fibers, waiting to be spun into yarn, sat beside the fireplace. Mimi and Burt couldn't keep up with the spinning that needed to be done, so hired spinners were necessary to keep Lambspun stocked with yarns. The wooden table had winding spools on each corner. Behind the high wooden counter Mimi and the other shop clerk, Connie, took care of customers.

On the walls surrounding them was a forest of knitting, spinning, weaving, and crocheting accessories. Needles, hooks, buttons, jewelry, and other assorted items packed shelves and were stacked on tables. The upper walls were covered by hanging garments, from woven shawls and stoles to sweaters and felted purses. Felting was one of Mimi's favorite art forms.

Kelly scrutinized everything, and saw all sorts of new items. But they were all shop-related. She scanned the shop again slowly, checking to make sure she hadn't overlooked something. If this new item wasn't for the shop, why would Burt tell her to come to the front room to see it?

Giving up, Kelly approached Rosa, who was still winding a variegated green merino wool yarn into a big ball. "Okay, Rosa, I give up. Burt told me to come up front and see what he and Mimi bought on their shopping trip the other day. But I've looked all over the room twice, and I can't figure out what it is. Burt said it wasn't anything for the shop. Can you give me a hint, please?"

Rosa looked up at Kelly with a devilish grin. "You're not looking in the right place. Go over closer to Mimi. Stand beside her, and you'll see it."

"Okaaaay," Kelly said, ambling over to the counter. Mimi was finishing up with a customer. Kelly inched closer to the back of the counter. Sipping her coffee, she scanned the shelves behind the counter and saw them filled with the usual office items—sales slips, pens, shopping bags, and file boxes. Kelly waited until Mimi had handed the customer her purchase before slipping beside her.

"Well, hi, Kelly," Mimi said. "Are you looking for something?"

"Uhhhh, actually I am. But I don't know what it is."

Rosa giggled from the winding table. Connie glanced over from the end of the counter where she was rearranging some custom-designed pins. "That's going to make it kind of hard to find, Kelly," Connie said.

Mimi leaned on the side of the counter. "Are you starting a new project?"

"Actually, I'm going to continue with the knitted

vest pattern that you showed me. So far, so good. I probably need to do another washcloth before attempting a crochet project."

"Are you looking for a different yarn or something?" Mimi continued to probe.

Kelly exhaled a sigh. "I'm looking for the mystery item that you and Burt bought the other day. I asked him what it was, but he wouldn't answer. He said it wasn't for the shop. Then he told me to come up front, and you'd show me." She drained her mug and placed it on the counter. "I gotta tell you, Mimi, I've looked all over this room twice, and all I see is shop stuff. Beautiful shop stuff, of course, but no mystery items in sight. Burt said I would see it, and I don't."

Mimi's eyes danced. "Oh, did he now?" Her smile spread. Connie was grinning at Kelly from the corner.

"What's so funny?" Kelly asked. "Is Burt playing a joke on me or something?"

Mimi leaned on the counter and rested her chin on her hand. Her left hand. "There's no joke, Kelly. Actually it's something really beautiful."

Kelly frowned and glanced around the room again. "Then where *is* it? Would somebody please tell me?"

Connie guffawed. "Oh, Kelly, it's right in front of your eyes."

Kelly frowned, thoroughly annoyed now. "*Where?* I don't see anything different!"

Rosa walked over to the counter, the wound green yarn ball in hand. "You'd better show her, Mimi, before she explodes."

Mimi extended her left hand and wiggled her fingers. Kelly stared and for the first time saw the diamond ring that now graced Mimi's hand. A lovely solitaire surrounded by diamond clusters on each side. Kelly's eyes popped wide.

"Oh my gosh! It's . . . it's beautiful, Mimi," she exclaimed. "I can't believe I didn't see it right away."

"Thank you, Kelly. Burt and I both loved the ring the moment we saw it."

Kelly's smile claimed her face. "Oh, Mimi, I'm so happy," she said as she enfolded Mimi in a big hug. "You and Burt belong together."

Mimi squeezed Kelly tightly before releasing her. "Well, both Burt and I are kind of old school, so we thought it was time we made it official, so to speak."

Kelly chuckled at Mimi's description of her relationship with Burt. With the exception of Jennifer, Kelly and her friends were each living with their boyfriends in intimate relationships. No rings in sight. Mimi and Burt were definitely following tradition.

"Usually a ring means you're officially engaged," Kelly teased. "Does that mean there's a wedding in the future?"

"Sometime." Mimi smiled slyly as a customer approached the counter.

Kelly backed away from the counter so Mimi and staff could take care of business. She retrieved her mug and headed for the back hallway which led to the café. Client accounts required caffeine. She noticed Jennifer, knitting bag over her shoulder, coming from the other direction. Kelly decided now would be a perfect time for a quiet chat.

"Hey, Jen, let me get a fill-up, and I'll join you on your break," she said.

Jennifer gave her a smile, which Kelly took as a good sign. "Let me get that for you, Kelly. Julie's busy in the other section." She took Kelly's mug and sped to the coffee counter, returning in less than a minute with a full mug.

"Wow, you're fast. I always forget how fast you can move around this café. Too bad you can't do it on the ball field," Kelly teased.

This time Jennifer smiled wider. "Yeah, I remember when you guys were trying to recruit me for spring training. Like that would ever happen."

Kelly laughed softly, then sipped from the mug as they headed toward the shop again. Now, *that* sounded like the old Jennifer. She was coming back slowly, Kelly could tell.

Jennifer plopped her knitting bag beside Kelly's laptop and pulled out a chair. "Pete's pacing outside again," she said quietly, shaking her head. "He'd stopped last month. But now, after he heard about last weekend, he's started up again." She sank into her chair and poured a cup of tea from Mimi's floral teapot in the middle of the knitting table. "I wish he wouldn't do that."

Kelly hesitated, then decided to plunge into this conversation in her usual fashion. "He worries about you, Jen. He told me that was his way of handling it."

Jennifer caught Kelly's gaze. "Did he really say that?"

"Yep." Kelly nodded.

Exhaling a sigh, Jennifer sipped her tea. "It makes me feel guilty whenever I see him out there. He worries me."

Kelly paused. Pete was worrying about Jennifer, and Jennifer was worrying about Pete worrying about her. There had to be some way to sort through this.

"Pete can't help it, Jen. He cares about you."

Jennifer closed her eyes. "I know, I know."

Kelly hesitated, toying with bringing up the subject she'd been dying to broach with Jennifer for the last year—Pete's feelings for her.

"Pete more than cares for you, Jennifer. He—"

Jennifer's hand flew up in "stop" mode. "Don't say it, Kelly," she said, her voice sharp.

"Say what?" Kelly dodged.

"You know what. The *L* word."

"Why?"

Jennifer leaned back into her chair. "Don't go there, Kelly."

"Why?"

"Because I don't want to talk about it, that's why."

"Why?"

"Jeez, Kelly! Lisa's right. You really *are* a Rottweiler."

Kelly grinned and relaxed into her chair. Humor was

always helpful. It made people relax. "Hey, I live with one. It rubs off."

Jennifer sipped her tea. "I swear, when you're focused on something you're like a dog with a bone. You don't leave it alone."

"It's called tenacity, and I've been told it's an admirable character trait."

"Ha!"

"Spoken by the Queen of Evasion."

Jennifer shot her a look. "I beg your pardon."

"Beg it all you want, Jen, but I've watched you ignore, avoid, and pretend not to notice Pete's obvious affections for you for over a year now. There's no way someone as savvy as you could miss those looks he throws your way, especially when he thinks no one else is watching. Heck, a blind man could see it with a cane, as Aunt Helen would say."

Jennifer's mouth quirked into a smile. "It's been a long time since I heard that expression. Probably since Helen used it."

"You couldn't help noticing how Pete feels about you, Jen. Why are you ignoring him?" She leaned forward over the table between them. "Give me a straight answer, and I swear I'll never ask you again."

Staring out into the yarn room, Jennifer held her teacup to her chest. "A straight answer? Okay. I've only had one rule that I follow when it comes to men I get involved with. Or, rather, used to get involved with." She paused, and took a sip of tea. "And that rule is never date someone from your workplace. No exceptions. Period. I may have pretty lax standards in all other areas, but I pride myself that I've followed that rule ever since I left college years ago."

Kelly stared at her friend, totally surprised by her answer. "You're kidding."

"No, I'm not. Workplace romances are nothing but trouble, and they always end badly. And . . . and I don't want to do anything that would ruin our friendship. Sex changes everything."

Kelly blinked, not sure she'd heard correctly. "Wait a minute, I want to make sure I understand you. You don't want to get into a serious relationship with Pete even though he *cares* for you deeply and even though he might be the *perfect* guy for you and even though *you* care for him deeply, and all because you're afraid sex will screw up everything. Is that right?"

"Pretty much."

"Jeez, Jen . . . do you realize how crazy that sounds? Pete is a fantastic guy, and you've known him for years. I can't believe you'd rather go out with those salsa-dancing sleazeballs than date a wonderful guy like Pete, just because you work with him."

A real grin spread on Jennifer's face. "Salsa-dancing sleazeballs, huh? That's pretty good. I've gotta remember that."

Kelly leaned back in her chair and took a deep drink of her coffee. Another thought had wiggled forward. *Maybe in Jennifer's book the strangers were safer. No commitment necessary. Pete was actually more danger-*

ous. A man like Pete was someone you could build a life with.

"I don't buy it," Kelly said at last.

Jennifer shot her an inquisitive look. "Buy what?"

"Your answer. I think there's something a lot deeper going on there, Jen. You're not being completely honest with yourself." She paused. "Have you ever talked about this with Dr. Norcross?"

Jennifer gazed into Kelly's eyes. "You can stop digging, Sherlock. Dr. Norcross and I are working at the edges of it right now."

Kelly felt a smile start inside. "Okay. I'll put my shovel away." Taking another sip, she switched directions. "By the way, have you seen the rock on Mimi's hand?"

Nine

Kelly polished off the last bite of huevos rancheros and chased it with Eduardo's coffee. Glancing through the café window beside her, she watched the dark thunderheads forming over the mountains, heading their way. Thunderstorms this early in the morning usually meant it would be raining all day and maybe into the evening. One never knew. *Capricious* was the word for Colorado weather.

"Hungry, were you?" Jennifer teased as she refilled Kelly's cup.

"Oh, yeah. Would you fill up my mug, please?" She pulled the mug from her bag. "Those clouds look like it'll be raining all day."

Jennifer stared out the window. "Yeah, Pete's had a

cancellation already. We were scheduled for an outdoor event tonight, but the woman just called and switched to the rain date tomorrow night."

"Hey, that means you'll be free to join all of us for pizza and beer." Kelly watched the stream of black nectar fill her mug. "You've missed the last two Friday nights because you've been working so many catering jobs."

"Have to. Real estate has slowed down to a crawl. Clients are just sitting and waiting. They search the listings and call and ask questions, but they don't even want to go out and look." She shook her head. "I tell you, the increase in Pete's business came at just the right time for me. It's steadier income."

"That's for sure. People will always eat," Kelly said with a laugh as she rose from the table, her bag over her shoulder. "We're gathering at our place right after work. So bring some chips until the pizza's delivered."

"Better put Carl outside. We'll be cheek by jowl in that cottage. You guys should think about moving into one of Steve's houses."

"That's a thought." Her cell phone jangled then, and Kelly dug into her jeans pocket. Lisa's voice came on the line.

"Hey, Kelly, I wanted to tell you that Greg and I won't be able to make it to your place tonight. We're up to our necks with boxes and want to do a final push at packing so we can start moving into the house tomorrow."

"Wow, you two have really been working. You only started packing a few days ago."

"After Steve took us to the subdivision to pick out a house, Greg and I couldn't wait to get there. We went to the box store that night and started packing."

"Would you like us to help?" Kelly offered, saluting the grill cook, Eduardo, with her mug as she walked through the café. He replied with his friendly smile. "Hey, why don't we have the pizza delivered to your condo? We'll gather over there and help you guys."

"Are you sure? That would be great. I'll tell Greg to buy the beer. We'd be guaranteed to finish by tonight."

"I'll spread the word. Looks like Jen's gonna be free because Pete's catering job was canceled by rain. Hey, I'll ask Pete, too. He needs to get out more."

"I'm not sure this will be Pete's idea of relaxing away from work, but we can use all the hands we can get."

"Okay, I'll have the pizza delivered to your place. See you tonight." Kelly clicked off and headed toward the kitchen area. Both Pete and Jennifer were working behind the counter. "Hey, guys, I just heard from Lisa, and she and Greg are really swamped packing boxes for their move. So I thought we'd all go over tonight and help them out. We're ordering pizza and beer, and I figured both of you could come since your catering gig got postponed."

"Sure," Jennifer agreed. "I'll go over right after I've checked the office. That won't take long, because nothing's happening. Unfortunately."

Pete glanced toward the kitchen. "I'd like to, Kelly, but maybe I should stay here and get some things prepared. You know, work ahead."

Kelly gave him an indulgent smile. "Pete, if I know you, you've already worked ahead. You need a break. Now, I know that packing boxes sounds like work, but it'll be a lot of fun with all of us. Plus, you don't have to cook."

Jennifer gave Kelly a "I-know-what-you're-up-to" glance, then added, "She's right, Pete. Everything's ready for tomorrow night. You can relax."

Pete's ingratiating grin spread, and he swept that errant lock of blonde hair off his forehead. "Okay, I'm in."

"Would you grab another slice of pizza when you bring the boxes?" Steve called to Kelly as she wove her way around the already-packed boxes that filled Lisa and Greg's living room.

"Will do," she said as she maneuvered past Jennifer in the small, cramped kitchen. "Whoa, you've cleared practically all the cabinets, Jen. Fantastic." Kelly grabbed some pizza and napkins and loaded two more flattened boxes under her arm.

"Kitchen duty is slow, but you simply can't throw all these spices and small stuff into a box."

"Why not?" Marty asked from across the living room where he was packing books from the two tall bookcases along the wall.

Megan tossed a roll of packing tape his way. "Now you know why I don't let you in the kitchen." She returned to loading compact discs and DVDs into a box.

"Remind me never to let Marty downstairs with the fridge and freezers. Too much temptation," Pete added with a grin as he packed silverware in towels and linen napkins.

"Got that right," Jennifer called from the kitchen.

Greg wrapped newspaper around dinner plates before loading them into a box. "Maybe we should put one of those electronic collars on Marty. That way we can zap him when he tries to open a fridge."

"I think we need two collars," Megan said, clearing another shelf. "One for you, too."

"Comin' through," Kelly said as she made her way back to the hallway where Steve was almost finished with a storage closet. The linen closet was hers. She handed Steve his pizza, then sank her teeth into a double-cheesy slice. "Ummmm, I love cheese." She glanced over her shoulder. "Where's my ale?"

"I drank it," Steve said before devouring his pizza slice.

"Man, I can't trust you."

"Helped get me through the closet," he said, folding the next box into shape.

"Greg, could you hand me another Fat Tire, pretty please?" she called down the hall.

"Coming up," Greg said, flipping the cap off the dark brown bottle then handing it to Pete who handed it to Megan who walked it down the hall to Kelly.

"Thank the assembly line," Megan said as she handed it over.

Kelly upended the bottle and let the tasty microbrew slide down her throat. *Okaaaay*. "Thanks, guys," she called out.

"It looks like the storm has let up," Lisa said, carrying two large garment bags from the bedroom.

"Finished loading the clothes already?" Greg asked.

"Yep. Everybody's working at fever pitch, and we're almost finished." Lisa laid the garment bags on the edge of the sofa. "Boy, we don't have any more room to stack boxes and stuff. We can barely get around each other now."

"I've got an idea," Marty said as he cleared the last bookshelf. "Why don't we start taking stuff over now while the rain's let up? It'll clear space here, plus save time tomorrow."

"Inspired suggestion," Steve said. "Let's do it. I've got my truck, and Greg's got his SUV. If everyone loads up, we can probably get most of this over to the house tonight. That'll leave the furniture for tomorrow."

"Then we can come back and finish the pizza and watch the latest DVD I got last week." Greg glanced up. "Unless Megan's packed it."

"Too late," Megan said as she taped the box shut. "All done."

"Not to worry, I've got some DVDs in my car," Jennifer offered.

"Okay, sounds like a plan," Marty said. "I'll bet we can be finished packing in ten minutes."

"Five bucks says fifteen," Greg countered.

"You're on." Marty's smile spread.

"Quick, before it pours!" Kelly yelled to Steve, Greg, and Marty as they hastened across the new green lawn.

A huge crack of thunder shook the sky, causing shrieks and laughter from the rest of her friends who had already reached the safety of the garage. The sky lit up with jagged forks of lightning. Rocky Mountain thunderstorm.

Steve and Greg sped into the open garage just as the heavens opened up. A deluge of rain poured down. "Boy, that was close," Greg cried, raindrops dripping down his face.

"Close, my butt, you're both soaked," Kelly said, running her hand over Steve's hair.

"Hey, is it raining in here?" he joked as droplets fell into his eyes. "I'd better check the roof."

"To heck with the roof, let's get this stuff inside," Marty said, heading toward the door that lead into the house.

"Wait a minute." Megan held up her hand. Everyone else had picked up their boxes again and clustered after Marty. "Where does this door lead?"

"The laundry room, why?" Lisa said.

"Good. We can all take off our shoes so we won't track mud and yuck all over the new carpets," Megan said, stepping to the doorway. "Who's got the box of towels? We can use those to dry off Steve and Greg."

"Better do as Megan says. She's got her fierce face on," Kelly said, shifting the load in her arms. Setting the box on the concrete floor, Kelly slipped out her Swiss Army knife and slit the tape then pulled out two fluffy towels.

"Man, I ought to hire you to supervise the showings, Megan," Steve said as he accepted a towel.

Lisa and Megan held the door wide as the crew trooped into the house and complied with Megan's orders. After removing shoes they wandered barefoot into the empty house, exclaiming as they explored each room.

"Wow, Steve, this is so pretty," Megan said, glancing up at the vaulted ceiling of the spacious great room.

"Cool kitchen," Pete observed, setting his box on the counter. "Gorgeous granite. Boy, I'm impressed."

Jennifer set her box on the tiled foyer floor. "Notice the details . . . the decorative tiles over the fireplace, glass-top range, brushed stainless appliances," she said in a singsong real estate agent cadence as she gestured around the great room and kitchen.

"Jennifer's shown several of these houses, bless her," Kelly said, setting her box beside Steve's on the foyer floor.

"And sold a couple before the slowdown got bad." Jennifer glanced around. "These are great, Steve. You've really put in good stuff here."

"Thanks, Jen. The guys and I are proud of them."

Marty strolled through the foyer, glancing into the adjacent dining room with bay window that led into the kitchen. "Beveled glass, cool tile. Like the carpet, too. Really nice, man."

"Uh, guys . . ." Lisa said. "We've got a slight problem. Since we haven't brought the furniture over, we can't unpack the boxes yet. There's no place to put this stuff. Except the garment bags, which we can hang in the bedroom closet."

"Ooooops."

"So much for the brilliant idea."

"Oh, the rain'll let up in a few minutes, I bet," Megan said, glancing toward the great room wall that was lined with windows.

Another sharp crack of thunder made everyone jump with nervous laughter.

"Then, again, maybe not," Kelly said.

"We can pass the time by trying out their master bath," Marty suggested with a devilish grin. "There's a cool Jacuzzi tub. And we've got a box of towels."

"Dude, no way you're getting in my tub."

"Why don't we relax and wait till the storm lets up," Jennifer said, settling on the great room floor, cross-legged.

"Is there a pack of cards in one of those boxes?" Greg asked, plopping onto the carpet.

"No cards, but I think this is the box with board games." Steve slipped out his pocketknife and opened the box he brought to the foyer. "Yep. There's Speedy Trivia, Monopoly, and Battleship."

"The Speedy Trivia is mine," Lisa said, slipping to the carpet beside Greg. "I forgot I still had it."

"Hey, I love that game," Marty said, sinking to the floor. "I used to play it in college. Late night sessions instead of studying."

"You weren't out chasing girls?" Kelly teased as she joined the semicircle that was forming on the floor.

Marty grinned. "No, the only things I chased in college were tennis balls. Had to keep my grades up to keep the scholarship."

"I can relate to that," Steve said as he sat on the floor beside Kelly and placed the board game in the middle of the circle. "I had to do the same to keep the baseball scholarship."

Lisa opened the box and scanned the directions. "Okay, it's coming back to me. There's a different category of questions each round, and everybody starts with a hundred points. Then one person at a time reads the question and works the timer." She pulled out a small gadget. "The reader winds up this buzzer thing, and everyone has about ten seconds to answer. The first person with the right answer gets twenty points. The next person with the answer gets ten. Everyone else loses ten points. Except the reader. Whoever is ahead at the end of the round of ten questions is the winner."

"Hey, I remember that game," Pete said, settling beside Jennifer.

"Wow, you gotta move fast," Kelly said.

"It's kind of like the television show *Jeopardy*, but you don't have to answer in a question," Jennifer explained. "I used to watch those quiz show reruns when I was working my first real estate sales agent job. I was at a builder's site south of town, and no one came in. Talk about bor–ing. So, I turned on the kitchen television while I waited for clients to show up."

"Man, I hope this market doesn't come to that." Steve closed his eyes and leaned his head back.

"Okaaaay," Greg said, grabbing the lined score pads and pencil in the box. "Looks like the reader keeps score. This box is pretty worn. How old is this game?"

"Pretty old. I remember playing it with my dad and mom when I was growing up. Maybe that's why I've never thrown it away." She examined the outside of the box, smiling. "This box brings back a lot of memories."

"Okay, I'll start off as reader, then we go clockwise after that," Marty instructed, reaching for the buzzer.

"How do we choose the categories?" Megan asked, leaning back on her elbows.

Lisa studied the inside of the box again. "Uhhh, I think you start off. Yeah, that's it. The reader makes the first choice, and we go straight down the list of categories." She pulled out a dog-eared piece of paper. "Here they are. And here're the category cards." Her eyes lit up. "Wow, do I remember these. I used to study up on the category cards when I was a kid, hoping I'd remember the answers. My mom and dad were super at this game."

"Okay, so we know who's gonna win," Kelly said, relaxing back on her hands.

"Not necessarily." Marty took the stack of cards from Lisa. "It's not enough to come up with the answer.

You've got to come up with it fast. That's the tricky part."

"Okay, this time limit has peaked my interest. Let's get started. See how fast we all are."

Steve grinned. "Spoken by the bike racer."

"All right," Marty said, checking the category list. "I pick World History to start off."

"Uh-oh, I only took a couple of those courses in college. Accounting ate up my schedule." Kelly looked over at Steve. "I don't think I'm gonna be very good at this, partner."

"Well, I took several courses, but I've probably forgotten everything by now," Steve said.

"Everybody understand how this goes?" Marty asked, shuffling a deck of blue cards. "I'll read the question and push the timer. We've got ten seconds." Placing the shuffled cards beside Megan, he said. "Cut."

"Sure thing." Megan obliged. "Can I take a peek?"

Marty looked shocked. "No! That'd be cheating."

"I was only *kidding*." Megan rolled her eyes, then put the cards beside him.

"Megan, I hope you know this, because I can't answer. One of the most successful rulers of the Holy Roman Empire during the eighteenth century had a forty-year reign, sixteen children, and is credited with being the savior of the Hapsburg Dynasty. Okay, here goes." He pushed the timer. A metallic whirring noise sounded.

Kelly could barely understand the question and turned to Steve. "Do you know—"

"Empress Maria Theresa of Austria," Pete and Jennifer answered together. They both looked at each other and burst into laughter. The buzzer buzzed.

Greg's mouth dropped open. "Whoa! That wasn't even five seconds. Were you guys History majors or something?"

Pete gave a modest smile. "History and Literature."

"Hey, same here," Jennifer said. She and Pete grabbed hands in a jock handshake, laughing softly.

Steve looked at Kelly. "We're in deep trouble, partner."

"Don't I know it."

"Didn't you take any History courses?" Marty teased Megan as he handed her the stack of cards.

"Yeah, but it wasn't *Speed* History," Megan said. "I had the name, but I just couldn't come up with it that fast."

"So, twenty points each for Jennifer and Pete, and minus ten for the rest of us." Marty scribbled on the score pad. "Darn it! I knew that one, too," he said with a frown.

Megan made a face at him while she shuffled the cards. "Let's see how fast *you* are." She set the deck in front of him.

Kelly smiled to herself, watching supercompetitive Megan and equally competitive Marty react to losing a game. Neither one of them had much experience at losing.

Greg clapped his hands together. "Okay! Now, that we all see what we're up against, let's get serious. I had that name on the tip of my tongue, too. Couldn't get it out fast enough."

"Well, Kelly and I were clueless," Steve admitted.

"All right, here's the next question," Megan announced, holding up her hand for emphasis. "Which American president was responsible for the United States completing the Panama Canal?"

"Teddy Roosevelt," Pete said, even faster than the first time. Jennifer echoed his answer a second or two behind. Marty came in third.

"Whoa," Kelly said, laughing as she watched Greg's astonished expression.

"Man, we've *got* to move faster." Greg shook his head and turned to Lisa. "I thought you said you used to study the questions."

Lisa gave him a look. "That was ages ago! I can't remember any of it now."

"Fat lot of help you are."

Lisa gave him a poke.

Megan scribbled on the score pad. "Well, Pete's still in the lead, and Jennifer is right behind him." She handed the buzzer and cards to Kelly. Then she gave Marty an evil smile. "Not fast enough Mr. Smarty Marty."

Marty gave a sheepish grin.

Greg cackled. "You are *so* sleeping on the sofa tonight."

"And you're *not*?" Lisa said, arching a brow.

Steve collapsed on the floor laughing. Steve, Kelly, Jennifer, and Pete all joined in, watching their overly competitive friends goad each other. After Kelly shuffled, she cut the deck and read the next question.

"One of the greatest rulers of Russia in the 1700s—"

"Man, what is it with the eighteenth century?" Greg grumbled.

"This monarch was also one of the most controversial. She collected art from all over Europe, founded schools and universities, reformed the Russian legal system, and made war on Prussia, Turkey, and the Crimea. Who was it?"

"Beatrice the Wise," Megan piped up, laughing.

"Hannah the Humble," Lisa joked.

"Catherine the Great," Pete and Jennifer chorused again, then started to laugh.

Once again, Marty was too late. "Damn, you guys are scary."

"I remembered that name. Just not fast enough," Greg said.

Kelly handed the deck to Steve, who was still laughing. "Hannah the Humble? I don't think I remember hearing about her."

"She used to hang out with the monks a lot," Pete quipped.

"That's because she had really bad hair," Jennifer added, then burst into laughter.

"Okay, you guys are getting way too cocky," Greg said. "Let's see if we can beat you on one question. I mean, one out of ten. You'd think the rest of us would know at least one."

Kelly watched as Steve read the next question. Once

again, Pete and Jennifer were the first to answer. And so it went, question after question. Either Pete and Jennifer answered together or nanoseconds apart. Marty was always right behind them. But at least Greg beat out Marty once with a response. Meanwhile, Kelly and Steve watched their respective scores steadily drop to the basement.

Finally it was time for the last question. Megan held up the blue card. "The Ottoman Turks, led by Suleiman the Magnificent, stormed the gates of which European city in 1529?"

"Ohhhh, I know this, I read a novel," Greg sputtered. "Vienna!"

Marty was right behind.

Kelly and her friends turned to Jennifer and Pete, who sat quietly smiling at everyone. "What's the matter? Didn't you guys know that one?"

"We thought Greg and Marty deserved to win a round," Jennifer replied.

Greg screwed up his face. "Ooooh, charity points. That is so cruel."

Marty shook his head. "Sad. Really sad."

"Guys, get a grip, it's a board game," Kelly said.

"Yeah, just accept Jennifer's and Pete's charity and admit that you guys stink," Steve teased.

"Give up? *Never*!" Greg declared melodramatically. "We have just begun to fight. Quick! Who said that?"

"John Paul Jones," Jennifer answered with a wicked smile.

Greg sank his head into his hand. "Man, we *do* stink."

"I think we're outgunned, that's all," Marty offered. "I know. Let's switch partners. I get Jennifer."

"*What!* You're ditching me?" Megan exclaimed. "Boy, you're not even getting close to the sofa. You're sleeping on the floor."

"Okay, then I get Pete!" Greg declared, gesturing for Pete to join him.

"Then you can stay here tonight and sleep with the towels," Lisa said, giving her boyfriend a shove. "Kelly, you wanta team up?"

"Hey, we're on a roll," Pete said. "We don't want to mess it up."

"Steve and I are no help whatsoever. We didn't know any of the answers."

"Kelly and I should go get some beer. That, we can handle," Steve volunteered.

Kelly looked out the tall windows. Still raining. "We're going to get soaked."

"All we have to do is get to my truck. There's an umbrella there. We're already wet."

"*You're* wet, I'm not," Kelly teased as they both scrambled to their feet. "Okay, beer run, it is."

"Actually, I checked the pizza before we left and there's only a couple of slices left, so I think you'd better pick up some takeout," Jennifer suggested. "Anybody up for Chinese?"

"Oh, yeah," Lisa said.

"Always."

"Could you get Indian, too?" Greg asked, reaching for his wallet and pulling out some bills.

"Definitely."

"Are we going to have heartburn tonight, or what?" Kelly predicted as she watched her friends toss cash into the center of the carpet.

Ten

"Give it up, Carl. They're too fast," Kelly yelled to her dog, watching him chase after the fleet-footed squirrels that raced along the top of her chain-link backyard fence. Carl never seemed to weary of the chase, even though his nemesis Saucy Squirrel—or one of his relatives—always won the day. Or at least the race.

Saucy and friends leaped to the ground and skittered across the grass to the nearby cottonwood tree which provided the lion's share of shade for the cottage and yard. Once atop a branch Saucy turned and chattered at Carl, then shook his tail in what Kelly took to be a rude gesture. Carl didn't seem to care. He woofed up at Saucy like he always did when bested. A sort of "Wait till next time" bark. Saucy simply ignored Carl's threats and scampered up the tree to higher realms.

She closed the glass patio door as the jangle of her cell phone sounded. Retrieving it, she strolled into the kitchen and checked the coffeepot. Empty. *Rats.*

"Hey, Kelly," Burt's voice came over the line. "Did I get you before you burrowed into your accounts?"

"Perfect timing, Burt," she said as she leaned against the kitchen counter. "I was about to get Eduardo to fill my mug and dig into the accounts. What's up?"

"I need your help with some phone calls. Mimi and I are arranging a little casual get-together after the shop has closed tonight and everyone's off work, so we can announce the engagement to close friends. We've already told our families, of course. Rosa and Connie were the first to notice." He chuckled. "I heard you were going nuts up front trying to see something 'new' the other day. Rosa said Mimi had to wave the ring in your face." This time, he laughed out loud.

"Yeah, she's right. I felt so lame. Maybe I should turn in my junior detective badge, what do you think?"

"Don't worry about it, Kelly. Listen, could you call up Curt and Jayleen, please? Ask them if they'd like to swing by Pete's café this evening after five thirty. Since it's Monday, Pete doesn't have a catering job tonight, so Mimi and I grabbed him and sent him downstairs to start baking pies."

"Oh, wow. Now I'll be thinking about those pies all day." Kelly could almost taste the succulent blueberry and cherry, yummy pecan and lemon custard. "I'll call

Steve and make sure he doesn't work late. We can have pie for dinner. He'll love it."

"Great. I'll call the rest of the crew. I'm heading out on errands now. Thanks, Kelly, I really appreciate your help."

"Anytime, Burt." She chose a clean mug from the dishwasher. Might as well get that fill-up and sniff those pies right away. Maybe it was still early enough to put in a request.

"Oh, by the way. I heard from my friend in Peterson's department. Vern said the guy who was number one on Peterson's list, that rancher named Bill . . . well, he's been able to come up with a good alibi. Seems he was with his girlfriend all night. So, it looks like he's off the list."

"Really?" Kelly slipped the coffee mug into her shoulder bag and headed to her front door. "Well, so much for the medical examiner's suspicions, right? So, are the police going back to accidental death?"

"Well, not yet. My friend said Peterson is going to start questioning everyone again. To see if they remember anything else."

Uh-oh. That meant Peterson would be questioning Jennifer, and he'd probably do it alone this time. Kelly felt a little squeeze on her heart. There would be no way for Jennifer to truthfully answer Detective Peterson's probing questions without revealing how she had first met Everett. And the ugly rape that followed.

"That means he'll be interviewing Jennifer, too," Kelly said. "Damn." She slammed the door behind her and sped down the concrete steps that led to the walk-way through her cottage's small front yard. The tulips she had planted last November had risen vibrant and healthy. Crimson reds and canary yellow. Daffodils dotted another planter, alternating with purple crocus. Spring flowers.

"Yeah, I thought about that, Kelly. I know you were trying to protect Jennifer, but you really can't. You know that, don't you?" Burt's kind voice reminded.

"Yeah . . . I know," Kelly admitted as she walked across the driveway toward the shop and café.

"I don't think there's any reason to worry. I can't imagine Peterson would consider Jennifer a suspect. No matter what she felt about Everett, we all know Jennifer couldn't murder someone."

Kelly's little buzzer went off inside. *I have to tell him.*

She let out a breath as she slowly made her way through the breakfast crowd seated outside the café. Deliberately taking the flagstone path away from the tables, she said, "Yeah, Burt, we all know that. But the problem is Jennifer took a walk alone that night after we all left the campfire. Lisa and I went right to sleep in our cabin, so we don't know how long Jen was out there alone. There's a path that winds along the edge of the river, and it passes right by Everett's ranch house."

Burt was quiet for nearly a minute. "Ohhhh, my," he said with a tired sigh. "That does change things, I'm afraid."

Kelly paused by the small pond near the café's front door. "It sure does, especially with an investigator as thorough as Detective Peterson. I've watched him work twice now. Once he learns that . . . well, I'm afraid he'll put Jennifer at the top of his empty list of suspects."

"Well, let's not jump to conclusions yet, Kelly. Peterson's a reasonable man and not a hothead."

"I'll try not to, Burt. But it's not Peterson I'm worried about. It's that medical examiner who's so hot to turn this accidental death into a murder."

"Whoooeeee, I can sure smell those pies, but I can't see 'em," Jayleen announced in a loud voice as she entered the café. "Where're you hiding them, Jennifer?"

"Pete's bringing them up from the warming ovens in the basement," Jennifer said as she set out silverware on the alcove tables.

"Grab a chair," Kelly said as she set coffee mugs on the tables. "Megan's outside playing with Carl, and Lisa and Greg are on their way."

Curt Stackhouse followed Jayleen to a corner table. "I sure hope one of those pies is lemon custard. That is some kind of good," he said as he dropped his Stetson to the table and settled his tall rancher's frame into a chair. "Is my nephew dropping by? I haven't seen him for nearly a month now."

"He's finishing up a big case," Kelly said. "Megan said he's been putting in some long hours. Jen, is more coffee brewing?" Kelly asked, glancing toward the coffee bar behind the counter.

"I'm on it," Jennifer said, opening drawers.

"Don't get close, I'm covered in dog slobber," Megan said as she entered the café.

"Don't tell me you rolled around with him in the yard like Steve does," Kelly said.

"No, but I went inside the yard to pet him."

"Big mistake," Jennifer said.

"Oh, yeah." Megan laughed. "Boy, he was all over me. I gotta wash up," she said as she went down the hallway.

"Look who I found in the parking lot," Steve said as he rounded the corner, pointing to Lisa and Greg behind him. "Boy, I'm starving, so I hope Pete made a lot of pies. Kelly said this was dinner." He gave Kelly a kiss as he passed.

"Me, too, but I grabbed some pizza on the way over," Greg said as he straddled a chair.

"We're out of pizza," Kelly said. "In fact, our fridge is looking kind of bare except for coffee."

"Staple of life."

Curt snorted. "I swear. Don't you kids go shopping? You're getting way too busy."

"Well, you're right about that," Lisa said, holding out her mug so Jennifer could pour coffee. "Once we decided to move, we've been going a mile a minute."

"How's that going?" Jayleen asked. "Kelly told me you two were moving into one of Steve's houses."

"Smart decision," Curt said with a nod. "For you

kids and for Steve. Tight times require some juggling to make it through."

"That's for sure," Steve said, nodding his head.

"Well, thanks to everyone's help this past weekend, we got all the furniture moved and all of the boxes."

"And managed to have a furious game of Speedy Trivia," Megan added as she pulled out a chair beside Curt and Jayleen.

"Hey, don't remind me. I haven't had time to read up," Greg said.

The sound of metal on countertops told Kelly that Pete had returned from the basement ovens. The aromas that wafted out of the café kitchen announced the pies.

Greg sat up straight and sniffed the air. "Pete, if that's you in there, I'll forgive you for busting my butt the other night if you'll let me have first crack at those pies."

"Not on your life," Steve threatened over his cup. "You don't know how hungry I am."

"Take it easy, guys." Jennifer stood in front of the pies, knife in hand. "The engaged couple gets first cut. They can practice for cutting the wedding cake."

"I'm not about to argue with a woman holding a knife," Steve said.

Mimi and Burt came around the corner at the same time. "Hey, everyone's here," Mimi said, face flushed with obvious pleasure. "Well, almost everyone. We can wait."

"Nope. No waiting," Jennifer decreed, handing Mimi

the knife. "You and Burt have the honors of first cut, pie of your choice. There's lemon custard—"

"Now, you're talkin'."

"Strawberry, blueberry—"

"There goes my willpower."

"And chocolate cream."

"Oh, Lord."

"Let me be the first to officially congratulate you two on your engagement," Pete said with a broad smile.

"Why, thank you, Pete. You're a sweetie," Mimi said. "I'm not sure I'll be able to fit into my new dress if I try all of these."

"Don't worry, Marty will be here in a few minutes," Megan warned.

"Ohhhh, decisions, decisions." Mimi hesitated before choosing the blueberry pie.

"Jayleen and Curt, you two go next," Jennifer said, gesturing. "Then the rest of you hungries."

"Age before beauty, right?" Jayleen joked.

"When are you folks tying the knot?" Curt asked as he followed Jayleen to the kitchen.

"We thought Sunday June first would be good." Burt held out Mimi's chair before he settled at a table. "Early summer weather should cooperate. If we're lucky, we can hold the ceremony outside in Mimi's backyard, and then have a small gathering with friends."

"You mean a reception, right?" Lisa asked as she followed behind Greg to the pie line.

"Well, not really a big reception, just close friends and family." Burt brought another forkful of chocolate cream decadence to his lips, then paused. "All of you folks are invited, of course."

"Uh-oh." Greg glanced to Lisa as they waited for Curt to make his selection. "No reception means no food."

Mimi laughed. "Don't worry, Greg. Pete will be catering, so there will be plenty of food."

"Oh, good. My social calendar just cleared," Greg said as he served himself a heaping portion of strawberry pie.

"Why don't you let us help you with the reception," Kelly suggested, following behind Steve. She had her eye on that strawberry pie, providing Greg left some.

"Oh, you girls don't have to do that. Like Burt said, we're not planning much. It's going to be very low-key. Just our families and very close friends."

"Still, Mimi, that adds up to a lot of people," Megan added. "Have you made a list of guests yet?"

Mimi waited until she'd savored the strawberry pie before answering. "Well, I've started a list—"

"Why don't you and I get together over coffee tomorrow morning and get that list completed? That way you'll have an idea what size event this will turn out to be."

"Better do as she says, Mimi," Lisa said, settling at a table with a slice of blueberry pie. "Megan's got her organizing hat on, I can tell. She can organize the daylights out of anything."

"Thank you, thank you." Megan gave a fake bow before choosing her pie.

"Well . . . maybe I should," Mimi said.

"Not a bad idea, Mimi. That way we'll know how many are coming, and Pete will have a better idea of what to make," Burt added.

"I can help with setup," Kelly volunteered. "I'm a whiz at arranging chairs, tables, all sorts of stuff. And I'm good at cleanup, too."

Mimi and Burt looked at each other. "You know, we hadn't even thought about all that. Maybe we do need to make some plans."

Kelly savored the delectable flavors of fresh strawberries and delicate pie crust melting over her tongue. *Yum.* "Plans are good, Mimi."

Curt rose from his chair and raised his coffee mug high. "To Mimi and Burt. Two of the nicest people I know. Who were also smart enough to find each other the second time around. To many more years of happiness together."

Kelly and all her friends raised their mugs and echoed their congratulations while Burt beamed and Mimi teared up.

Dabbing at her eyes, she said, "Curt, that is so sweet. It was so romantic."

"The next time we say a few words, it'll be over champagne," Curt said with a smile. "My treat."

Eleven

"Kelly, can you hand me that tangerine-colored yarn, please?" Mimi reached over the table where she was surrounded by students focused on their individual crochet projects.

Kelly looked into the bins behind her and found the vibrant wool and mohair yarn Mimi was seeking and handed it over.

Mimi's Easy Crochet class was filled. Kelly had been lucky to find a seat at the table as an observer. All she wanted was some quick run-through on basic technique.

Now that she'd managed to crochet an edge around the knitted washcloth at the retreat, Kelly wondered if she could move up to another project. Mimi's Easy Crochet class would be the perfect place to start.

Kelly's cell phone jangled, and she turned in her chair to answer. Clearly, crochet would have to wait for another day.

"Kelly, are you over at the shop right now?" Burt asked.

"Yeah, I'm in Mimi's crochet class," she said in a lowered voice so as not to bother the other class members.

"Well, I think you'd better get back to your place because you'll be receiving a rather important phone call pretty soon."

This time, Kelly left the table. There was something different about Burt's voice. It was sharper than usual. "Who's calling?"

"Detective Peterson wants to talk to you."

"So he's started interviewing people, huh?"

"Oh, yes. And imagine his surprise when a couple of the people he was questioning said they witnessed you threaten Cal Everett."

"*What?* That's crazy! I didn't threaten him—"

"Apparently they say you did." Burt's voice acquired a disappointed-parent tone. "Is there something you'd like to tell me, Kelly?"

"I had a conversation with Everett, that was all," Kelly admitted, feeling decidedly uncomfortable.

"What kind of conversation?"

"Well . . . it was . . ."

"Was it about Jennifer?"

"Uh . . . yeah."

"And, what did you say?"

"Well, I can't remember exactly," she hedged. "I kind of told him what I thought about him."

"Uh-huh." Burt's tone turned skeptical. He could always tell when she was straying from the truth. "Did you 'kind of' tell him in a forceful way?"

"Weeeellll . . ."

"Kelly, stop dancing," Burt scolded. "Tell me what you said."

"Okay, I told him that he'd better not get anywhere near Jennifer again, or he'd have to deal with me. And Jennifer's friends."

"That sounds like a threat to me, Kelly. Did you also happen to tell him that one of those friends was a former police detective who would be watching for his license plate if he drove in Fort Connor?"

Oooops. She had said that, hadn't she? Oh, well. Better 'fess up. "I might have."

A long sigh came over the phone, and Kelly could picture Burt shaking his head. "Kelly, that also constitutes a threat and harassment."

"Okay, so I got a little carried away—"

"A *little*? You threatened Everett in front of witnesses. Don't you realize that makes you a possible suspect in Peterson's eyes?"

"What! He can't be serious."

"Try telling that to Peterson. Threatening someone *is* serious, Kelly."

"I was only trying to protect Jennifer."

"I know you were, but that was not the way to do it. Your intentions may have been good, but they were misguided, and now you'll have to explain to Peterson. I'm just glad he already knows you."

"He can't seriously think I'm a suspect, can he?" Kelly didn't think that was logical at all.

"It's his job to consider everyone who might have a grudge against Everett. So, you'd better get over to your place where there's some peace and quiet. You've got a lot of explaining to do."

"Okay, okay."

"Call me when it's over. Bye." Burt clicked off.

Kelly quietly made her way back to the crochet class, retrieved her barely started project, and left the shop. Burt was right. She'd need a quiet place to find the right words for Peterson.

Unfortunately, she didn't have much time to practice. Her cell phone rang as soon as she entered the cottage living room. Recognizing the county policeman's phone number, Kelly took a deep breath and answered.

"Kelly Flynn, here."

"Good afternoon, Ms. Flynn. Lieutenant Peterson, here. If you have a few moments, I'd like to ask you some more questions about the weekend that Cal Everett died."

"Certainly, Detective Peterson. What would you like to know?" Kelly started a slow stroll about the small room. She thought better when she was moving.

"We have your statement describing the confrontation between Everett and the rancher named Bill," Peterson said, his voice relaxed and folksy as usual. "What I'm wondering is why you neglected to tell me about your own confrontation with Cal Everett earlier that afternoon."

Bull's-eye. Peterson didn't waste time beating around the bush. He went straight for the target. Kelly took a deep breath before giving Peterson her version. "Well, I wouldn't call it a confrontation exactly."

"We have two witnesses, ranch staff workers, who were standing within earshot of this exchange, and they both stated that you threatened Cal Everett. Would you like to elaborate on their version, Ms. Flynn?"

Kelly knew from her earlier conversation with Burt that any hedging or "dancing about the facts" would only make her look worse in Peterson's eyes. It was time to come clean.

"I wanted to make sure that Everett stayed away from a friend of mine. A friend he had . . . he'd hurt a few months ago. So I told Cal Everett that if he ever got near my friend again, he'd have to deal with me. And all her friends felt the same way. Now, I admit that my actions may have been clumsy, but I was only trying to protect my friend." She paused. "Cal Everett was a predator, Detective. I'm sure if you started looking into his background, you'd find he was a nasty piece of work."

Peterson was quiet for half a minute. "We have investigated Everett, and I agree, he was definitely no Boy Scout."

Kelly gave a derisive snort in reply.

"But, nevertheless, Ms. Flynn, threatening someone with bodily harm is a crime in itself. I'm sure you're aware of that. And according to the witnesses, you threatened Everett with physical beating at the hands of some of your friends. Would you like to elaborate on the identity of those friends? Could one of them be the young man who came to your defense last year in Bellevue Canyon?"

She wasn't sure, but Kelly thought she detected a slight trace of amusement in Peterson's tone. "Yes, I was referring to my boyfriend."

"I figured as much. From what I heard, he flattened a suspect who was under police custody at the time."

"Knocked him out cold, Detective. One punch."

"I see. Well, I think you'll agree that was an entirely different situation, Ms. Flynn. And threatening Cal Everett with the same fate would not be treated with the same leniency."

"I understand, Detective. Rest assured, that situation will never be repeated."

"Rest assured? I certainly hope so." He paused. "Would you like to tell me the name of the friend you're so valiantly trying to protect?"

Kelly hesitated. "Uhhhh, I'd rather not."

Peterson paused again. "Never mind, Ms. Flynn. I think I have a pretty good idea of whom we're talking about."

He probably does, Kelly figured. "Was there anything else, Detective?"

"Not for the moment, Ms. Flynn. But don't make plans to leave the area anytime soon, all right? I may need to speak with you again."

The unsettled feeling returned to Kelly's gut. "I'll be here, Detective Peterson. I'm not going anywhere."

Kelly sipped the delicious butternut squash soup. A perfect choice for a rainy spring night. Glancing at friends around the restaurant table, she noticed no one had ordered pizza this time. It was definitely a soup and sandwich night.

"Burt told me Detective Peterson is questioning everyone again about that retreat weekend. Has he contacted you yet, Kelly?" Lisa asked before tipping back her microbrew.

Kelly took a drink of her favorite ale before answering. She figured she might as well tell the truth. Her friends would find out anyway and be annoyed if she withheld information. Might as well ease into it.

"As a matter of fact, he called this morning."

"Did some new information turn up or something?" Marty asked after polishing off his sandwich.

"Not really. Burt told me he'd heard that Peterson reopened the investigation at the request of the medical examiner." She tasted her soup again. *Delicious.* "He wants to make sure Everett's death was accidental. Apparently he was concerned about the angle at which Everett fell off the deck."

"What's to worry about?" Lisa said, reaching for the

baguette in the bread basket. "He was plastered and took a dive over the rail."

"Good riddance," Greg added, then upended his beer.

"So, what did he ask you this time?" Steve asked, taking the baguette Lisa offered. "Did you remember something that you hadn't told him before?"

Kelly leaned back in her chair and swished her ale, watching it foam in the brown bottle. "Yeah . . . kind of."

Steve turned and eyed her. "There's something you're not saying. What is it?"

Leave it to Steve. He was as bad as Burt. Both of them could tell when she was hiding something. *Brother*. Was she that easy to read?

Lisa leaned over the table. "Did you see something? Or someone sneaking around that night?"

"No, I didn't see anybody sneaking around."

"Then what aren't you saying?" Steve probed.

"Spill it, Kelly, now you've got us curious," Greg said, finishing his soup.

Kelly released a dramatic sigh, and decided to play it nonchalant. "I'd forgotten to tell Detective Peterson about the conversation I had with Everett that afternoon," she said, trying to sound casual. "Apparently two of the ranch workers saw me talking with him and told Peterson. That's all." She shrugged, hoping they would buy it. They didn't.

Steve's hand came up in "stop" mode. "Wait a minute. You had a conversation with Everett?"

"Yeah. And it got a little heated, so those staffers thought it was a confrontation—"

Both hands up now. "Hold it. How 'heated' are we talking about here?"

Lisa's eyes popped wide. "Kelly, you didn't tell me that!"

Marty leaned on the table. "I'm curious as to why those staffers would call it confrontational."

Kelly took a sip of ale before continuing. Fortification. If Attorney Marty was weighing in, she was in trouble. "Maybe because they heard me tell Everett to stay away from Jennifer. And if he didn't, he'd have to deal with me."

"Jeeeez . . ."

"Kelly, what were you thinking?"

"She wasn't."

"Go, Tiger."

"Hey, guys, I was just trying to protect Jennifer, and I went a little overboard."

"You think?" Steve stared at her incredulously.

"Let's ask the House Lawyer," Greg teased. "Does that constitute a threat?"

"Yeah, technically," Marty replied with a grin. "But I doubt Peterson would get too excited about it because this Everett was a big guy, and it's kind of unlikely Kelly could beat him up."

Kelly stared at her empty bottle. Maybe she could order another one and deflect their concentration. She could feel them all staring at her.

No such luck.

"Unless . . ." Marty continued, "she threatened Everett with something else."

"I need another one," Kelly called to the passing waiter.

"Oh, God . . ."

"She needs another beer. This is gonna be good."

"Kelly!"

"She's gone quiet. It's gotta be bad."

"What did you say, Kelly?"

Kelly looked around the table and gave her friends a disarming smile. "I simply told him that he'd also have to deal with a couple of Jennifer's friends who wanted to beat him up."

Greg arched a brow. "That would be us, I take it?"

"That would be us," Steve said, shaking his head. "Damn, Kelly . . ."

Marty sank back into his chair, hand over his eyes. "And that would be a threat. In front of witnesses, yet."

"Hey, guys, Everett is dead, so it's not likely he's going to press charges, right?" Kelly countered, accepting the replenished ale.

"That's true," Megan said. "So, Kelly won't be charged with anything."

"Unfortunately, Peterson is now investigating this as a murder," Marty explained. "Which means Kelly has just gone to the top of his list of people at the retreat who may have wanted Everett dead."

"No way!" Megan retorted.

"Yeah, way," Marty, Steve, Greg, and Lisa chimed in unison.

Kelly listened to her friends argue about her fate while she sipped the delicious ale. Deciding there was no way she could allay their concerns, she decided on the only possible end to this conversation. Total surrender.

"Okay, guys, you're right. I screwed up. Big-time. But before they haul my butt off to jail, can we get an order of chocolate chip cookies?"

Twelve

"I was hoping I'd find you here this morning," Lisa said as she approached the knitting table. "What's that you're working on?"

"It's supposed to be a small rectangular table topper," Kelly replied. "But if I screw it up, it'll turn into a place mat for Carl. I sat in on Mimi's crochet class and thought I'd try a practice piece. I figure if it turns out really awful, I'll unravel it and reuse the yarn."

"I'm glad to see you do crochet. It's about time you tried something different." Lisa settled into a chair and removed a skein of Mimi's hand-dyed rose pink yarn. She began casting stitches onto her knitting needles.

"You didn't have physical therapy clients this morning?"

"No, I rescheduled because Detective Peterson dropped by the clinic for my interview."

Kelly smiled. "How was it? Better than mine, I'm sure."

"It wasn't bad. I simply repeated everything I'd told him before." Her smile faded. "However, after your experience, I started looking back with new eyes, and I remembered something."

"What?"

"You weren't the only one at the retreat who had a confrontation with Everett that night. Remember Jane telling us that she 'called him out' when she saw him on his front porch?"

Kelly had forgotten. "Oh, yeah, she did. But that sounded like she gave him a piece of her mind, that's all."

"Still, a confrontation is a confrontation in my book," Lisa said with an emphatic nod. "And I wanted to make sure Peterson knew about it."

Kelly could tell her friend was sticking up for her just in case Marty's dire prediction proved true. The idea of being on Detective Peterson's Most-Likely-to-Do-Something-Bad list was not pleasant.

"Thanks, Lisa. I appreciate your efforts to make sure I'm not alone on Peterson's list. That was sweet of you to come to my defense."

"Yeah, yeah, yeah."

Kelly smiled to herself. Lisa hated the idea of being "sweet." She liked to think of herself as the take-charge leader, organizing everything in sight. In reality, Megan was the hard-as-nails Trail Boss, and Lisa was the Worrier and Caregiver. The Warrior role Kelly had taken for herself.

"Did he say if he'd interviewed Jennifer yet? I haven't had a chance to talk with her because they were swamped at the café when I came in a little while ago."

"He asked me where would be the best place to catch Jennifer to ask questions, her real estate office or the café. I told him she worked mornings at the café, so I wouldn't be surprised if he showed up." She glanced out the window. "Actually, that's another reason I rescheduled everybody. I wanted to be here in case he does talk to Jen today. That's bound to be hard for her."

"You're right. I'm glad I took my break early. I'd rather be here for Jennifer. Even though Burt always reminds me that we can't protect her."

"Jen wouldn't let us anyway."

"Did he say who else he's interviewed?"

Lisa shook her head. "Not a word. But he did get to talk to Greta before she left for class. So that's one more down." Lisa knitted another row of rosy pink stitches.

The sound of tires crunching gravel drew Kelly's attention, and she glanced through the window in time to see a black car driving into Lambspun's parking lot. She didn't get a good look at the driver, but instinct told her it was Peterson.

"A man driving a black car passed by. I'm betting it's Peterson," she said and dropped her crocheting onto the table.

Lisa looked up, concern already on her face. "I bet you're right. Let's head over to the café."

"We'd better stay in the background," Kelly said as she left the main room. "Peterson might get annoyed with us hovering around, like Mother Hens."

Lisa followed Kelly. "Yeah, not to mention how aggravated Jen would be."

Kelly headed through the hallway toward the café and down a narrow passageway only the kitchen staff used. "We can hide out here in the corner." She pointed to the windows that overlooked the patio garden outside and the parking lot beyond.

The outside tables were still filled with breakfast customers. Warm, sunny mornings brought out the crowds even on weekdays. Kelly looked beyond the customers and over the garden fence with flowering vines and spotted Peterson exiting his car.

"You were right," Lisa said. "Where's Jennifer?"

Kelly scanned the garden area outside, not spotting her friend, then turned to Eduardo, who was working at the grill. "Is Jennifer working inside or outside this morning?"

"She and Julie are covering both," he said, flipping a cheesy omelet onto a plate.

"Look, there he goes," Lisa said, pointing out the window.

Kelly followed Lisa's direction and saw Jennifer approach Detective Peterson by the gate to the garden patio. Peterson gestured toward an empty table away from the others. Jennifer nodded, then followed behind Peterson to the secluded spot.

"Who's that guy with Jen?" Pete's voice came from right behind Kelly's shoulder.

Kelly hesitated for a second before answering. She couldn't protect Pete, either. "That's Lieutenant Peterson from the county police. He's interviewing all the retreat attendees again. He interviewed me yesterday and Lisa this morning."

Pete's normally smiling face sobered quickly. "Why? Did they miss something?"

"Apparently the medical examiner wants to make sure Everett's death was accidental. So he's asking more questions."

Pete's eyes popped wide. "Please tell me you're kidding."

Kelly gave a rueful smile. "I wish I were. He even questioned me because I'd had a discussion with Everett myself. I told him to stay away from Jennifer or else."

"Oh, God, you didn't." Pete looked appalled.

"That's precisely what we all said last night."

Pete looked from Lisa to Kelly and back again. "It's no accident the two of you are here, right? You're here because of Jennifer." He glanced through the window toward Jennifer and Peterson, clearly engrossed in conversation at the shady table. "And that means . . . oh, God . . . Jen didn't tell him, did she?"

Kelly shook her head. "Nope. When he was questioning us at the retreat, I kind of danced around and distracted him so he wouldn't ask her straight out if she had ever met Everett before. I mean, I figured he'd dived off the deck himself, so it didn't matter if Peterson found out. I—I just wanted to protect Jennifer."

They all stared out the window again, watching Peterson clasp his hands together and lean forward over the table. Jennifer folded and refolded a napkin in her lap as she spoke.

All three friends watched in silence for several minutes.

"Oh, God . . ." Pete whispered.

Kelly leaned her arms on the café table in the quiet alcove. "What did Peterson say? I mean, what questions did he ask?"

Jennifer stirred the coffee in her mug and took a sip before answering. "Actually, he did more listening than questioning. He started out by asking if I'd ever met Everett before the retreat." She ran her index finger around the rim of the mug. "I said 'yes,' then I told him . . . everything."

"Was he understanding? I mean, how did he act?" Lisa probed, worry lines furrowing her brow.

"Oh, he was very understanding . . . and very kind," Jennifer replied, clasping the mug. "But then, we've had a chance to talk before." A small smile tugged at the corner of her mouth. "In fact, he gave me some fatherly advice over a year ago. If I'd taken it, I probably never would have met Cal Everett." She took a long drink.

"Did he ask anything about the retreat?" Kelly continued. "Or the night Everett died."

Jennifer nodded slowly. "Yes, he did. I told him that after the campfire, I took a walk alone around the grounds while you and Lisa went back to the cabin."

Lisa looked pained. "Did he focus on that?"

"No, he simply asked me how long I walked and where and did either of you two see me return." Jennifer held the mug tightly between her hands. "I told him that I walked for about an hour around the grounds and near the creek, not the ranch house, and you and Kelly were asleep when I returned."

That meant neither she nor Lisa could corroborate Jennifer's version of what time she returned. Kelly kept her worries to herself. She knew Peterson would be drawing his own conclusions after speaking with Jennifer. There was nothing any of them could do to help her now. No dancing around, no distractions would keep Peterson from putting Jennifer at the top of his list. She placed her hand on her friend's arm.

"It'll be all right, Jen," she said, trying to calm the worries that must already be forming in Jennifer's brain. "Peterson is a reasonable man." She found herself repeating Burt's line.

Lisa placed her hand on Jennifer's other arm. "We're here for you, Jen. All of us are, and so is Dr. Norcross."

Jennifer looked up and smiled at the two friends across the table. "I know, guys, and believe me, I appreciate it. Even the hovering. Don't think I didn't spot you two looking out the window."

"Busted," Kelly said in mock irritation. "Man, I'm gonna have to turn in that junior detective badge."

Pete approached the table then and placed his hand on Jennifer's shoulder. His face clouded with concern. "It's okay for you to leave now, Jen. The rush is over. Julie can handle it now."

Jennifer glanced up at him. "That's okay, Pete. I can stay and help her."

He shook his head. "No, no . . . you go ahead and take some time. Drive over to your office, go up into the canyon, go sit by the Poudre. Whatever. Take some time for yourself. It's a beautiful day."

"Okay, I'll go to my office," Jennifer said with a knowing smile. "The chairs are more comfortable than those rocks beside the river."

Kelly watched her friend give a goodbye wave and leave the café. Kelly, Lisa, and Pete stared after her, then exchanged a look with each other. Kelly recognized the same worry in their eyes as she felt inside herself.

"Is that Pete out there in the garden?" Steve asked, peering out the cottage front window. "It's after five. The café has been closed for hours. What's he doing out there?"

"He's pacing," Kelly said, lacing up her baseball

cleats. "He's been pacing ever since he learned what happened at the retreat."

"You're kidding."

"I wish I were. Eduardo told me that Pete paces two or three times in the morning. And Mimi and I see him pace every afternoon after the customers leave." She joined Steve by the window. "And now that Peterson has heard Jennifer's story, she'll go to the top of his suspect list, and poor Pete will pace himself to death."

"Damn . . ." Steve said softly.

"My sentiments exactly. I wish I could help him," Kelly said as she grabbed her spring jacket. Spring nights were chilly once the sun dropped behind the mountains. "Mimi said he confided to her that he has borderline high blood pressure."

Steve grabbed his jacket and headed out the front door, Kelly following behind. "Not good. All that worrying about Jennifer is probably sending his pressure sky-high."

"What he needs is some way to channel all that worry into something that would actually help him, like running," she said as they reached Steve's big red truck.

Steve clicked the lock and opened the door. "I agree. But Pete's a workaholic. He'd never take time to work out."

"Hey, we're workaholics, too, but we take time to run in the morning." Suddenly an image flashed before Kelly's eyes. Pete running beside her along the golf course. An idea wiggled from the back of her mind. "Wait a minute, maybe we can help him."

"How?" Steve asked as he climbed into the driver's seat. "Buy him a membership in a health club?"

"Better than that. I can go running with him."

Steve slammed the door, then started the engine. His window whirred down. "C'mon, we're gonna be late for practice. Our team is working out on the field next to yours."

Another idea danced in front of Kelly's eyes now. "You go on. Tell Megan I'll be a little late and tell her why. Hand me my glove, willya?" She pointed behind his seat.

"What are you gonna do? Run with Pete now?" he said, handing her the baseman's glove.

"No time like the present. I'm going to tell Pete I'll run with him every afternoon. Starting right now."

Steve grinned as the engine roared into life. "Okaaaay, but if Megan gives first base to someone else, don't say I didn't warn you."

"Hey, it'll only be a few minutes. It's a worthy cause," Kelly said, backing away as Steve drove off.

Heading toward her own car, Kelly popped the trunk and tossed her glove beside the two baseball bats inside. Louisville Sluggers, both. Beside them were bags of softballs and baseballs. Always prepared for a pickup game. It was springtime and ball games were in the air. She and her friends had been practicing with their teams for four weeks. The season started this weekend.

She waved to Pete as she headed his way. He was

still pacing in the empty café garden. "Hey, Pete, come here. I've got something to tell you." She motioned him over.

Pete strolled across the driveway, his familiar smile in place. Kelly noticed he was already wearing sneakers. *Good*.

"What's up, Kelly?"

Deciding that a no-nonsense approach would be best, Kelly took his arm. "Follow me, Pete, we're going to take a little jog around the golf course."

Pete stopped in his tracks. "What? I don't have time to jog, Kelly. I've got work to do in the kitchen, pies need—"

Kelly urged him forward again, pulling his arm. "You got time to pace, you got time to jog. Besides, jogging is better for you." She grabbed his arm again and pulled Pete forward once more.

Pete kept resisting, trying to pull away from Kelly's grip. "C'mon, Kelly, this is silly." He started laughing.

"I'm not joking, Pete," Kelly insisted and grabbed his arm with both hands.

A familiar car turned into the driveway at that moment, and Jennifer pulled to a stop beside them. "Where are you taking Pete?" she asked.

"Kelly has this crazy idea she wants to go jogging with me. Don't you have softball practice or something to go to, Kelly?"

"Yes, I do, but this is more important. We've all watched you out here pacing every day. Eduardo says you come out three times every morning."

"At least," Jennifer said, looking solemnly at Pete.

"Jogging is better for you than pacing. If you have time to pace, you have time to jog."

Jennifer looked from Kelly to Pete and back again, then pulled her car into a spot.

"C'mon, Kelly, the team needs you," Pete teased. "Let me get back to work." He turned to Jennifer as she approached. "Did you leave something, Jen?"

"No, I was coming back to make sure you weren't slaving away downstairs making more pies. We've got enough already."

"See?" Kelly insisted, taking Pete's arm again, glad for Jennifer's support. "C'mon, Pete, no more excuses."

Pete held up both hands, his genial smile still intact. "Guys, I appreciate your suggestions, but I don't want to take the time—"

"We're not giving you a choice, Pete." Kelly faced off with him, hands on hips. Serious Coach stare in place. "You have to do it for your health. Mimi told us about your blood pressure."

Pete's smile disappeared. "Man, a guy has no privacy around here."

"Give it up, Pete. The Lambspun network knows everything," Jennifer said.

"Yeah, so, give up any idea of resistance. I'm going to go jogging with you every afternoon unless there's a downpour. And don't try to hide. I know where you live."

Pete shook his head with a rueful smile. "You're serious about this, aren't you?"

"Oh, yeah."

"Trust me, Pete. You'd better do what she says. When Kelly gets her mind set on something, she's like a dog with a bone. She won't leave it alone."

Kelly had to laugh. "She's right about that, Pete. I'm relentless."

Pete stared off at the golf course. "Every day?" he complained.

"Monday through Friday. You get weekends off."

"Man . . ." He shook his head.

"Listen, Pete," Jennifer said, slipping off her jacket. "I'll come along with you guys. That way you'll have someone else to complain to who's equally miserable. And we can torture Kelly with stereo complaining."

Pete looked at Jennifer and started laughing. Kelly just stared at her friend.

"Wait a minute, wait a minute," Kelly said, leaning against Jennifer's car. "I gotta make sure I wasn't hallucinating just now. Did I actually hear you say that *you* were going to come jogging with Pete and me?"

Jennifer gave her a disarming smile. "Yes, you did."

Kelly stared at her friend in disbelief. "I've been asking you to join me running for two years now. How come you haven't done it before?"

Jennifer shrugged. "Pete's coming this time. That makes it different."

"Incredible," Kelly muttered as she pushed off the car and headed across the driveway. She noticed that Jennifer was wearing sneakers, too. "Okay, Pete, you heard it. You're the magic ingredient. Let's get to it, so

I can make ball practice before Megan gives away my base."

Pete and Jennifer followed after Kelly as she started a slow jogging pace around the cottage and alongside the golf course. Golfers were still doing their best to hit their balls in the approximate direction of the individual greens. Some succeeded, some did not.

Rounding a corner by the edge of the course, Kelly kept her pace slow. "We should be safe from most of the drives over here. But, no guarantees, so heads-up, guys," she warned.

"Oh, great, now we're threatened with injury," Jennifer teased.

"Some of those guys are my customers, too," Pete said, between pants of breath.

"Good, then they won't hit you."

They all jogged silently and slowly alongside the long stretch of greens. Then, Kelly heard Jennifer's voice pipe up behind her, like a preschooler in a car seat. "Are we there yet?"

Thirteen

"Hey, Kelly, did I catch you at a bad time?" Burt's voice came over the phone.

Kelly steered around the corner of an intersection. "Not at all. As a matter of fact, I'm driving to the mall to shop for a dress to wear to your wedding."

Burt's soft laughter sounded. "Mimi told me Megan wanted all of you to dress in springtime colors, like flowers."

"Ohhhh, yeah. That's Megan for you. Organizer par excellence. She even told us which colors would look best on each of us." Kelly slowed for a stoplight. "Lisa's violet, Jennifer's light green, Megan's pink, and I'm blue."

"Megan is something else. Once she started helping

Mimi with the guest list, next thing we knew, she started giving Mimi and me daily lists of things we had to do before 'M Day,' as Megan calls it."

Kelly laughed out loud this time. "Trust me, Burt. You'd better do what she says. Megan gets fierce if you don't follow through on her marching orders."

"I'll bear that in mind. Meanwhile, let me tell you why I called. I heard from my friend in Peterson's department. Vern said they've finally finished interviewing everyone at the retreat except for one woman who's out of town on business."

"Did they learn anything new? I mean, other than Jennifer's story."

"Well, a couple of things got their attention, he told me. Naturally, Jennifer's story stood out the most. Unfortunately."

"I was afraid of that."

"Yeah, well, we knew that would spark Peterson's interest. I mean, it would spark mine if I was investigating. You have to be impartial. So, even though Peterson knows Jennifer and obviously likes her, he can't help but see her as the one person at the retreat who had the most reason to wish Cal Everett ill, so to speak."

"Yeah, I know, I know. Did they interview Jane what's-her-name? Jane admitted to several of us on Sunday morning that she'd confronted Everett the night before, just like I had. Apparently she called him a scumbag and some other colorful terms."

"Yeah, he did mention that they interviewed a Jane

Kirchner, and she readily admitted confronting Everett." Burt's voice revealed amusement. "In fact, she repeated the entire colorful conversation."

"Hey, then she should go on Peterson's list next to Jennifer, right?"

"Well, it seems Jane has an alibi. She and her cabinmate, Sue, left the campfire and played cards in their cabin the rest of the evening. They went to sleep about midnight. So, I'm afraid that still leaves Jennifer alone at the top of Peterson's list."

"Damn," Kelly breathed, merging her car into another lane.

"I know, I know . . ." Burt commiserated. "But there was one other bit of information that surfaced. Dr. Norcross said she remembered hearing the sound of a large engine, like a truck, late at night. She heard it when she got up to use the restroom. She doesn't remember what time it was. But she did glance through the curtains and said she saw bright headlights coming up the driveway, and a big truck pulled into the barnyard. Then Cal Everett went out to meet whoever it was."

"How'd she know it was Everett? It was pitch-black outside. I know, because I checked out the door before Lisa and I went to sleep."

"Apparently Everett was carrying a lantern, that's how she recognized him. So, that's some good news. Everett had a nighttime visitor. Now, all they have to do is find out who he was."

Kelly pondered that new information as she turned

her car into the mall parking entrance. "A big truck, huh? Sounds like Rancher Bill, but it couldn't be him because he was with his girlfriend all night."

"Yeah, well, I have a feeling that Peterson is going to go back and interview Rancher Bill again, given Dr. Norcross's statement."

Kelly remembered something. "Speaking of Dr. Norcross, I recall her saying that she had her own discussion with Everett. After she learned he was the one who assaulted Jennifer. According to Jen, Dr. Norcross warned Everett to stay away from all of her retreat attendees that weekend. She told him to 'stay out of sight.' Yeah, I think that's what she said."

"Hmmmm, my friend didn't mention that. Maybe I'll call him and find out if Dr. Norcross told Peterson about that conversation."

"Don't get me wrong, Burt. I really admire Dr. Norcross," Kelly backtracked, feeling slightly guilty. "She's really great. I had a chance to see her in action. But, we're trying to make sure all confrontations with Cal Everett are accounted for, right?"

Burt chuckled. "Right you are, Junior Detective Flynn. I'll get on it and report back to you. Meanwhile, enjoy your shopping excursion."

Kelly nosed her car into a parking space as she flipped her phone closed. Somehow springtime colors didn't seem as bright. Not with her friend Jennifer still at the top of Detective Peterson's Most Likely list.

She flipped the car's electronic lock as she crossed the mall parking lot and was about to shove her phone into the pocket of her new summer cropped pants when she remembered something. She punched in Lisa's number.

"Hey, do we have practice tonight?" Kelly asked when Lisa's voice came on the line.

"We sure do. You'd better not be late again, or Megan will kick your butt."

"As Marty says, she'll have to catch me first," Kelly teased as she entered the air-conditioned chill of the sprawling mall. "I've got Pete pretty well trained to the routine after three days, so I could leave before he's finished. Jennifer's another story, of course."

"Of course," Lisa chuckled. "I still can't believe she's actually running with you and Pete."

"Well, running would be an exaggeration. Slow jogging is more like it, but that's okay. It's a start. I'm hoping Jen will actually get used to it and keep doing it every day. I've pretty much convinced Pete that we'll all swoop down on him like avenging Mother Hens if he stops working out."

"Avenging Mother Hens? Aren't you mixing your metaphors, there? Mother Hens are supposed to nurture, not avenge. That's for eagles or angels or somesuch."

"Whatever. I usually slept during Lit classes. They were too early in the morning," Kelly said before turning serious. "I just had a phone call from Burt. He told me Jennifer's still alone at the top of Peterson's list. It seems Jane bragged about confronting Everett, but she's got an alibi. She and her roommate played cards all night, then fell asleep."

"Darn. I was kind of hoping she could deflect attention from Jen."

"Me, too. But there is some good news, I guess. Apparently Dr. Norcross said she heard a truck engine late at night when she got up. She saw a big truck pull into the barnyard and Cal Everett went out to meet it."

"Whoa, that's interesting."

"Yeah, I thought so. Let's hope it leads to something. Burt thinks Peterson will go back to Rancher Bill for more interviews."

"I thought that guy Bill had an alibi, though."

"He does. According to Burt, Bill says he was with his girlfriend all night. But we all remember Everett arguing on the phone that night. Not once, but several times. Maybe he was arguing with Bill. Maybe Bill came back to settle the score like he promised. Who knows?"

"You're right. Say, what's that noise?"

"It's the mall announcement," Kelly said, pausing in front of a boutique she particularly liked. "I'm doing my Megan-authorized spring bouquet dress purchase. Wish me luck."

"Good luck, and thanks for reminding me. I'd better shop tomorrow night. No practice. Listen, gotta go. Client coming in."

Kelly clicked off and scanned the shopwindows again. Where-oh-where had all the spring flowers gone?

Fourteen

Kelly fingered the bamboo and silk yarns as they tumbled from the bins. Soft and smooth. She noticed the pretty lacy vest that hung above the bins. Maybe she should have used that pattern for her vest. She could picture herself wearing it over a white shirt. She'd seen that lacy, open pattern in countless magazine pictures.

Of course, most of those patterns were a lot more complicated than the simple one Mimi had recommended for Kelly. But then, Mimi knew Kelly's propensity for making nearly fatal fiber errors. Mimi never used the word *mistake*. She called those knitting missteps "learning experiences." After two and a half years of working with yarns, Kelly had learned and experienced a lot. *Ohhhh, yeah.*

Shifting her empty mug to her other hand, Kelly sank her free hand deep into a bin of seductively soft yarns, letting their silky fibers caress her fingers. Kid mohair—lavender, yellow, and pink balls of fluff. Skeins of merino wool, silk, and cashmere. Sinfully soft.

Burt's voice broke through the fiber trance. "Hey, Kelly, good to see you early in the morning."

Kelly glanced up. Burt was holding his coffee mug as he leaned against the archway that led into the adjacent yarn room dominated by the Mother Loom. That was the large loom Mimi and her most advanced weavers used. Shelves of novelty yarns, spools of embroidery floss, and sewing thread lined two of the walls.

"Actually, I came over for my morning coffee fill-up, but got sidetracked by these new yarns Mimi put out. They are scrumptiously soft."

"Aren't they now?" Burt said with a smile.

"How does Mimi expect us to finish projects when she keeps distracting us with new yarns? Some of us have short attention spans, you know. I'm struggling with my crocheted place mat."

Burt chuckled. "You know Mimi. She can't help sharing everything new she finds." His smile faded. "Why don't we head into the café, Kelly? We can chat while you load up with caffeine."

Kelly left the yarn temptations and followed Burt down the hallway leading to the café. She could tell he had something to tell her, and from the expression on his face, Kelly sensed it wasn't good news.

She plopped her bag on a table and sat down, then

lifted her mug to the waitress in a silent signal. "You've got something on your mind, Burt, I can tell. Somehow I sense I won't be happy to hear it."

Burt settled into a chair across the table and leaned forward over his folded arms. "Your instincts are as good as ever, Kelly."

"What have you heard, Burt?"

He took a sip of coffee before starting. Not a good sign. "I got a call from my friend, Vern. He said Peterson went to Jennifer's favorite bar, The Empire Room, and started interviewing to see if anyone remembered seeing her with Everett."

Kelly's stomach tightened. "And did they?"

"It seems Ted, the regular bartender, didn't remember the night Jennifer met Everett, but he does recall his coming into the bar a couple of months ago. Apparently, Everett sat at the bar one night and told Ted that he'd 'had' Jennifer the month before in what he described as a bout of rough sex. Ted recalled Everett saying Jennifer liked it 'rough.' But when he got rougher than she wanted, she got mad and . . ." Burt paused. "And Everett claimed Jennifer threatened to kill him."

Kelly felt every muscle in her body tense. If Cal Everett wasn't already dead, she'd go after him right now. *Damn him.* "That lying bastard. If he wasn't dead, I swear—" Her threat went unfinished when Julie appeared to fill her mug.

Once the young waitress moved to another table, Burt continued, "I know, Kelly. I feel the same way."

He wagged his head in the way he always did when he was perturbed about something. "But our feelings about Jennifer don't count, and you know it. It's Peterson who makes the call. And this new information gives him even more reason to suspect Jennifer. Everett's assault gave her reason to hate him. Now, there's a witness who can testify that Everett claimed Jennifer threatened his life."

"But, Burt, that's a crock, and you know it," Kelly protested.

"Remember, Kelly, it doesn't matter what we think."

"I know, I know, it's Peterson who decides." Kelly expelled an exasperated breath. "It's just the idea of his showing up at that bar and saying all those things about Jennifer. *Bastard*."

"I don't think it's necessary to tell Jennifer about this, Kelly."

She nodded. "I agree. She doesn't need to hear this ugly gossip and Cal Everett's lies. She's gone through enough, thanks to him." Kelly sniffed the dark rich aroma, then took a sip and felt the coffee's burn as it slid down her throat. "But I am going to tell Lisa and Megan. We can vent in private."

"I think that's a good idea. No need to spread this ugliness around."

Kelly glanced at her watch. She had a full morning's work on her clients' accounts. Then, perhaps she could meet Lisa for coffee or something. See if she had some time between physical therapy clients.

"I'll see if Lisa has some free time this afternoon. Meanwhile, I've gotta get back to my clients." She scraped back her chair. So much for the mellowing yarn effect of a few minutes ago. Her mood had turned considerably darker now.

"See you later, Kelly. Take care," Burt said as he held up his mug for Julie to refill.

Kelly was about to head toward the café's back door and walk through the garden to her cottage when she paused. She wanted something to dissipate the bad taste of Cal Everett in her mouth. Even dead, he seemed to be tormenting Jennifer.

"Has Megan given you your daily list yet?" she teased.

Burt's smile finally reappeared. "Mimi said it's waiting for me up front. So, I guess I'd better get to it."

Kelly gave a low laugh. "I'd say so, Burt. Megan's a tough taskmaster. Coffee break is over."

"Do you want me to wait till you get home for dinner?"

"Naw, you don't need to wait," Steve's voice came over the phone. "That meeting could run late."

Kelly steered into the parking lot adjacent to the Sports Health facility. "That's okay. I can wait. We can meet at the Wine Bar and have tapas and wine for dinner."

"That'll work."

"Okay, give me a call when you've finished, and I'll go over and grab a table."

"Sounds good. See you later." He clicked off.

Kelly quickly parked her car and walked toward the ever-opening glass entry doors to the sports facility. Heading toward the patient waiting area, she found a chair and pulled out her daytimer. Lisa wouldn't be finished with her last appointment for a few minutes, so Kelly might as well make some business calls. Then a woman's voice sounded close by.

"Hi, Kelly. Are you waiting for Lisa?" Greta Baldwin asked.

"I sure am. How're you doing, Greta? I haven't seen you since the retreat."

Greta shrugged. "I'm doing okay. Professors want longer and longer papers, and we have shorter and shorter amounts of time to do them."

"That brings back memories of university life," Kelly said with a wry smile.

Greta's smile faded. "How's your friend Jennifer doing? I hoped the retreat would help her start to put her life back on track."

Kelly looked over at the huge indoor swimming pool where therapists were working with patients. "Well, she was making progress on that, until Cal Everett came back to life, so to speak."

Greta stared at Kelly, clearly confused. "What do you mean?"

"You know. The medical examiner's suspicions about Everett's death. That's why Peterson came back to question us again, remember?"

"I remember."

"Yeah, that," Kelly said. "Well, it was during that second round of questions that Detective Peterson learned about Jennifer's assault. So, naturally, that makes her the number one suspect on Peterson's list."

"*No!*" Greta exclaimed, looking shocked.

"Oh, yeah." Kelly nodded. "And Jennifer has no way to prove she didn't do it, because she went out for a walk after we left the campfire that night. Lisa and I were back in the cabin, sound asleep. So, we can't give her an alibi." She shook her head disconsolately. "I wish I hadn't let her go walking alone that night."

Greta stared at Kelly for a few seconds. "You can't blame yourself, Kelly. Jennifer probably wanted some time alone that night. It was a pretty intense weekend for her . . . you know, sharing and all."

"Yeah, I hear you. I simply worry about her," Kelly said, still staring off.

"Have you been waiting long?" Lisa called as she hurried down the wide hallway, which was filled with clients and therapists standing and talking.

"Only a few minutes. Greta and I were chatting."

Lisa gave Greta a warm smile. "Hey, Greta, Kelly and I were going for coffee. Would you like to join us?"

Greta shifted her backpack over her shoulder and shook her head. "Thanks, but I've got to finish a paper for that other Psychology professor. Maybe another time," she said, backing away.

"Okay, I'll hold you to that," Lisa said.

"Good to see you again," Kelly called as she watched Greta hurry away.

"Boy, her workload must be way heavier than mine, because she just disappears lately. She's either in class or in the library studying. We used to always have time for coffee, but no more."

"Grad school can do that to you," Kelly said as she shoved her daytimer into her shoulder bag. "Do you still have time for coffee?"

Lisa checked her watch. "Yeah, no clients until five. Where do you want to go?"

"Someplace quieter where we can talk. Burt gave me another update this morning, and it wasn't good news."

Lisa ran her finger along the rim of the ceramic coffeehouse mug. "That is so unfair. That bastard is dead, yet he's still hurting Jennifer. With his lies, this time."

Kelly took a deep drink of the extra dark roast. This coffeehouse, with its Old Town atmosphere, was one of her favorite boutique coffee shops. Non-chain, non-corporate, and not a speck of chrome in sight. Just warm and intimate and cozy.

The century-old building in Fort Connor's Old Town still had the architectural details that made it distinctive, like the beaten tin ceiling. Now the walls were painted sunset red and mustard yellow, the better to highlight the constantly changing art displays. On one wall was a mural rendition of van Gogh's *Starry Night*, which gave the coffeehouse its name.

She stared at the black brew, choosing her words

carefully. They would almost sound like heresy if she spoke them. But she had to. Lisa had been at the retreat with them. No one else would understand like she would.

"Lisa . . . I know this sounds awful, but I keep thinking about Jennifer's long walk that Saturday night. And how upsetting that whole weekend was for her, you know?"

Lisa exhaled a long sigh. "Yeah . . . I know, Kelly. That worries me, too. Nobody saw her on that walk. Nobody knows when she returned."

Kelly swirled the coffee in her cup, hating herself for what she was about to say. "Lisa . . . do you think Jen went to confront him that night? Do you think something . . . something happened while she was there? I mean . . . maybe he tried to hit her or . . ."

Lisa put her forehead in her hand and closed her eyes. "I don't know, Kelly . . . I just don't know. But it's been haunting me, too. What if Jen did go to see him? I can't picture her doing that, but neither of us knows what she did on that walk."

Kelly stared at the colorful design beneath the table's laminated surface. "I keep wondering the same thing, Lisa. What if she did? Everett was pretty drunk that night. Maybe he tried to force himself on her again. She would fight him. We know she would."

"For sure."

"And maybe she pushed him. He was so drunk, he could have fallen over that railing and broken his neck."

Lisa looked up and met Kelly's gaze. Kelly saw the same fear there that she felt inside herself. Fear for their friend.

"And Jennifer would never be able to prove it was an accident. No one would believe her," Lisa said sorrowfully.

Kelly simply nodded. Those were the same words that Jennifer had spoken when Kelly went to comfort her devastated friend three months ago. "No one would believe me."

She was right, Kelly concluded with regret. *No one would.*

Kelly speared another bacon-wrapped date and popped the delectable morsel into her mouth. *Way too good.* She could eat an entire plate of the yummy little appetizers. That was the nice thing about tapas—she could dine like a queen on several different selections without overeating. And the wine flights made it all the more enjoyable.

Kelly looked around the wine bar and café. Booths lined one side, tables were set up in different groupings, and chairs and love seats clustered here and there, creating cozy spots. She and Steve were seated near the fireplace, and no one else was nearby, which gave the setting even more privacy.

Steve glanced around the main room. "Boy, they put a lot of work into this place. Hickory floors, beaten tin ceiling, vintage light fixtures."

Kelly sipped a smooth pinot noir. "Spoken like a builder with an eye for detail." She paused. "Would you like to do more remodeling of these older buildings? You enjoyed working on Baker Street so much. You know, preserving the historic details while modernizing the other features."

Steve leaned back in the upholstered chair beside Kelly and drained his glass of sauvignon blanc. The metal and glass hanging light fixtures sent a soft amber glow around the room. "That's what brought me the most pleasure at Baker Street. Transforming those special details into something entirely new and distinctive."

"Are there any more projects like that you could get involved with, Steve? That might help get you through this rough patch in the market."

Steve shook his head. "Even if there were, Kelly, I have no money to invest anymore. Everything's tied up in Wellesley and Baker Street. I can't start any new projects. I'm just trying to hang on to the ones I've got."

Kelly placed her hand on his arm, feeling the crisp weave of his cotton shirt. A different feel from his preferred denim work shirts. Denim and jeans and work boots. Steve's favorite attire when he was busy building new houses. Comfortable clothes.

Not anymore. Now he wore sport coats or suits with dress shirts. Better for meetings with bankers and investment types. His days were spent in his office in Old Town in the Baker Street building. Steve had taken one of the smaller retail shops as his own. No longer tromping through mud and worksite clutter.

The picture of Steve working inside an office instead of striding around a building site was hard to bring into focus. It didn't seem right. Steve had been building houses for eight years in northern Colorado, all around his hometown of Fort Connor.

Kelly decided to offer another suggestion, rather than her usual reassuring comments, since he'd heard them all before. "Have you considered signing on as an architect with one of the local firms? You know, as a consultant, maybe?"

Steve nodded, not even looking surprised by her comment. "Yeah, I have. If those Wellesley sites don't sell this summer, I may have to sign up with a company. I'll have to hustle up money somewhere to cover those new loan payments."

Kelly sought for something to say, surprised that he had never mentioned to her that he was considering a different course. "You may enjoy designing other people's projects, Steve. It could be challenging, even."

Steve gave a little rueful smile. "Right now, I've got all the challenge I can handle."

Fifteen

Kelly leaned against her patio screen door, watching a squirrel scamper across the grassy backyard within a few feet of her sleeping dog. Carl lay stretched out in the sunshine for his morning nap. Kelly sipped her coffee while Brazen Squirrel darted about the backyard, digging in the flower beds, acting totally unafraid of Big-Dog-on-Patrol. Clearly, Brazen Squirrel knew Carl's habits better than he did. Midmorning was nap time in the sunny corner of the yard. Carl was snoring peacefully as big dogs were wont to do, totally unaware that his nemesis was within easy reach.

Kelly smiled and didn't make a sound. She wasn't about to blow Brazen's cover. *Hey, if you sleep on the job, you're gonna miss out.* That was one of the big differences between dogs and cats, she'd noticed. Cats might look like they were sleeping, but one eye or their antennae or whatever was always paying attention. Cats were *always* on the job. Something small and tasty might be creeping nearby. There was no way Brazen Squirrel would scamper about so nonchalantly and carefree if Carl the Cat lived there.

Her cell phone jangled in her pocket, playing her latest music download. Burt's voice came on, excited.

"Kelly, I'm finally calling with good news. In fact, it's great news."

"I can tell from the sound of your voice, Burt." She pushed away from the door. Carl had stirred and raised his head, sending Brazen Squirrel into the bushes. "Quick, tell me."

"Rancher Bill's alibi just sprang a leak. His girlfriend confessed to Peterson that Bill wasn't with her the night of Cal Everett's death."

Kelly sucked in her breath. "You're kidding!"

"No, I'm not. Peterson went back to interview the girlfriend after hearing Dr. Norcross's statement that she saw a big truck drive into Everett's barnyard that night. Apparently the girlfriend acted real scared and broke down. In fact, she admitted her boyfriend Bill wasn't with her at all. He called her after the police interviewed him and begged her to lie for him. He said he was at his office all alone that night and had no alibi. And he knew everyone at the retreat saw him arguing with Everett."

"Ha! *Got 'im*!" she exulted.

"Well, not yet," Burt cautioned. "But he's definitely moved higher on Peterson's list."

"I'm curious. What's Rancher Bill's full name?"

"Ummm, let me check my notes. It starts with a *Z* I think. Yeah, it's Zarofsky."

"Okay. Next question. When's Peterson going to visit Zarofsky again?"

"Vern said they were headed out to his office this morning. He's a rancher turned developer or something and has an office listed under commercial real estate. Why don't you ask Jennifer if she knows this guy."

"Sure. But I doubt she knows him, or she would have said something when she saw him at the retreat. We were all standing right there, staring at the two of them yelling at each other."

"Vern said the girlfriend told them Zarofsky was really spooked about that. He knows that puts him right in Peterson's sights."

"They must have talked to the girlfriend yesterday, right?"

"Yeah, yesterday afternoon."

"Aren't they worried the girlfriend spilled everything to Zarofsky yesterday? That would give him time to find someone else to lie for him."

"Don't worry, Kelly. It won't be the first time Peterson's been face-to-face with a liar. He finds ways to trip them up."

Kelly heard the amusement in Burt's voice. "Yeah, you're right. I'm just being paranoid, I guess."

"No, you're right on. Most criminals will keep look-ing for someone else to bail them out of trouble. Now, we don't know if this Zarofsky is a criminal or not, but his behavior certainly doesn't inspire trust."

"I'll bet that's why Peterson questioned the girlfriend first after he'd heard from Dr. Norcross. He was hoping she'd admit Zarofsky was lying. That way, he'd have more leverage when he questioned Zarofsky next."

"And you'd bet right, Sherlock."

"Boy, I can't wait until Peterson gets ahold of Zarof-sky this afternoon. You've got to let me know as soon as you hear something, Burt. Promise?"

Burt chuckled. "I promise, Kelly. You know me. I will always keep you in the loop."

"You've made my day," Megan said, smiling at Kelly across the knitting table. She was working a turquoise bamboo and silk, turning it into a lacy top. "Now maybe Jennifer will be off the hook."

Kelly slid her right knitting needle under the left side of the next stitch on the other needle, wrapped the red yarn around the needle, and slipped the stitch from the left needle to the right. Only two years ago, that simple maneuver—so natural to her now—had been fraught with much anxiety.

"I sure hope so, Megan. But it all depends on what this Zarofsky has to say. I mean, he may come up with another alibi, who knows? So, let's keep our fingers crossed that Detective Peterson breaks him down."

Megan giggled. "You've definitely been watching too many *CSI* and cop shows. By the way, where's your crochet practice project? Did you finish it already?"

"No, it's in my bag," she admitted sheepishly. "It started looking kind of uneven, and I got discouraged. So I returned to my vest."

"Well, don't give up. I can help you with it if you want me to."

"I'll take you up on that offer. But first I may edge another washcloth. Meanwhile, I want to finish this vest while it's still warm weather so I can wear it."

Kelly noticed two women entering the main room, laughing and gesturing as they examined the yarn bins. She recognized both women as two of Mimi's regular crochet group members. Once a month they showed up for an all-day yarn fix. They both lived in Poudre Canyon, consequently they didn't drive down to Fort Connor as frequently as other Lambspun regulars did.

An idea wiggled from the back of Kelly's mind. Watching the two women settle into chairs at the other end of the table, she whispered to Megan, "Do you remember their names? I only recognize faces."

Megan leaned over the table. "The gray-haired lady is Miriam, and the younger blonde gal is Eileen."

Kelly waited until both women had drawn their yarn projects out of their bags and settled into their chairs. "How're you two doing? We haven't seen you for a while. Eileen, isn't it? And Miriam?"

"You've got a good memory, Kelly," Miriam said with a maternal smile. "And you're right. I haven't been able to get into town for a month. There was way too much spring cleanup to do on the ranch. We've got alpacas, you know."

Kelly didn't know that. "I've heard a friend of mine talk about her workload. She has an alpaca ranch in Bellevue Canyon."

"It's pretty up there, but it's cold, cold, cold in the wintertime," Eileen said, crochet hook working a lavender yarn. It looked like a blanket was coming into shape.

"And icy," Miriam said as her smaller hook worked a purple scarf.

Kelly knew about wintertime cold. She'd experienced Bellevue Canyon's cold and ice one winter and almost lost her life.

"Don't mention icy roads," Megan said with a shudder. "I've been spooked ever since Kelly crashed while she was driving out of that canyon during winter last year."

"Oh, goodness, you're right," Miriam exclaimed. "That's when you had the cast on your foot, right?"

"I don't remember that," Eileen said, peering at her friend.

"I certainly do," Kelly said with a laugh. "I was clomping around the shop for six weeks, bumping into things, knocking over yarn bins. It was lots of fun, believe me."

"She exaggerates as usual," Megan teased, turquoise stitches forming another row.

Kelly waited for the quiet laughter to fade away before she brought up the topic she was aiming for—ranchers Everett and Zarofsky. "Did either of you two know that guy who died recently? He owned the retreat ranch and stables way up the canyon. I think his name was Cal Everett. The newspaper said he broke his neck in a fall."

Both Eileen and Miriam glanced at each other, then Miriam spoke. "I heard about his death. Both of us had met him, but neither of us had a very favorable impression, I'm afraid."

Megan shot a look at Kelly. "What do you mean?" she prodded.

Miriam kept working the purple yarn, hook busily stitching. "My husband and I worked with him on a fund-raising function when he first bought the canyon property. We were running a chili dog stand to raise funds for the mountain school. He was nothing but uncooperative. Everett wanted to stand in the crowd and smile and talk to people but didn't want to get his hands dirty inside the tent. So we wound up doing all the work, while Mr. Smiley worked the crowd. He said he was 'drumming up business.' When my husband suggested we could use his help, he became combative." She gave a matronly *harrumph* that reminded Kelly of Hilda von Steuben, one of Lambspun's elderly knitters and regulars. "An altogether unpleasant man."

"I remember him from the canyon property owners' association," Eileen weighed in, hook picking up speed. "He always challenged the homeowners' fee assessments, and he was always late in paying. In fact, he never paid for this year's assessment. We depend on that money to clear snow from the private roads and keep them repaired."

Kelly stitched quietly for a minute, then added her observations. "I didn't know him, but I was at a retreat at his ranch once. It was really pretty up there."

"Oh, it's a pretty place, all right. He does a lot of retreat business from what I've heard. Lots of cars coming and going, especially on the weekends," Miriam said.

Eileen gave a derisive snort, crochet hook moving even faster. "Not as many as my neighbor."

"You mean Zarofsky?" Miriam said with a chuckle. "Well, you're right about that."

Megan and Kelly exchanged looks. "Does he have a retreat business, too?" Kelly asked innocently.

Eileen shook her head. "I asked him that very question after he'd moved into the ranch. He'd been living there about six months, and I'd noticed how many cars were always going and coming into his place. So I asked him when I spotted him at a local coffee shop. He said he had a lot of business clients, that's all." She scowled a little. "Problem is, our bedroom is on the same side of the property as Zarofsky's driveway, so the sound of car and truck engines wakes us up at night."

"Boy, that would get old real fast," Megan volunteered. "Have you thought about filing a noise complaint or something?"

"We try to solve things without the help of the legal

system if we can," Miriam said with a wry smile. "Lawyers tend to complicate things, we've found."

Megan grinned. "Well, you're certainly right about that."

"She should know." Kelly couldn't resist. "She's dating one."

"Oh, you poor thing," Eileen teased.

Megan laughed so hard, she spilled her coffee.

"What's so funny?" Mimi asked as she entered the room, a customer trailing after her.

"Marty. People laugh at the mere mention of his name," Kelly replied as her cell phone rang from her cutoff jeans pocket. "Excuse me for a moment." She headed into the adjacent yarn room, which happened to be empty. Burt's name flashed on her phone screen.

Checking her watch she flipped open the phone. "Hey, Burt, I didn't expect to hear from you until tomorrow morning. What's up?"

"I just heard from Vern, so I thought I'd update you now. Mimi and I have a whole new to-do list of errands for tonight, so I figured I'd never get around to calling you later."

"I see Megan's organizing skills are in high gear."

"Ohhhh, yeah. She's got us working overtime."

"So what did Vern say about Zarofsky? Did he have a new alibi?"

"Actually, no. That surprised me. Like you, I thought he'd try to rustle up another one. But Vern said Zarofsky acted real contrite and said he'd been at his office all alone that night, working late. He admitted he'd panicked when Peterson showed up the first time to question him. He knew a lot of people saw him arguing with Cal Everett that weekend. That's why he called his girlfriend and begged her to lie for him."

Kelly pondered Zarofsky's latest version. It sounded plausible. *But was it true?* "What do you think, Burt? Is he telling the truth, or is he trying to weasel out of it with a plausible-sounding lie? You know . . . the 'I know it was stupid, officer, but I just didn't think' excuse."

Burt laughed. "I don't even want to know if you ever used that line before."

"Me? *Never.* But I've had friends who've reportedly used it to great effect."

"I believe you. But as for Zarofsky . . . I don't know, Kelly. I wasn't there to watch him when he was questioned. That's when I used to pick up signals from people. They always reveal themselves."

"What will Peterson do now? Question more people?"

"Yeah, and put more pressure on Zarofsky to come up with a way to prove he was working that night. You know, e-mails from his office computer, maybe. Let's see what he comes up with."

Kelly thought for a moment. "What does your gut tell you, Burt?"

Burt didn't answer for a few seconds. "My gut thinks he's lying."

"Mine, too."

Sixteen

"**How** do you spell his name again?" Jennifer asked as she grabbed a notebook and pen from her bag.

"Z-a-r-o-f-s-k-y." Kelly leaned back into the chair at the corner café table and sipped the fresh mug of coffee Jennifer had provided. After polishing off one of Pete's delicious omelet breakfasts, she figured this was the perfect time to pick Jennifer's real estate brain. Burt had said Zarofsky was a commercial developer. Maybe Jen knew something about him. Kelly's antennae had been buzzing on this guy ever since her conversation with Burt yesterday.

"And he's developing commercial properties?"

Kelly shrugged. "According to Burt, that's what Zarofsky told the cops. But my buzzer is going off on this guy. His girlfriend blew his alibi for that Saturday night, and he admitted to Peterson that he lied. Apparently he lied because he was working all alone at his office that night. But you know, my gut tells me he's lying about that, too."

Jennifer quirked a brow at her. "Okay, Sherlock. I'll check him out and start asking around. His name doesn't sound familiar, but he could be working part-time with some small company. Let's see what I can find."

"Thanks, Jen. I figure if he *is* telling the truth, maybe someone who works in the same building would have seen him there."

"Where's his office?"

"I think Burt said it was in the Commercial Bank Building on College Avenue."

Jennifer pushed away from the table. "Okay, I'll check it out and give you a call later. We've got a commercial broker in the office who knows everyone who's working in this town. He'll give me a lead, I'm sure." She slipped her bag over her shoulder, turning to go. "And I appreciate what you're doing, Kelly. I know you're trying to keep me out of Peterson's sights."

"Hey, what are friends for?" Kelly teased. "By the way, congratulations for hanging in there with the workouts. It's been over a week now, and you're still showing up every afternoon."

Jennifer gave her a wry smile. "Well, I have to admit, it hasn't been as bad as I thought it would be."

"*See!* I told you." Kelly made a face.

"And . . . I've noticed I'm not as tired after working an evening catering job."

"*Ha!*" Kelly crowed.

Jennifer rolled her eyes. "So, yes, you were right. It does make me feel better. But I'm not sure I could do it without you and Pete along. That makes it endurable."

"Pete's doing really well. I told him so this morning. I'm so proud of both of you." Kelly beamed like a proud mother.

"Yeah, yeah, yeah," Jennifer said with a dismissive wave. "I've gotta get to the office. I'll call when I have some info on that guy."

"Thanks, Jen," Kelly called before draining her coffee. Reaching into her briefcase, she pulled out her laptop computer. This morning, Kelly felt like working in the café. The yummy smells of breakfast and cinnamon rolls and fresh coffee helped distract her from the repetitive nature of her work. Updating the accounts of her alpaca rancher clients.

It had been a year and a half since she'd given notice to the Washington, D.C., corporate CPA firm where she'd been steadily climbing the ladder for seven years. She'd been aiming for an eventual partnership position. Zeroing in on it.

But all of that changed two years ago when her aunt Helen was found murdered in her little cottage across from Lambspun. The same cottage Kelly inherited. The same cottage where she and Steve lived now. Kelly had taken an extended family leave to return to her childhood home and wound up uncovering the real killer. Someone the police never suspected. Kelly also found new friends in the knitting shop her aunt loved so well. And in the process, those friends became her new family.

The warmth of those new relationships plus the inheritance of a substantial amount of family property tempted Kelly to leave the big city corporate life behind and create a new life in Fort Connor. She took over her friend Jayleen's alpaca rancher bookkeeping clients and traded designer suits for jeans, tee shirts, and sneakers. Now she worked in the relaxed setting of her sunny cottage or amidst the sensuous world of color and texture that was Lambspun.

At first, keeping track of the alpaca rancher accounts had held her interest. The alpaca business was demanding of its owners, who both showed and bred the sweet-faced creatures with the to-die-for-soft wool. Kelly also enjoyed getting to know all of her clients personally and meeting with them face-to-face. She'd become a financial consultant to many of them.

But now, the daily monotony of the work was beginning to wear on her. It was too easy. There was no challenge. Kelly had been involved in difficult corporate mergers and sorting out challenging financial accounting issues when she was with the D.C. firm. Now, she was dealing with breeding fees and exhibition expenses, shearings and vaccinations. She was bored.

Two months ago, she had finished a week in Denver at continuing education classes for her CPA license.

For five days she was immersed in corporate financial issues once more, challenging herself. Her financial juices were flowing again.

She had to find a way to continue to work with the more challenging accounting issues. Thanks to Curt, she'd started consulting with a Fort Connor rancher/ developer who needed a CPA's higher level of accounting skills to handle his businesses. Now, *those* spreadsheets were way more interesting and much more to Kelly's liking.

Moving her cursor over the laptop's icon-filled screen, Kelly was about to click on the folder containing each of her clients' spreadsheets when she paused. Instead, she clicked on the familiar Internet browser icon which opened the portal to the Web.

Why not check out this Bill Zarofsky? She hadn't done it yet. She could find out the name of his commercial development business and the actual address. That would help Jennifer, and it would keep away the monotony of too simple accounts. She could distract herself for a while longer.

The familiar colorful logo of the powerful search engine website flashed on the screen, and Kelly entered Zarofsky's name, using *William* instead of *Bill*, and adding Fort Connor, Colorado, afterwards. Thanks to Google, no one could hide anymore.

Within seconds several entries flashed on the screen. Kelly scanned them. Each one related to William Zarofsky, giving his ranch address in Poudre Canyon. One entry was a listing from the alpaca breeders' association, and another was a listing of his name as an exhibitor in the Alpaca Extravaganza held in northern Colorado every February.

Kelly scrolled down, checking other entries. They were similar to the previous ones in that they each referenced Zarofsky's alpaca ranch or his breeding business.

That's curious, Kelly thought. Zarofsky said he worked in commercial real estate development, yet there was no mention on any of the listings about real estate. Shouldn't there be at least one reference?

Kelly's buzzer in the back of her head got louder. *There's something wrong with this guy. What is it?*

Signalling Julie for a refill, Kelly leaned back in her chair and stared at the laptop screen still holding Zarofsky's alpaca ranch listings. She dug out her cell phone and punched in Jayleen's number. Jayleen knew every alpaca breeder and rancher in northern Colorado. She was bound to know if Zarofsky was developing real estate on the side.

Nodding her thanks to Julie as she refilled the coffee mug, Kelly listened to the ringing, waiting for voice mail to come on. Instead, Jayleen answered.

"Hey, Jayleen, I've got a question for you."

"Well, I hope I have an answer. How're you doing, Kelly?"

"I'm doing fine, but I'm a little curious right now. I'm trying to check out a guy who has an alpaca ranch in Poudre Canyon, name of Bill Zarofsky. Have you heard of him?"

"Sure have. He's been in the business for about five years or so. His herd isn't as big as mine, but he seems to be doing okay. I've checked out his stock at the shows, and he's got some good breeders. He hasn't won any prizes yet, but he's getting close. Why're you asking?"

"He came up to Everett's ranch during that retreat weekend, and we all witnessed him having a big argument with Cal Everett."

"You're kidding."

"No, I'm not. They were fighting over a loan Zarofsky made to Everett. Everett was behind on his payments, and Zarofsky threatened to put a lien on Everett's land. They both got pretty hot."

"I bet. Threatening a rancher with a lien on his land, well . . . those are fightin' words."

"Well, they were fighting, all right. And the police are investigating Everett's death again to make sure it was an accident."

"Damn . . ." Jayleen breathed. "Does that Lieutenant Peterson know about Jennifer's connection with that bastard Everett?"

"Yes, he interviewed her last week. We're all worried Peterson will suspect Jennifer of helping Everett over the rail, so to speak."

Jayleen interjected some choice and colorful invectives describing how she would have helped speed Cal Everett's demise.

"Well, we're all hoping this Zarofsky will be Peterson's new suspect because his girlfriend admitted she lied for him by saying he was with her that night."

"Damn."

"Burt says Zarofsky claimed he was scared because he was alone in his office here in town. Claimed he's working in commercial real estate development. That's why I'm calling. I wondered if you'd ever heard him talk about working in real estate."

"No, matter of fact, I haven't. I know most all the breeders who've gone into real estate, and none of them have ever gone into commercial. They usually concentrate on finding large ranch or farm acreages they can buy or sell."

Kelly's little buzzer rang again. "You know, Jayleen, I just checked out Zarofsky on the Web, and I didn't find any mention of real estate in any form. Only his alpaca business. So, I'm a little curious why he'd tell Detective Peterson he was working in another business if he wasn't."

Jayleen chuckled low. "You sleuthin' again, Kelly?"

"Yeah, maybe. Just a little. Gotta satisfy my curiosity, you know." She sipped her coffee.

"You know what curiosity did to that old cat, doncha?"

"Yeah, yeah, but I'm trying to be good now."

Jayleen guffawed. "That'll be the day."

"I know, my reputation precedes me," Kelly admitted with a laugh. "I can only be so good. Would you do me a favor and check with some of your rancher/developer friends and see if any of them know about Zarofsky going into real estate?"

"Sure, I will, Kelly. Who knows? Maybe he's starting out. Hey, I've got another call coming in. Talk to you later, Kelly girl."

The affectionate nickname that Jayleen had picked up from Curt always made Kelly smile. She was about to drop her cell phone onto the café table when it rang again. This time, Megan's voice came on.

"Hey, Kelly, don't forget ball practice tonight. And you need to be on time. We've got our first game tomorrow night. Pete and Jennifer don't need you to babysit them jogging around the golf course anymore."

Kelly listened politely to Megan fuss at her, then replied sweetly. "Yes, ma'am, Miss Megan, ma'am. Whatever you say, ma'am."

"I'm serious, Kelly. You don't want me to give away your base, do you?"

Kelly could tell Megan was bluffing, but played along anyway. "*No! Not my base!*" she wailed loudly, causing Eduardo and Julie to turn around in the kitchen. "Please, Megan, don't give away my base! *Oh, noooooooo!*" She took the wail up the scale in the manner of a former Lambspun knitter who was known for her histrionics.

"Oh, brother . . ."

"Oh, noooo," Kelly let her voice drop from its upper register cry.

"I can tell you've had waaaay too much caffeine already this morning. We're gonna have to talk with Eduardo."

"You leave Eduardo and his coffeepot alone," Kelly said with a laugh.

"Okay, just promise you'll be on time tonight."

"I swear, Imperial Commander." Kelly dutifully saluted a grinning Eduardo. Then an idea popped from the back of her head. "Hey, Commander, can you do me a favor?"

"Not if it involves running errands. What with trying to organize Mimi and Burt's reception, I'm too busy."

Kelly laughed. "And you've got Mimi and Burt going in circles and bumping into each other. You'd better cut them some slack, Megan, or they'll be exhausted by the wedding. Not a good idea."

"Hey, they can relax on the cruise ship," Megan teased.

"You are merciless. But really, this won't take more than a few minutes of your time. I need you to check someone on those special no-access-allowed-except-Megan websites of yours."

"Sure. Who're you checking?"

"Zarofsky. William Zarofsky. I was hoping you'd check to see if he has had any problems with the law or any legal entanglements of any kind."

"You mean the guy who threatened Everett? The one we were talking about yesterday?"

"Same one. Can you check him out, please? I've already Googled him and the only thing that comes up is his alpaca ranch in the canyon. Nothing else."

"Okay, will do. I'll slip it in when I have a moment and see what I find."

"Thanks, Imperial Commander. I'll be ever so grateful."

"Save the gratitude. Just be on time tonight."

* * *

Kelly trailed her hand across the yarn bins on the way to the main room and the knitting table. Client accounts were finally finished, and she deserved some relaxing time. Fiber relaxation. Her vest project was going slowly. It would never be ready for summer at this rate.

Turning the corner, she saw Lisa sitting alone, knitting quietly. The rose pink cotton vest was nearly finished. Clearly Lisa had more time to knit. How did she do that? Lisa's schedule was as busy as hers.

"Did you just come in? I've been working on accounts in the café." She plopped her shoulder bag on the table and pulled out a chair.

"Yeah, I thought I'd drop by and knit a little." Lisa didn't look up, keeping her attention focused on the rose-colored yarn.

Kelly picked up on her friend's subdued mood. "Are you okay? You sound kind of down."

Lisa knitted for a few seconds without answering. "Yeah, I guess I am. I—I'm trying to figure out some things. You know, 'knit on it,' like Mimi says."

Kelly pulled out her knitted vest, which still looked halfway finished. It seemed stuck at halfway forever. It didn't look like she was making any progress at all. Maybe her vest was like Jennifer's sweater that wouldn't end. Would she have to hide the vest in the back of her closet for a year? Maybe it would finish itself.

"What's up? I can tell something's bothering you," Kelly asked her friend.

Lisa let out a long sigh. "The receptionist in Dr. Norcross's office went to a dentist's appointment, so I covered at the front desk. Answered the phones and made appointments. And while I was entering dates on the calendar, I noticed that Greta had scheduled appointments with Dr. Norcross three times this week and three times last week and three times the week before. That completely floored me."

"Wow. That does sound like a lot. What's happening with Greta?"

"I don't know. That's just it. She's been acting weird lately, preoccupied more than usual. Not her regular self at all. She doesn't want to talk anymore. I've asked her several times if anything's wrong, but she only shakes her head and says 'no,' then rushes off." Lisa frowned. "That's so frustrating. We used to be pretty close. Or at least I thought we were."

Kelly moved her needles through the familiar movements, knitting another row. "Has anything changed with her job or her classes?"

"Not that I know of."

"Have you mentioned anything to Dr. Norcross?"

Lisa focused on her knitting again. "Well, we're not allowed to discuss anything regarding staff, so I couldn't ask her straight out."

Kelly glanced up. Lisa was still focused on her knitting, adding more pink rows of stitches. There was something Lisa wasn't saying.

"What is it, Lisa? There's something else, I can tell."

Lisa gave Kelly a crooked smile. "You'd be good in our business, Kelly. Your antennae are razor sharp."

"They don't call me Sherlock fer nuthin'," Kelly teased. "You found out something else, didn't you?"

"Yeah, I did." Lisa exhaled a sigh. "And I'm feeling guilty about it."

"Why?"

"Because I overheard a private conversation between Greta and Dr. Norcross, and I shouldn't have listened. I should have turned the other corner and left the room. Instead, I stayed."

"You didn't plan on eavesdropping, Lisa, so don't beat up on yourself."

"Yeah, but now . . . now I'm feeling really unsettled."

"Exactly what did you overhear?"

Lisa screwed up her face. "That's just it, Kelly. If I tell you, then I'm compounding the invasion of privacy."

Kelly considered Lisa's dilemma. Clearly, her friend was conflicted over telling Kelly something she'd overheard. That would only happen if she overheard something disturbing. That made Kelly's little buzzer go off.

"Listen, Lisa. You didn't take an oath of doctor–patient confidentiality or whatever it is. You're not a doctor, and you're not a psychologist. So there are no professional or legal restrictions binding you. It's clear to me you overheard something that bothered you. And I know that you wouldn't have mentioned it if you didn't want to tell me, right?"

Lisa wagged her head, a wry smile curving her mouth. "Man, you'd make a good lawyer, too. You been taking lessons from Marty or something?"

Kelly smiled. "No, I simply pay attention. If something's bothering you, there's always a reason."

Lisa knitted several more stitches before answering. "They must have been standing outside Dr. Norcross's office because I heard their voices in the hallway around the corner. Dr. Norcross was talking to Greta, and she said, 'I know the retreat brought back lots of disturbing memories from the past. That's to be expected.' Then Greta said something I couldn't hear, and they closed the door."

Kelly pondered the scene her friend recounted. "Disturbing memories from the past" that were triggered by the retreat. Many things happened on that retreat in Poudre Canyon. A lot of them disturbing.

"That could refer to all sorts of things, Lisa. It was an emotional roller coaster of a weekend for a lot of people. And on top of everything, we discovered Everett's dead body at breakfast. That episode alone would bother most people."

"I know what you're saying, Kelly, but something tells me Dr. Norcross wasn't talking about Everett's death. She was talking about all the stories the women were sharing about their experiences." She knitted another few stitches. "And now I'm wondering if Greta was a victim of sexual assault herself. Maybe she didn't share it with anyone except Dr. Norcross."

Kelly considered what Lisa said. "You know, you

may be right, Lisa. Maybe those are the 'memories' Dr. Norcross was speaking of. And maybe that's why Greta went into martial arts. Maybe she didn't ever want to be a victim again."

Lisa stared at the yarn bins for a moment, then nodded. "That's possible."

"Has she ever given you any indication that she was assaulted?"

"No, she hasn't. The only thing I've ever heard Greta say was that women need to protect themselves. And I've seen her get very concerned when college girls come in and talk about some of their experiences at parties."

Kelly knitted another row. "I wonder why she didn't choose to share at the retreat. Do you think she simply wanted to keep a kind of professional distance or something? You know, since she's trying to become a psychologist herself."

"That could be it. Maybe—"

Lisa was interrupted by a mini-hurricane that resembled Mimi, hurrying through the doorway, fluffy balls of yarn in her arms. "Lisa, Kelly, could you give me a hand, please? Burt and I have got to run off and do errands before dinner, and the delivery truck has dropped off three boxes of new yarns. Connie is too busy with customers at the front to unpack."

"New yarns? I'm on it," Kelly said, dropping her vest onto the table. "I take it you want them in the center room. These bins are already full."

"I'll help, too, Mimi," Lisa said, shoving her knitting back into her bag.

Mimi dumped the colorful fluff balls onto the library table, sending them scattering. "You girls are lifesavers. I feel like that proverbial chicken running around with its head cut off. I swear, I'm running so fast I'm meeting myself in the middle." She pointed to the central yarn room. "All of these yarns go into those bins along the wall, Kelly. I'll bring some more in a minute. Burt's already loading the shelves on the other side of the room. Lisa, you can help me unpack and load the shelves in the back room." Mimi hurried from the room.

"See you tonight at practice, Kelly," Lisa said as she followed after Mimi.

Kelly gathered up all the fluff balls and headed to the central yarn room, where Burt was opening another box of yarn. An empty box lay at his feet.

"Hey, Burt, I see Megan's got you two running so fast you're meeting yourselves in the middle."

"You're right about that, Kelly," Burt said without turning around. "Mimi and I are seriously considering running off to elope this weekend."

"Too late for that, Burt," Kelly said as she started filling bins with fluff balls on top of fluff balls. "Dresses have been bought, cakes are being baked, or will be. You're stuck now."

Burt chuckled. "But you know what?" He turned to eye Kelly. "I like being stuck with Mimi."

Kelly laughed softly as she continued to load the balls of colorful yarn into bins. Mimi brought out another box, and Kelly started loading those yarns as well. The bins and shelves fairly spilled over with the abundance of fiber. Merino wool, cotton and silk, eyelash, crinkly ribbons.

"Anything new on that investigation, Burt? Any word from your friend?"

"Nothing new, according to Vern," Burt said, reaching deep into the box. "They were finally able to interview the last retreat attendee. She'd been away on business ever since Peterson started the second round of investigations."

Kelly looked up with interest. "Did she say anything different from the others?"

Burt shook his head, then emptied the box. Two fluffy balls and crinkly skeins fell onto the floor. "Not really. She did mention something about Greta hearing a noise in the middle of the night."

"Really? Well, that's something. I don't recall Greta saying anything about that."

"It doesn't sound like anything, though. Edie is the woman's name, and she and Greta shared a cabin. She said she awoke in the middle of the night and saw Greta standing in the open doorway. Anyway, she asked if anything was wrong, and Greta said she thought she heard something and got up to check outside. She didn't see anything, though."

"Maybe she heard Bill Zarofsky's truck engine like Dr. Norcross did. What do you think?"

Burt shrugged. "I don't know, Kelly. Maybe." He glanced over his shoulder and gave her a smile. "But it really doesn't matter what we think. It's Peterson's ball game. He calls the plays, and we're not on his team. Officially, that is."

Kelly's bat hit the ball with a loud crack. The sweetest sound in the world to Kelly's ears. She watched the ball sail up, up, and away as she dropped the bat and took off, rounding first base in a loping stride. Good-natured teasing and cheers sounded as she ran.

They were all hitting well tonight. Everybody connected with line drives, even home runs. "Outta the park," as one of Kelly's summertime teenage baseball players would say.

If this were a game rather than a practice, they'd be burying the other team with their bats. *Oh, yeah.*

"Lookin' good," Megan called, giving Kelly the high sign as she rounded third.

Boy, were they ready. The season started tomorrow night. *Bring it on.*

Seventeen

Kelly slammed the door of her cottage and raced down the steps. The light showers predicted for this morning had appeared exactly on schedule. She ran through the rain, across the driveway, and into the flowering patio garden behind Pete's café. Since spring's showers had been abundant in April and May, the garden was already lush and green with plants.

Flowering lilac bushes threw their wet scent into the air, peonies burst into bloom, and vinca vines covered the flower beds with green leaves and purple flowers. Yellow and pink irises edged the fence, and the blossoming crab apple trees were heavy with pink and white flowers.

Kelly scampered up the wooden back steps to the

café and burst inside, shaking raindrops off her clothes. "Boy, it's chilly today," she declared, brushing droplets out of her hair. "I really need that coffee now."

Jennifer took Kelly's mug from her outstretched hand and poured a stream of Eduardo's black brew. "One of these days, you'll learn how useful jackets are on rainy days. I thought you had a jacket with a hood."

"I do, but I always forget to wear it," Kelly said as she eagerly accepted the refilled mug. She sniffed the heady aroma trailing upward. "Did you learn anything about Zarofsky yesterday?"

"A little. There wasn't much to learn," Jennifer said as she headed back into the busy café.

"Did your commercial broker friend know him?" Kelly asked as she settled at a table in the alcove along the side of the café.

Jennifer paused at Kelly's table, scanning the seated customers before answering. "Ralph never heard of him. He checked his associations' lists, and Zarofsky isn't there. So, the only thing Ralph and I can figure out is maybe Zarofsky is a 'wannabe.' You know . . . he pretends to be a developer when in reality, he doesn't do squat."

"Maybe so," Kelly said, sipping her coffee. "I had a feeling he was lying."

"Well, that's what I figured after I talked with Ralph. Then yesterday afternoon I took some paperwork over to another real estate agent who has an office in the Commercial Bank Building. While I was there, I checked the directory, and sure enough, Zarofsky has an office in the building. And he's listed as 'Commercial Real Estate.'"

Kelly stared at her. "What? But he's not working in commercial. Your guy said so."

"Yeah, I know. I thought that strange, too, so I went up to his office. His name is on the door, all official, but it was closed and locked. Not a soul in sight."

"That is so bizarre," Kelly said, shaking her head. "This guy is lying. I can feel it. But why?"

"I know, it doesn't make sense. There's a possibility he's getting started in the business and hasn't joined the associations yet. But, that's kind of unlikely. Real estate is a business of networking. Everyone knows everyone else in the business. You've got to work with people to be successful. Maybe he's so new at it, he simply doesn't know what he doesn't know."

"Yeah, riiiight. I still think he's lying, but I can't figure out why."

A customer on the other side of the café lifted his cup, and Jennifer turned away. "Gotta go, customers calling. But there was one other thing. I checked the county real estate records and found out Zarofsky did put that lien on Everett's ranch."

"He did?" Kelly exclaimed. "Whoa, now that's something serious, according to Jayleen. When did he do it?"

Jennifer started to walk away. "The Monday following the retreat. Talk to you later."

Kelly's thoughts sped up. Monday was the day after they found Cal Everett's dead body. Boy . . . Zarofsky sure didn't waste any time, did he? Why would he put the lien on Cal's property so soon after their fight? Unless . . . unless Zarofsky already knew Everett was dead. And if he was the one who "helped" Cal over the railing, then Zarofsky knew Everett would no longer be a problem.

Her mind buzzing, Kelly pulled out her laptop and set up on the café table. She had client accounts to enter. Work to do. Boring, yes, but necessary.

Gray, rainy days were actually unusual in Fort Connor, since it boasted approximately 320 sunny days a year. So, those days were conducive to snuggling in a warm, cozy spot and working. She flipped open the laptop and powered it up. Her hand moved the cursor over the screen as she tried to force her mind into accounting mode. It wouldn't go. Instead, the cursor stopped over the Web browser icon. Always so tempting.

She paused, staring at the icon. Kelly's last search on Zarofsky revealed nothing except alpaca associations. Maybe Megan had learned something. She dug out her cell phone and punched in the familiar number.

Megan answered quickly. "Hey, there, I was about to call you."

"Why? Did you find something on Zarofsky, I hope?"

"Well, yes and no. Like you, I didn't find anything about a commercial real estate connection—"

"Neither did Jennifer," Kelly interrupted. "But she did find his office in the Commercial Bank Building. All closed and locked. Nobody there."

"That's bizarre."

"Isn't it, now? I know that guy is up to something. I can feel it. Did you find any legal problems or stuff like that?"

"Not on William Zarofsky, but I did find some past history on a Kevin Zarofsky. He was arrested several years ago for selling drugs."

"Whoa! I wasn't expecting that. He must be related to Bill Zarofsky, don't you think? I mean, with that same last name. 'Zarofsky' isn't exactly common."

"I think that's probably a good bet."

"Way to go, Megan! You are fantastic. You and those special websites of yours. How long ago did this happen? Was he convicted? How long was he in jail?"

"Hold on, let me check my notes." Megan paused. "He was convicted seven years ago on two counts of possession with intent to distribute methamphetamines. Looks like he served five years in the Colorado State Department of Corrections in Buena Vista."

"How old is he?"

"That information wasn't listed."

"Was he arrested here in Fort Connor? I mean, was he doing drugs here?"

"It looks like he was arrested in Denver. Yep, Denver. And he was tried in Denver District Court and sentenced to serve five to eight years. He got out in five."

"So he's finished his sentence. Can you find out where he is now?"

"Nope. No can do. That's all I've got."

"Man, you are fantastic, Megan. A superstar sleuth."

"Yeah, right. Listen, I hate to state the obvious, but the fact that Bill Zarofsky has a scumbag relative who's a convicted felon doesn't prove anything about Zarofsky himself. Kevin could be the black sheep in the family, that's all."

Kelly considered Megan's point. "You're right. But my instinct is still buzzing about Bill Zarofsky, separate from his criminal relative. He's proved himself to be a liar once already. And I think he's lying again about Cal Everett."

"So, what are you going to do now?"

That was a good question. Kelly thought for a minute. *What can I do?* She had nothing on Bill Zarofsky except an empty office. That was less than nothing. People closed offices all the time. And having a felon for a relative didn't prove anything.

"Right now, I'm going to call Jayleen and see if she's learned anything about Zarofsky. She knows him from the alpaca associations and exhibitions."

"Well, good luck. I've gotta get back to my own work because I'm hoping we'll still have a game tonight. It's not looking too good right now."

"Do we have a rain date?"

"Yeah, tomorrow night. Meanwhile, keep your fingers crossed that those clouds blow away."

"Will do. Thanks again, Megan," Kelly said as her friend clicked off.

She immediately paged through her cell phone's directory until she found Jayleen's number and punched it in, anxiously waiting as the phone rang.

"Hey, Jayleen, did you find out anything about Zarofsky?" she blurted when her friend's voice came on the line.

"Hey, Kelly, slow down and take a breath," Jayleen said with a laugh. "I was going to give you a call later."

"Did you learn anything?"

"Not much. All I heard were some comments about his dealings with other breeders. Seems he's had some disputes with a couple of them over breeding fees and stuff. Apparently this guy has a short fuse."

"Short fuse and lying to the cops. Not a good combination. You know, Megan did a Web search and found out that Zarofsky has a relative who was convicted of dealing drugs a few years ago in Denver. He served five years in Buena Vista."

"*Damnation!* Well, that sure puts a new light on things. Was Zarofsky connected to any of it?"

"Megan didn't see his name mentioned at all, so there's no proof he's connected with Kevin Zarofsky. But with a name like that, it's likely they're related."

Jayleen paused. "You know, Kelly, Zarofsky might not be involved at all. Whether Kevin is a relative or not. Zarofsky might be clean as a whistle."

Kelly mulled over what Jayleen said. Of course it was possible Zarofsky was innocent of all wrongdoing. But Kelly's little buzzer kept going off. Something was up with this guy. Something made him lie to the police about the night of Everett's death. *What was it?* Was he involved in Everett's death? Was he involved in Kevin's drug dealing?

Suddenly a memory surfaced from the back of Kelly's mind. Something she heard around the Lambspun table when she and Megan were talking to the two women who lived in Poudre Canyon. They both had strong opinions about Cal Everett, but one woman also mentioned something about Zarofsky. Something that bothered her. What was it?

Cars. The noisy cars in his driveway regularly woke her up at night. There were lots of cars, she said, coming and going at all hours. Kelly's little buzzer rang louder.

Why would Zarofsky have so many visitors? Maybe those cars weren't coming to see Bill Zarofsky. Maybe they were coming to see ex-con Kevin. Was Kevin Zarofsky up to his old habits? Was he dealing drugs from the canyon ranch?

Kelly felt her pulse speed up at that thought. Assuming Kevin Zarofsky was related to Rancher Bill, wouldn't the police know about it? Wouldn't he be under supervision or on parole or something? *Who knows?* Maybe he jumped parole and slipped away from Denver. The canyons surrounding Fort Connor were heavily wooded and filled with rugged crags and ravines. Someone who wanted to hide out could do so easily in the canyons, especially if they had a relative nearby who provided food and shelter.

Her mind racing, Kelly let the images and scenes she was scripting in her head swirl. Then, another thought flashed in front of the rest. One of her crazy ideas, of course. Most of her best ideas were a little bit crazy and often a little bit risky.

"Kelly, I can hear you thinking all the way over this phone line," Jayleen said with a low chuckle.

Her friends knew her too well. "Yeah, I am, Jayleen. There's something I want to do, but I could use your help. That is, if you don't mind doing a little sleuthing after lunch."

"Ha! I knew you were up to something. What's going on in that fertile mind of yours?"

"Is there a way we can go up to Zarofsky's ranch and take a look? Slip in a side way, so we can see without being seen?"

Jayleen paused for a moment. "What're you looking for, Kelly?"

"I'm just curious. One of Lambspun's regulars has a place next to Zarofsky's. And she mentioned that cars were coming and going down his driveway all the time. Even at night. She said it kept her awake."

"You don't say."

"Yeah. I didn't think anything of it at the time, but now that we know Zarofsky's got a relative who was selling drugs, well . . . it makes me wonder."

Jayleen was quiet for a moment. "You know, Kelly, you've got me curious, too. Why don't we take a little drive up there. I know that area around his ranch real well, because it backs up into national forest. We can drive down a forest road, park, and hike up to his property line and take a little look-see."

"That's exactly what I had in mind. When can you go? I can be up there whenever it suits you," Kelly said, once again pushing off the accounting routine until another day.

"How about you be at my ranch by noon? We'll head off then, okay?"

"Works for me."

"We'll take my truck. Your little red car can stay parked here. It sticks out like a sore thumb."

"Good point. I see you've done surveillance work before," Kelly teased.

"You mean spying on people? Hell, yes. Back when I was still drinking and paranoid. Usually checking on my cheating husband. By the way, you'd better bring a jacket. It's still raining up here."

"Wow, you really have done this before."

Jayleen chuckled. "I'll bring my binoculars."

Kelly stepped through the pale spring green foliage, wet grass clinging to her khaki pants. This high up in Poudre Canyon spring was only now making its presence known. The buds on the bushes were starting to open, and tiny leaves were clasped together like praying hands. Everything glistened. The earlier rain had dropped to a light sprinkle.

Mountain rain showers, however, were deceptive. They may appear light, but they soaked you through unless your rain gear shed water well. One of Kelly's first shopping trips after she'd decided to make Fort Connor her home had been to the local outdoor gear retail store. She'd needed to stock up.

"Looks like there's a good spot up ahead," Jayleen said, walking in front of Kelly.

Pushing back a pine branch, Kelly followed. Droplets of water fell from the branch onto her pants and hiking boots as she walked through the dark, wet soil of the forest floor. The smell of damp earth rose like perfume. Pine branches caught at her jacket but slipped away, unable to grasp its wet surface.

Jayleen paused behind a stand of evergreens and brushed aside a long branch. Kelly joined her and peered through the opening Jayleen had created. The land sloped down from this spot and ended in a rolling green pasture.

There below, Kelly spotted a sprawling one-story white farmhouse. Pastures with alpaca bordered both sides of a gravel driveway that ended in a clearing beside a large reddish brown barn. A smaller gray-colored garage was set back from the barn. She could see alpaca grazing in the pastures, and several clustered in the corral leading into the barn. From here, Bill Zarofsky's place looked like a typical mountain canyon ranch. Nothing special and nothing suspicious.

Jayleen lifted the binoculars that hung around her neck and adjusted the focus as she peered down into the ranch below. "Looks pretty normal to me."

Noticing two trucks parked in the barnyard, one

black, the other light blue, Kelly squinted. Zarofsky drove a light blue truck. "Do you see anyone walking around?"

"Nope, not yet. But we know at least two people are there because there're two trucks parked."

Kelly and Jayleen stared at the ranch without speaking for a couple of minutes. Then, Kelly saw a door opening to the smaller garage building. A man exited and strode across the barnyard to one of the trucks.

"Well, looky here. I knew someone would turn up," Jayleen said, and adjusted the binoculars again.

The man opened the door to the black truck, got inside, and started the engine. Even from this far away, Kelly could hear the engine's rumble. The man wore a dark jacket and what looked like jeans. He proceeded to turn the truck around in the barnyard and drive over to the garage. Then he parked, got out, and walked to the back of the truck, where he lowered the tailgate before disappearing into the garage.

"Looks like he's going to load something," Jayleen said.

Kelly moved another pine branch out of her line of sight and stared at the gray building, waiting for the man to reemerge carrying something. It was all she could do to contain her impatience. Finally, he appeared, carrying two boxes, one stacked on top of the other.

"Now it's getting interesting," Jayleen said, leaning forward.

Suddenly another man appeared from the garage, and he was carrying two boxes as well. Both men walked to the truck, where they loaded all four boxes. Then, the first man pulled what looked like a tarp from the corner of the truck bed and spread it over the boxes. The other man returned to the barn.

"I wonder what's in those boxes." Kelly said, pushing back her jacket hood, now that the tree branches provided rain cover.

"They looked like regular old cardboard boxes to me. I guess he's covering them in case the rain picks up again."

The second man emerged from the barn again, this time carrying a large sack. He dumped it on top of the boxes in the back of the truck and returned to the barn. Meanwhile, the first man secured the tailgate while the second man returned with another large sack and dumped that into the truck as well.

"Can you tell what's in those big sacks they brought out?"

"Looks a lot like bags of feed. Almost exactly like it. Those are pretty heavy sacks. I wonder why they're not covering them with the tarp, too. Those feed sacks will be ruined in the rain."

"Looks like they're more interested in covering up the cardboard boxes. Kind of makes you wonder what's in those boxes."

"Here," Jayleen said, slipping the binoculars over her head. "Take a look and see for yourself. For what it's worth, the guy in the blue jacket looks like Bill Zarofsky. I can't be sure."

Kelly adjusted the focus of the powerful binoculars,

amazed how far the vision field extended. Now, the barnyard was close and she could see the men as they walked around the truck, loading more sacks of live-stock feed. Glimpsing one of the men, she agreed with Jayleen. The man in the blue jacket resembled the man she saw arguing with Cal Everett at the retreat, but she couldn't be sure. And the truck looked like the one Bill Zarofsky had been driving.

"You know, Jayleen, I'm really curious why they're covering up those boxes with feed. They've already got a tarp over them. And you're right, the rain would de-stroy those sacks of feed. Do you think they're simply trying to conceal the boxes?"

"Yep, I think that's about the size of it."

Kelly pondered. Not having any personal experience with the drug world, she didn't have a clue how much any of these substances weighed. Like everyone else, she'd seen television news reports and movies showing bags of cocaine, and they always seemed packed pretty tightly in their contraband containers.

She decided to defer to a more knowledgeable au-thority. Jayleen's former life of alcohol addiction had exposed her to a fair slice of the shadowy world. So, Kelly asked outright.

"What do you think they're hiding in those boxes, Jayleen? I figure it's drugs. What kind, do you think?"

"I'd bet it's most likely crystal meth. I've heard how easy it is to hide a meth lab in the mountains. In fact, my warning bell is ringing like crazy right now. And that's always a sure sign of trouble."

"Mine, too. In fact, I'd put money on it. I'm gonna give Burt a call."

"Good idea, Kelly," Jayleen said, accepting the binoculars again as Kelly dug out her cell phone.

Checking for a signal, Kelly punched in Burt's number. Her pulse was racing with the excitement of the chase. And the catch. Burt would be proud of them. Her sleuthing may have solved Cal Everett's murder and busted a drug operation all at the same time.

Burt's voice came on. "Hey, Kelly, what's up? Would you like to help me run some errands this afternoon?"

"Maybe, Burt, but first I think there's something else that deserves your attention. Did you know that Bill Zarofsky had a relative who served five years in Buena Vista for dealing drugs? He got out three years ago. Name is Kevin Zarofsky."

Burt was quiet for several seconds. When he answered, Kelly noticed his voice lacked all the fatherly warmth she was used to. "How'd you find out about Kevin Zarofsky?"

"Megan found out for me," Kelly blithely replied. "I asked her to search some of her restricted access sites, and she found out about his conviction and sentencing. Now, you know how suspicious I've been of Bill Zarofsky. Well, I've got a strong suspicion that Bad Boy Kevin is up to his old tricks again and involving Rancher Bill with him."

Another pause. "And what gave you that idea, may I ask?"

"Because I'm standing here with Jayleen on the

edge of Zarofsky's ranch, watching two men load several cardboard boxes into the back of a pickup truck."

"*What!* Where are you again?"

"I'm up here on the edge of Zarofsky's ranch, watching him and this other guy who's probably his brother hide boxes under a tarp in the back of his truck. Then they weighted them down with sacks of feed," Kelly rattled on. "Jayleen thinks the boxes are probably full of crystal meth, and they'd need—"

"*Damn it, Kelly! Get your butt off that ranch right now!*"

"Wha—?"

"Peterson's guys are ready to swoop down on Zarofsky this afternoon. If you screw up his operation, I swear . . . even I can't save you. Peterson will be so mad, he'll throw you in jail, too!"

That got her attention. "I–I'm sorry, Burt. I didn't know . . ."

"Move out of there now before Zarofsky sees you and gets suspicious. You'll blow Peterson's plans to bits."

"Don't worry, Burt, we're up here in the trees. They can't see us," Kelly said, motioning to Jayleen, who was shaking her head already. Savvy Jayleen had clearly picked up the gist of the conversation.

"Just get your butt out of there now and pray that you didn't blow this thing."

Backing away from their surveillance spot, Kelly said, "We're leaving now, Burt. Nobody in sight. We parked Jayleen's truck down on the forest service road. Tell Peterson he'd better hurry up. Those two guys look like they're ready to drive away in that truck any minute."

Burt uttered a few more exasperated rebukes before he hung up.

Jayleen held back a pine branch as they hastened through the green forest, returning to their path. "I have a feeling we just stepped into something we shouldn't have, Kelly girl."

"Ohhhh, yeah. And I'm up to my waist."

Kelly turned the windshield wipers to high as she maneuvered her car around the corner into a favorite shopping center. Meanwhile, she waited for Steve to answer his cell phone. Finally he picked up. "Hey, I was thinking about ethnic for dinner tonight. Since our game was rained out, I just feel like staying home and staying dry. How about you?"

Steve released a long sigh she could hear over the phone. He sounded tired. "Yeah, that's fine. Damn rain. I was really looking forward to playing tonight."

Kelly could hear a level of frustration in his voice she hadn't heard before. "Feel the need to knock it out of the park, huh?"

"Oh, yeah."

"Well, tell me all about it tonight while we curl up and eat and stay warm and dry."

"Sounds good."

227

"So, what do you want? Indian, Chinese, Thai, Italian, what?"

He sighed again. "I don't care. You choose."

Kelly heard that frustration creep into his voice again. "Okay, Indian it is."

Eighteen

Kelly peered around the corner of the Lambspun foyer, hoping to spot Burt. No sign of him. She walked through the yarn rooms toward the knitting table, listening for the sound of his voice. Nothing.

Rats! She was hoping to catch Burt here at the shop before he left to run errands this morning. With the wedding only days away, Mimi and Burt had rarely been seen at the shop this week. Kelly wanted to apologize to her mentor and partner in crime investigations for stumbling into the Zarofsky business without checking first. She should have known Peterson and his guys were suspicious of Zarofsky's black sheep relative, Kevin. After all, the cops were privy to all sorts of information from informants. Hadn't Burt once told her they kept intelligence files on people they were suspicious of? Watching and waiting for them to make a mistake. Of course he did.

She was also dying to know how Peterson's raid on Zarofsky's ranch went. Did they find a drug lab in that garage as Jayleen suspected? Were those boxes filled with crystal meth, all packaged and ready to sell? She had hoped Burt would call her last night with an update, but she hadn't heard a word. Kelly wasn't sure if Burt was still annoyed with her or had simply spent the evening doing more errands with Mimi.

Kelly plopped her bag on the library table and took a big sip of Eduardo's coffee. Maybe she should sit and work on the knitted vest for a while, on the chance Burt might appear. Or, she could open her laptop and catch up on her accounting clients. Kelly pulled the vest from her bag.

Then, she heard a familiar voice coming from the classroom area outside Mimi's office. *Burt.* She hastened to the doorway. Burt stood in the middle of the room, talking on his cell phone. She waited until he finished his call before apologizing.

"Mea culpa, Burt. I'm majorly sorry," Kelly said in a contrite voice. "I didn't mean to cause trouble yesterday."

Burt glanced over and smiled. His regular warm, fatherly smile again. Kelly felt better seeing that. "I didn't mean to bite your head off yesterday, Kelly. But you caught me at a bad time. Behind a traffic jam, behind on errands, and way behind on patience."

"You and Mimi still running ragged? I'm going to have to talk to Megan about those lists. She's outta control."

"Well, she's a taskmaster, I'll say that. But Mimi and I are almost finished. Today and tomorrow should be the last of it. We're scheduling downtime for Saturday, the day before the wedding. In fact, we may even turn our cell phones off." He gave her a devilish smile.

Kelly feigned shock, hand to her mouth. "Turn off your cell phones? Why . . . that's heresy!"

"Yeah, I know."

Now that she was back in Burt's good graces, she had to ask. Her curiosity was killing her. "Can you tell me what happened, Burt? On Peterson's raid, I mean. What did Vern say? Did they find any drugs?"

Burt chuckled. "I wondered how long you could last before asking." He checked his watch. "Looks like about sixty seconds."

"Okay, okay, okay, so I'm impatient," Kelly admitted. "So tell me, please! I'm dying of curiosity."

"I can tell. Let's go find a quiet place."

"No one's at the knitting table right now," Kelly said, heading toward the adjacent room.

"I'll give you the details quickly before I have to leave for errands." Burt pulled out two chairs next to each other.

Kelly settled beside Burt and leaned forward, so they

could speak softly without their voices carrying. "Okay, what happened?"

"Well, we were right about Kevin Zarofsky getting back into his drug business. Those boxes were filled with plastic bags of crystal meth, ready to sell on the street."

"*Yes!*" Kelly hissed in triumph, fist clenched. "Jayleen and I were right."

Burt nodded. "Yes, you were. Good instincts, Kelly. And you were right about them starting to leave. It sounds like Peterson and his boys roared down the driveway just as the Zarofskys were ready to drive off. Caught them red-handed with the drugs in the truck. And that garage was their meth lab. Pretty slick setup, too. No neighbors close by who could see what they were doing and get suspicious."

"Actually, Zarofsky did have one neighbor who lives across the road from his place, and it was her comment that made me suspicious. She said he had lots of cars going down his driveway."

"You're kidding? Who was it? Where'd you find her?"

Kelly smiled. "Right here in Lambspun. She's one of the regulars who comes down for the crochet sessions and workshops. Her name's Eileen. Mimi's bound to know who she is. She was here at the table one afternoon with another gal who lives up in Poudre Canyon, and we started talking about Cal Everett's death. Then, she mentioned this neighbor of hers, Zarofsky."

"Well, I'll be damned. Good sleuthing, Kelly."

Kelly acknowledged his praise with a nod. "Thank you, sir. Now, enough about Kevin. What about Bill Zarofsky? Were they able to find anything that connects him to Everett's death?"

Burt shook his head. "That, I don't know. Vern didn't say a word about Everett. It was clear they were focusing entirely on busting the Zarofskys' drug business. It seems they've been keeping an eye on them ever since our old friend, Deputy Don, got suspicious last year. Apparently he'd noticed a lot of different cars coming and going, so he paid a visit." Burt smiled. "Don said his nose started itching the way it does when something's not right. That, plus the fact that Bill Zarofsky acted kind of jumpy when Don was talking with him. That was enough to get Don's report in their file. Then, they started hearing from other sources that some dealers were bringing meth into Denver from northern Colorado. That's how cases are built, Kelly. One bit of information at a time."

"Didn't they keep track of Kevin when he got out of prison?"

"They tried, but he jumped parole after six months. Apparently he's kept a low profile ever since he's been holed up in the canyon. No one's spotted him."

"So Peterson and the guys put all those little pieces together and decided that Kevin Zarofsky was on the scene. Hiding out in the canyon and cooking up crystal meth."

"Yeah. But they really caught a break when they questioned Bill Zarofsky's girlfriend the second time. That's when she got scared and admitted he wasn't with her that night and had begged her to lie for him. Peterson asked if she had any idea where he might have been that night, and who his other friends were. Apparently she told them Zarofsky had frequent cell phone calls from his *brother*." Burt's smile spread. "That's when they knew they had him."

"Ha! So Kevin really was the Black Sheep Brother."

"Apparently so."

Kelly leaned back in her chair and took a sip of coffee. "Good job, guys. You give Vern my congratulations, okay?"

"Will do," Burt said, rising from his chair. "Now, it's back on my horse I go. Wish me luck."

"Good Lord, Burt, what does Megan have you doing now? Are you sure you don't need any help finishing up with those errands?"

"Actually, I'm in pretty good shape. Mimi and I are down to little stuff now, like paper plates, napkins, and cups."

"I'm so glad you two are doing this casual, rather than formal. It's going to be so much nicer to relax in Mimi's pretty backyard with the gazebo."

"Well, thank Mimi. Megan was about to order linens and china and the whole nine yards of fancy, when Mimi put her foot down."

"Good for her!" Kelly exclaimed. "Megan gets wound up sometimes."

"Tell me about it," Burt said as he headed toward the archway.

"Oh, and don't forget to let me know if Zarofsky admits to anything else, okay?"

"I'll call you as soon as I hear something," he said over his shoulder.

Kelly took another long sip of coffee, processing everything that Burt told her. She picked up her vest and started another row, still pleased that she had been right on top of things, discovering clues just like the police. She finished one row and started another when her cell phone rang. *How will I ever finish this vest?* She was always starting and stopping.

She spotted Lisa's name on her phone screen. "Don't forget to be on time tonight," Kelly warned when she answered. "Megan will have your head. You know how she gets."

"Yeah, I do, but that's not why I called," Lisa said.

"What's up?" Kelly settled back in her chair. She heard that confidential tone in Lisa's voice.

"I want to tell you what happened this morning. Greta came up to me and asked how Jennifer was doing. That kind of surprised me, so I told her that Jen appeared to be doing okay. Her appointments with Dr. Norcross had helped a lot. Then I decided to use the opportunity to try and get Greta to open up. So I asked her if she was all right, like I have so many other times. And she got this funny look on her face and told me she was fine. Then, she grabbed her backpack and tore out of the office."

"I remember you saying she does that every time you ask her, Lisa. She probably doesn't want another therapist probing around in her past, especially if she was assaulted."

"That's what I thought, too. And then, I ran into one of the research assistants, Mary. She's another grad student. I remembered her mentioning that she and Greta had gone through undergrad studies together and had known each other for years. So, on a whim, I asked her straight out if she'd noticed that Greta was acting differently, nervous and not wanting to communicate. Then I told her what happened at the retreat, and that I was worried about Greta. And you'll never believe what Mary said."

Kelly paused, taking another sip of coffee, waiting for Lisa to continue. "Okay, what was it?"

"Mary got a worried look on her face and said that sounded exactly like the way Greta acted after her sister died. Well, I gotta tell you, that floored me."

"Greta never mentioned she had a sister who died. I wonder why."

"Well, that's not all. I asked Mary what the cause of death was. Was the sister younger or older? And Mary beckoned me over to a corner and told me that Greta's younger sister, Bonnie, committed suicide. She drove up into Poudre Canyon, parked in a secluded spot, and took an overdose of sleeping pills. She wasn't found until the next morning."

Kelly set her mug on the table. "Oh, my God . . . that's awful."

"I know. Now, I feel really terrible about trying to force Greta to talk."

"You couldn't know, Lisa. Greta obviously didn't share with anyone except her old friend and Dr. Norcross, no doubt." Kelly thought for a moment. "Does Mary think Greta blames herself for her sister's suicide?"

"Yes, she does. She thinks what's bothering Greta is that she didn't find the right therapist for Bonnie when she really needed help. Greta found several different therapists, but Bonnie's depression kept getting worse. After Bonnie committed suicide, Greta blamed herself. According to Mary, Greta believed that since she was studying psychology, she should have recognized Bonnie's signs earlier."

"Whoa, that's one heavy load of guilt Greta's carrying around. She couldn't possibly have recognized all of Bonnie's signs."

"Absolutely. Besides, family members become quite adept at hiding their symptoms from their families."

"When did Greta find Dr. Norcross?"

"Mary said it was about a year after Bonnie's suicide."

"That is so tragic. Is Mary going to take her concerns to Dr. Norcross?"

"She said she would." Lisa paused. "I told Mary my first thoughts were that Greta had been sexually assaulted, and the retreat brought back all those memories. But Mary thinks everything that happened at the retreat and Everett's death must have shaken loose some of Greta's old traumatic memories. She said that Greta withdrew from friends after Bonnie died."

Kelly mulled over what Lisa told her. "Well, it appears Dr. Norcross was able to help Greta years ago. So, I'm sure she'll be able to help her again. It sounds like she already is, given that comment you overheard."

"Yeah, you're right. I'm sure Dr. Norcross is on top of it . . . it's just . . ."

"Just what?"

"I keep thinking about all those appointments I saw on the calendar. Greta has been seeing Dr. Norcross three times a week, and she seems to be getting more and more agitated every time I see her. She doesn't seem to be getting any better."

Kelly didn't have an answer for that. So she told her friend the only reassuring thing she could think of. "You don't know that for sure, Lisa. Maybe Greta *is* doing better. Only Dr. Norcross knows. Why don't you leave it for her to decide?"

Lisa released a long sigh. "Yeah, you're right, I know you're right."

"Wow, can I tape that? I want to play it back again when you're giving me a hard time."

"Okay, okay . . . listen, I have to get to a physical therapy appointment. See you tonight."

"Right. And bring your game. We need a pitcher on the mound, not a therapist," Kelly teased before she clicked off.

Picking up the vest again, Kelly knitted another

three rows, thinking over everything Lisa had said. Poor Greta. Losing a family member to suicide was horrible from what she'd heard. The surviving family members worry that they should have been able to prevent it somehow. It was a double tragedy to Kelly's way of thinking.

Another row and another formed on her knitting needles, as Kelly wondered what on earth had happened in Bonnie's young life that would have caused her to end it all. She couldn't have been out of her twenties, because Greta was in her early thirties now, just like Kelly and her friends. What had happened?

After another few moments of pondering, Kelly's curiosity overcame the knitting. *I'll never finish this vest.* She slid her laptop out of her bag and fired it up, listening to the whirring electronic purr. When the icons popped up on her screen, Kelly clicked the browser, then the familiar search engine, where she entered the name "Bonnie Baldwin."

Various listings and items appeared and Kelly perused them all, but none of them referred to Greta's sister. These other people were older or lived in different places. Kelly scrolled farther, then closed the screen and flipped open her cell phone again. Punching in Megan's number.

"Hey, Megan, can you do another quick search for me?" she asked when her friend answered.

"Actually I'm right in the middle of a spreadsheet. Can I do it later tonight?"

The mention of spreadsheets reminded Kelly she had some waiting for her, too. She continued to ignore them. "It'll only take you a moment on one of your restricted sites. I've already tried to find this person on Google and got nothing. Please, pretty please. I'll never be late to practice again, I promise."

"Yeah, right."

"Promise, scout's honor, cross my heart . . ."

"Okay, okay . . . give me a second while I log in."

"You're a jewel. A pearl."

"Yeah, yeah."

"Even if you're giving Mimi and Burt ulcers with those lists."

Megan laughed softly. "You've been talking to Burt."

"Oh, yeah."

"Okay, I'm in. Who're you looking up?"

"A young woman named Bonnie Baldwin who died about three years ago here in Colorado. Committed suicide in Poudre Canyon."

"Oh, no . . . that's awful."

Kelly heard the sound of Megan's fingers entering information on the keyboard. "Yeah, apparently she drove up there and took an overdose of sleeping pills."

"Poor thing. I wonder what made her do that."

"That's what I'm wondering. I hoped there might be something listed, some information, maybe."

Megan was quiet for a couple of minutes and Kelly was, too, not wanting to interrupt her friend's concentration. Finally, Megan spoke. "Well, all that shows up are her car registration, her registration at the university, and her obituary. Looks like she'd gone through her junior year, studying agricultural economics."

"What does her obituary say? How old was she?"

"She was twenty-two. Wow, so young to die."

"Anything else?"

"Not really. Obits never go into detail about suicides. It simply says there'll be a private family graveside service. Lists family members. Greta Baldwin. Is that the Greta who's Lisa's friend at the university?"

"Yep, the same. And Lisa's been worrying about her. Seems like the retreat stirred up painful memories, and she's getting depressed like she did after her sister died."

"Oh, that is too bad."

"Thanks, Megan, I'll let you get back to work. In fact, I need to do the same. See you tonight."

"Be ready."

Kelly clicked off her phone and returned to her laptop. She quickly moved the cursor to open her client accounting files before she was tempted away again. Avoidance only worked for so long.

"Heeeey, batter, batter, batter, batter, batter," a man's voice called.

Kelly glanced over at the bleachers. Spouses, boyfriends, relatives, and friends sat clutching soft drinks and coffee cups, encouraging Kelly's team. Fan support definitely helped, but it couldn't make up for dropped balls, missed throws, and cold bats.

Nothing worked tonight. Everybody on the team was playing poorly. *What was the matter with them?* They'd been practicing for a month and were looking sharp. Kelly expected they'd take this game easy. Instead, they all looked like they'd just walked on the softball field for the first time since winter. They were lousy.

Maybe it was the rain, Kelly mused, looking for an excuse. They'd been rained out of the game last night. But that didn't make sense. They'd played in the rain before and won.

And it wasn't the other team beating them, either. They'd beaten this Windsor team before. But tonight, they were beating themselves. Once they started making errors—dropped balls, missed catches—the mistakes multiplied, spreading like wildfire throughout the team. Contagious.

Megan missed a catch in right field and had to run it down while three players scored for the other team. Lisa's pitching arm deserted her, and she could only throw easy-to-hit balls which arrived right over the plate. And Kelly dropped the ball trying to tag a runner out. She couldn't remember the last time that happened.

It was depressing to watch.

"Heeeey, batter, batter, batter!" another family member called to Liz, their shortstop, who was at bat.

Liz is a strong, consistent hitter, Kelly thought as she stood waiting for her turn at bat. Maybe Liz would get a hit. Meanwhile, Kelly was hoping she'd get a line drive this time. She'd struck out the last two times at bat. Just like the rest of the team. Nobody was hitting tonight.

"C'mon, Liz, knock it out!" she called to her teammate.

The pitcher's ball flew over home plate. Liz swung and missed.

"Yer out!" the umpire yelled, jerking his thumb to the bench.

Kelly dropped the bat and went to retrieve her baseman's glove again. Three batters in a row. Three strikes each. Three outs. Kelly's team was back on the field.

It was going to be a long night.

"Hey, another Fat Tire over here." Greg held up the empty bottle with the colorful label. A nearby waitress nodded and handed him a bottle from her tray.

Kelly tipped back her ale and sank into the chair at their favorite outdoor café in Old Town Plaza. The sky was velvet blue, the crescent of a new moon hanging over them. The night couldn't be more perfect, with balmy temperatures and just the hint of a breeze. As the month of May drew to a close, the weather had warmed to the low eighties.

Summer was almost here. Summer days stretched

out before Kelly in a comfortable vision of nights filled with ball games and good friends. Trips to the mountains, hiking, camping, sleeping out under the stars like last summer. She and Steve coaching their favorite teenagers in summer ball leagues. Cookouts and canoe trips. Good times . . . or, they should be.

The cloud in that sunny picture was the uncertainty about Steve's business. Worry nibbled around the edges.

Kelly glanced around at her teammates and friends scattered at various tables, consuming pizzas, sandwiches, fries, soups, wings, and drowning their disappointments with a variety of Colorado microbrews. If only they hadn't played so lousy tonight. Even Steve's team lost to Greeley, its archrival.

"Boy, did we stink tonight," Megan said, slouching over her half-eaten sandwich.

"Don't remind me," Lisa said, sinking back in the metal chair.

"You think *you* stunk?" Greg challenged. "Trust me, we reached a whole new level of stench tonight."

"I don't wanta think about it," Steve said, looking morose as he nursed his beer.

"To Greeley, yet. Man, that hurts," Marty added before popping a French fry into his mouth.

"Why don't we simply chalk this one up to first game screwups?" Kelly offered. "We'll get our rhythm back. You know we will. The season's just started."

"First game screwups? I'll drink to that," Greg said as everyone leaned forward to clink beer bottles.

"While we're waiting to get better, let's order more wings," Marty suggested.

"Batting practice would help more," Megan countered. "Who's up for extra practice tomorrow? We can use the cages at the university."

"I'm in," Kelly said, raising her hand as her cell phone rang. Digging in her pocket, she recognized Burt's phone number flashing on her view screen.

"Hey, Burt, what's up?" she asked as she left the noisy table.

"Hi, Kelly. I'll bet I got you in the midst of you guys celebrating in one of your favorite Old Town pubs."

"Well, you're half right. We're in an Old Town pub, but we're drowning our sorrows after playing really lousy tonight."

"I'm sorry to hear that, Kelly. And I'm afraid I'm not bringing good news, either."

Kelly stepped to the edge of the café, away from customers so she could hear better. "What's happened, Burt?"

"I heard from Vern tonight. Bill Zarofsky finally admitted he did return to Everett's ranch later that night—"

"*Yessss!*" Kelly exulted.

"Hear me out, Kelly. Everett paid Zarofsky the past due amount he owed on the loan and promised to pay off the balance early. Zarofsky said he didn't believe him and threatened him with a lien. Then he went back to his own ranch. He and his brother Kevin spent the rest of the night cooking up meth. He can verify that he returned before midnight, because Kevin called him on his cell phone as he was turning into the driveway. So the cell phone calls will be able to corroborate the time Bill returned and the location through GPS coordinates. So, he's no longer considered a 'person of interest' in Everett's death."

"But why?" Kelly protested, trying to keep her voice from rising. People were walking in Old Town Plaza; children were playing in the fountain. "He admitted he went to see Everett. Maybe they had a fight. Maybe he grabbed the check and ran for his truck . . ." Kelly stopped herself, knowing those arguments didn't make sense.

"He'd have no reason to kill Everett, Kelly, and you know it. Everett had given him most of the amount due, according to Zarofsky. So he had no motive. If Everett was dead, he'd never get the rest of his money."

Kelly turned away from the families strolling in the plaza. "I know, I know . . . it's just that I had all my hopes pinned on Bill Zarofsky being guilty. And now that he isn't, Jennifer goes back to number one on Peterson's list. *Dammit!*"

"I feel the same way, Kelly. Unfortunately, we can't change the facts."

"What will happen now, Burt? Is there anything we can do?"

"I'm afraid not. It's in Peterson's hands, and he'll keep investigating until he's satisfied, and there's no way to know how long that will take."

"*Damn,*" Kelly whispered again.

"We have to trust in Peterson's good judgment. Listen, I've got to hang up now. I'm beat. Talk to you tomorrow, Kelly."

"Thanks, Burt," she said, listening to him click off. She shoved her phone into her pocket and headed back to the café. Tonight kept getting worse and worse.

Nineteen

"**Jen,** when you have a second, could you fill up my mug, please?" Kelly leaned against the café's counter, dangling her empty coffee mug.

"Be right over," Jennifer said as she gathered dirty plates from an empty table. "How was your game last night? Did you guys win?"

"Naw, we lost. Boy, we're still rusty. I think we would have played better if we hadn't been rained out. We need to get our rhythm back. Our batting was lousy."

"Hey, summer is only beginning," Jennifer said as she dumped the plates into the plastic tub behind the counter. "You guys will be knocking it out of the park before you know it."

"I hope. Steve's team lost, too, so we all went to Old Town and drowned our sorrows."

Jennifer poured a dark stream into Kelly's mug as the last two café customers in the alcove left. "How's Steve doing? It's getting worse out there. Foreclosures are starting to pop up all over town."

Kelly smelt the aroma drift toward her nostrils—strong and heady. Nerve cells snapped online. "He's holding on, hoping none of his Wellesley homes get hit. But, it's such a bad time now . . . people are losing jobs."

Jennifer nodded, with the expression of someone who had witnessed these boom-and-bust real estate cycles before. Jennifer had built up scar tissue. "And when they lose their jobs, then they lose their homes. It's inevitable, because they can't make the mortgage payments. I've got my fingers crossed that Northern Investments will weather this storm. They're a reputable lender. The riskier companies are already going belly-up."

Kelly searched her brain trying to place the company Jennifer mentioned. "Who's Northern Investments again?"

Jennifer smiled and patted her on the arm. "It's the mortgage company that's handling all the loans for Steve's Wellesley homes."

"Ooops, I knew that," Kelly said, feeling guilty.

"Don't worry. I'll keep you posted if I hear anything. Real estate agents are always the first to know who's going under and who's still afloat."

Kelly flinched at Jennifer's metaphor. She took a deep drink of Eduardo's rich brew as she watched Jennifer wipe off the alcove café tables. The warm spring morning had enticed most breakfast customers outside onto the patio. *Good.* She wanted some privacy.

"Jen, I wanted to give you a heads-up," she said, approaching her friend while she worked. "Detective Peterson may be paying you another visit. I'm not sure, but maybe."

Jennifer glanced up. "Something's happened, I can tell."

Kelly nodded, dropping her voice so the kitchen staff couldn't hear. Thankfully Pete was nowhere in sight. His antennae were so acute when it came to Jennifer, he would be homing in on Kelly's signal right now if he was nearby.

"Yeah, it turns out that Zarofsky has an alibi after all. Seems he was at his ranch with his drug-dealing brother cooking up meth."

Jennifer's eyes widened. "Oh, lovely. He was the one you were hoping would replace me at the top of Peterson's list, right?"

"Yeah, he's guilty, all right. Just not of murder."

Jennifer stared off into the café. "Don't worry about it, Kelly. There's no way I can prove I wasn't involved in Everett's death. Peterson will either believe me or not."

"I know, I know, but . . ."

"You wanted to fix it," Jennifer said, smiling at her. "Some things you just can't fix, Sherlock. Cal Everett's dead. I went out that night for a walk alone. You can't change that. It is what it is."

Kelly didn't like that. She was used to solving problems. Accounting problems, business problems, financial problems, even people problems. Now there was a great big problem involving her dear friend, and Kelly couldn't do anything. She felt helpless. Kelly hated that feeling.

"At least Peterson knows you. That's something."

Jennifer walked up and put her hand on Kelly's arm. "I have a feeling everything's going to be all right. So stop worrying, okay?"

Kelly sighed. "Okay, I'll try. But let me know if Peterson wants to talk to you again."

"Absolutely," Jennifer agreed with a nod. "Now, you go into the shop and finish that vest before it's too hot to wear it. I've got to check my outside customers."

Kelly raised her mug in salute. "Aye, aye, Captain." Then she headed toward the hallway that led into the knitting shop.

Lambspun customers were already prowling the bins and shelves, examining bright summer yarns. Kelly fingered some skeins of cotton and silk as she strolled through the rooms on the way to the knitting table. This would be a good time to catch up on her accounts. There was nothing like numbers to keep her mind occupied. Number problems were a lot easier to handle. You didn't worry about number problems. You solved them.

As she trailed her fingers across a bin of enticing

bamboo and silk blended yarns, Kelly noticed a woman exploring the skeins of novelty yarns in the corner. Something about her looked familiar. Kelly observed the woman, watched her sort through the bins. *Where had she seen her before?* Dark brown hair in a ponytail, looked in her thirties, maybe. Where was it?

Suddenly Kelly remembered. The canyon retreat. The woman was one of the attendees. One of Dr. Nor-cross's patients. *That's it.* Kelly searched her memory, waiting for a name to come. Her name started with an *E. Edie. That's right.*

Another memory popped into Kelly's head. Edie was the one who had been out of town. She was Greta's roommate.

That thought started more ideas churning. Maybe Greta talked to Edie about her sister and her suicide. After all, they shared a cabin while at that emotion-filled retreat. Maybe they talked and shared with each other when they were alone.

"Edie, is that you?" Kelly said, venturing closer.

The woman's head jerked up, and she stared at Kelly for a second before smiling in recognition. "Hey . . . Kelly, isn't it? How're you doing?"

"I'm fine. Weren't you out of town or something? I think I remember you mentioning at the retreat that you had to travel a lot with your job," Kelly fudged. Edie had mentioned her job, that was all.

"Yeah, I've been away on business for a couple of weeks. Consulting has its demands. But I put a re-minder on my daytimer to check out this shop when I returned. I remembered how you guys described it and the yarns." She gazed around in admiration. "Boy, you didn't exaggerate."

Kelly grinned. "Yeah. It has that effect on people. We call it the 'yarn trance' or 'fiber fever.'"

Edie laughed. "Well, you're right about that. I've picked out several yarns trying to decide which is best for my new project. I want to knit a triangular shawl. Maybe you can take a look at my pattern and see if I've got the right thing or not."

Startled that anyone would actually ask her opinion of knitting techniques or procedures, Kelly hesitated a beat. "Sure, I'll be glad to. Why don't we take your basket over to the table, and we can take a look." She plopped her bag on the knitting table, then gestured to the chair beside hers. "Make yourself comfortable."

Edie settled and began rummaging through her basket of yarns, then pulled out a pattern. "I was thinking of knitting the shawl with a lot of different yarns. Then I found this big ball of special yarns and wondered if it would work all right with my pattern. What do you think?"

Kelly looked over the page and inwardly sighed in relief. She'd made this shawl herself. *Whew!* "Oh, this is a nice pattern, and it's easy to knit. I've done it myself." She fondled the ball of yarns Edie had chosen. "Just to be sure, you'll want to knit a gauge swatch to see if these yarns will match the gauge the pattern recommends. Looks like you've got the right needles, circular size 15."

Edie looked doubtful. "How do I make a gauge swatch?"

Kelly recognized that look. She'd worn it a lot. "It's easy. All you have to do is cast on about twelve or so stitches, then knit about six or eight rows. Then you measure with a ruler. That will tell you if you're getting four stitches to the inch like the pattern says."

"I can do that," Edie replied, confidence resurfacing.

Kelly took out her vest-in-progress while Edie started to cast stitches onto her needles. Kelly deliberately let a couple of quiet minutes pass before speaking. Let the meditative and relaxing knitting "vibe" take over. Something about the relaxed knitting activity made conversation flow, just like it had at the retreat that weekend.

"Didn't you and Greta share a cabin at the retreat?" she ventured finally.

Edie nodded, keeping her concentration on her stitches. "Yeah. She's a really nice gal. Good martial arts instructor, too. I may take it up. If I ever find the time."

"Yeah, I liked Greta, too. That's why I'm concerned. Lisa says she seems to be going into some kind of depression lately."

Edie looked up. "Really? Ohhhh, that's too bad. She seemed okay at the retreat. Of course, I didn't know her before."

Kelly knitted another few stitches. "Apparently she's acting really nervous and jumpy and doesn't want to talk to people. She's withdrawn from everyone. Lisa said some of Greta's friends are really getting worried. One of the therapists has known her for a long time and said Greta got like that after her sister died a few years ago."

Edie shook her head. "I'm sorry to hear that. I know how traumatic that was for Greta because she told me. That evening after Jennifer had shared what happened to her . . . well, Greta and I started talking when we got back to the cabin. I wasn't able to share in front of the others, but somehow talking to Greta made it easier."

"Sounds like she'll make a great therapist." Kelly stitched to the end of the row. "So, she told you that her sister killed herself?"

Edie returned to her swatch, making slow, careful stitches. "That was so tragic. It sounded like Greta found the best counselors she could, but they must not have been a match because her sister didn't respond. I mean, none of us ever gets over being raped, but if we're lucky, we learn how to overcome and not let it define our lives. That's why I'm so grateful I found Dr. Norcross."

Kelly stared at Edie, momentarily speechless. Bonnie Baldwin had been raped? *Good Lord!* That had to be the reason she committed suicide. And Greta blamed herself for not saving Bonnie. No wonder Greta had spiraled into a depression after the retreat. Being surrounded by women who had suffered the same trauma was bound to bring all of those old memories swirling back.

"Good Lord, I didn't know her sister was assaulted," Kelly breathed. "How awful."

Edie nodded. "According to Greta, some guy followed her sister home from a bar in Fort Connor one night. Told her she'd left something at the bar, then forced his way in. Just like Jennifer described."

A cold chill rippled across Kelly's skin at the sound of Edie's words and the raw emotion beneath. Kelly sat in silence. There was nothing she could say which could express the revulsion she felt right now.

Her thoughts, however, were anything but quiet. They screamed for Kelly's attention. A guy followed Bonnie home, lied about her leaving something at the bar, then forced his way in. Bonnie's assault was exactly like Jennifer's. Could that be a coincidence? Was the same attacker responsible? Did Cal Everett rape Bonnie, years before he raped Jenifer?

Kelly's pulse started to race with the thoughts that zoomed through her mind now. She'd bet anything it was Everett. The attacks were so similar. Did Greta learn who raped her sister, or did she put it together when she heard Jennifer's story?

"Did Bonnie go to the police? Did they find out who did it?"

Edie shook her head, still stitching. "Apparently Bonnie didn't want to go to the police, even though Greta begged her. She never filed a report."

"So they never learned who the attacker was?"

"No. Greta said Bonnie swore her to secrecy about

the rape. She didn't want anyone to know. She simply withdrew from everyone, Greta said."

"Damn . . ." Kelly said softly. "If only she'd pressed charges, maybe . . . maybe that guy would have been found and caught."

"Maybe. Some attackers never are, Kelly. That's why Greta worked so hard to find good therapists for her sister. She said she kept watching Bonnie close off, and she didn't know what else to do. Greta said she must have taken Bonnie to five different therapists over two years."

"That is so sad," Kelly said softly, staring at her yarn. "And poor Greta is carrying such a huge load of guilt around." She started knitting once again, wondering how to ask the next question that pushed forward. "Did Greta ever try to find out who the guy was?"

"Yeah, she tried. She said she went to that bar and asked the bartender some questions, but he didn't remember seeing her sister, let alone the guy with her. Greta said she wanted to find out who he was so she could confront him. Tell him he was responsible for Bonnie's death. Hold him accountable. That's what she said."

Kelly knitted another row of stitches, sorting through her thoughts. They'd slowed down as well, no longer speed-racing like they did whenever a new scenario formed in her mind. Now, they played through her mind more deliberately, so she could consider each possibility.

It sounded like Greta had tried to learn the identity of her sister's attacker. Had she figured it out? Did she already know it was Cal Everett? Is that why she came on the retreat? Or, did she listen to Jennifer's account of her assault and suddenly realize the similarity? That must be it.

Kelly stitched another row, then another, as those possibilities played through her mind. Clearly Greta was sorting through everything she learned that weekend. *Is that why she shared her sister's story with Edie? Was she preparing herself to confront Cal Everett?* She'd told Edie that she wanted to face Bonnie's attacker and hold him accountable for what he did. He caused her sister's death.

Did Greta confront Cal Everett that night? When? She and Edie retired to their cabin about the same time as Kelly and Lisa. There were still women by the campfire. They would have told police if they saw Greta walking about.

Suddenly, a stray memory floated into Kelly's mind. Dr. Norcross had heard a truck engine and got up in the middle of the night to investigate. But there was someone else who was awake in the middle of the night. Burt said Edie told police she awoke at night to see Greta standing in the cabin doorway. She'd asked Greta what she was doing, and Greta said she'd heard a noise outside.

Kelly's thoughts began to race once more as another scenario formed in her mind.

What if Greta was lying? What if she had just come from confronting Cal Everett? Did she slip through the dark to find a drunken Cal Everett on the deck? Did she deliberately push Cal over the railing? Or, maybe . . . maybe she simply slipped up behind the drunken Everett and helped him over the rail.

Was that why Greta had been acting so depressed and agitated these last few weeks? She wasn't grieving over her sister again. She'd killed a man.

Kelly forced her thoughts to slow and let that scenario play in front of her eyes again, looking for things that didn't make sense. *Was that possible?* There had to be some reason Greta was seeing her therapist several times a week. Something was bothering her. They'd all assumed it was a return of guilt about her sister's suicide. Maybe this time, Greta's guilt was her own.

There was another question Kelly had to ask, but she had to work around it first.

"I was told that Dr. Norcross heard a truck engine in the middle of the night and got up to check it out. Apparently she saw Everett and that rancher Bill what's-his-name in the barnyard. Did you or Greta hear anything that night? It sounds like police are looking at this rancher guy more closely."

"Really?" Edie asked, glancing up. "Well, I didn't hear any truck engine but I think Greta heard something. I woke up and saw her standing in the open doorway. I'm a light sleeper, and I heard the door opening. So, I turned on the lamp beside the bed and saw her in the doorway, looking out."

Kelly paused before asking her next question. "Do you remember if Greta was wearing her clothes or was she in her pajamas?"

Edie peered at Kelly. "Hmmmm, that's a weird question."

"I was just wondering if she'd gotten up to investigate the noise."

Edie closed her eyes, as if remembering. "You know, I think she was dressed. Yeah, she was wearing that green Colorado State University sweatshirt."

Kelly's heart skipped a beat. "Interesting. Did she say anything else?"

"No, only that she'd heard a noise."

Her mind racing a mile a minute now, Kelly glanced at her watch. She needed to call Lisa. Gathering up the knitted vest, Kelly shoved it into her bag and rose to leave.

"Whoa, sorry, Edie, I just remembered a client call I've gotta make before ten this morning. So, I have to run. Your gauge swatch looks fine to me. Check it with the ruler on the table, and you'll be good to go."

"Great, thanks, Kelly," Edie said as she put her swatch on the table.

"Take it easy," Kelly called as she raced from the room. Digging out her cell phone as she sped to Lamb-spun's front door, she punched in Lisa's number, hoping to catch her between appointments and classes.

"Whoa, am I glad I caught you," she said when Lisa answered.

"You sound excited."

"*Excited* isn't exactly the word, but my instincts are on hyperdrive, and my little warning buzzers are ringing like mad."

"What's up?"

Kelly took a deep breath and launched in. "I just finished talking with Edie here at the shop. She was Greta's roommate at the retreat. Remember, she said Greta woke her up in the middle of Saturday night standing at the cabin doorway."

"Yeeeaaah . . ." Lisa replied in a careful tone.

"Well, she went on to say that she and Greta had a sharing session that Friday night after the campfire. And Greta revealed that her sister Bonnie was raped." Kelly paused for Lisa's reaction.

Lisa sucked in her breath. *"No!"*

"Oh, yes. That's got to be why Bonnie committed suicide. And, that's why that weekend was so traumatic for Greta."

"Oh, my God, yes! Poor Greta."

"Well, it gets more complicated. Edie repeated Greta's account of her sister's assault. Apparently a guy followed Bonnie home after meeting her in a bar in Fort Connor. Told her she'd left something at the bar, then forced his way in and raped her."

Kelly heard Lisa's slow intake of breath.

"She even said 'just like Jennifer.'" Kelly paused.

"Oh, no . . ."

"Yes. I think Greta heard Jen's story and put two and two together and came up with Cal Everett."

Lisa paused again. "Kelly...you can't be thinking—"

"You bet I am. Edie even told me Greta was dressed in her clothes in the middle of the night. That was after they had gone to bed earlier."

"Oh, no . . ."

"Oh, yes. I think Greta decided to confront Cal Everett Saturday night after everyone was asleep. Edie told me Greta said she wanted to 'hold the man accountable' who attacked her sister and tell him he caused Bonnie's death."

"Oh, God, she didn't . . ."

"I think she did, Lisa. As soon as I heard what Edie said, it started to make sense. Greta's been agitated and withdrawn ever since the retreat. We thought it was a recurrence of her depression over her sister's suicide, but I think it was the enormous guilt over her own actions."

"Kelly, you can't be serious!" Lisa protested. "Greta couldn't kill anyone. Not even Cal Everett."

"I'm not saying she did it on purpose. I think she went to confront him like she'd obviously pictured doing, and things got out of hand. Maybe they had a fight. Maybe she got mad and pushed him out of anger. He was so drunk, it wouldn't take much for him to fall over the rail."

"Kelly, I don't think Greta could do that . . ."

"Lisa, accidents happen all the time. And look at Greta. She's obviously wrestling with some enormous problem, right?"

"Right."

"Accidentally causing someone's death would cause a huge burden of guilt, don't you think?"

"God, yes."

"Well, that's what I think Greta's grappling with now. And I think we can help her. We need to talk to her as soon as possible. Today, if we can."

"Oh, Kelly . . . I don't know if we should."

"Lisa, I sense she's desperately calling out for help with these behaviors of hers. Wouldn't you rather we talk to her first and see if she'll open up and tell us what happened? Because the police are going to question her anyway. I mean, now that I've heard what Edie said, I have to tell Detective Peterson. I can't conceal information. You know that."

"I know, I know, I'm just not sure. Even if Greta did go out to confront Everett, maybe that's all she did. Maybe she said her piece, and he was so drunk he couldn't even talk straight. Maybe he simply sat and stared at her, and nothing happened."

Kelly considered that. "Maybe that's exactly what happened. And if so, then that's what Greta will tell us. Then she'll have to tell Detective Peterson. Because right now, she's concealing information from the police. Not only once, but twice, by not admitting she spoke with Everett that night. That's serious, Lisa. She needs to come clean. No matter what happened."

"You're right."

"Is there any time when she's free? Do you know her schedule?"

Lisa paused. "Actually, she and I are meeting this afternoon to go over some research results. Maybe you could come over then. We'll be in a secluded office. Room number four zero two, Clark Building."

"What time?"

"Why don't you come over at two thirty? That'll give Greta and me some time first."

"I'll be there."

"Oh, God, this is so awful."

"Yes, it is, Lisa, but it will only get worse and worse the longer Greta takes to tell the truth. Whatever happened that Saturday night at the retreat, she's got to come clean."

Kelly hurried up the fourth-floor steps of the Clark Building, situated at the heart of the university campus. Empty classrooms lined the hallway as her footsteps echoed down the corridor. The academic year was finished, exams completed, graduations done, and nobody was home. No one except dedicated graduate students and professors still doing their research. The summer session would start the following week. Until then, the university was quiet.

Spotting the office Lisa mentioned, Kelly gave a quick knock, heard Lisa's voice, and entered.

"Hey, there, I thought I'd stop by for a few minutes," she said with a big smile as she crossed the room. Lisa and Greta were seated beside each other at a large desk, papers spread out over the top. Greta looked surprised by Kelly's sudden appearance. Lisa looked subdued.

"Hi, Kelly. Have a seat," Lisa said, indicating the chair across the desk from them.

"Hey, Kelly," Greta said, looking at her curiously.

Kelly settled in the chair and took a sip from her take-out coffee with the familiar logo on the cup. "How's the research stuff going?"

"Umm, okay, I guess," Greta said, darting a quizzical glance to Lisa. Lisa was staring at the chart in front of her.

Kelly set her coffee cup aside and leaned both arms on the desk. She'd never had much patience for beating around the bush. Her natural instincts were to come directly to the point. She followed her instincts now.

"Greta, you probably wonder why I interrupted your meeting."

Greta looked at her, brown eyes wide. "Yeah, kind of."

"I came because Lisa and I care about you. And we've both been concerned about the obvious distress you've experienced ever since we returned from the retreat in Poudre Canyon."

Greta's gaze turned wary. "I—I don't know what you mean."

Lisa turned and placed her hand on Greta's arm. "Greta, you've scheduled therapy appointments nearly every day with Dr. Norcross. Now, that wasn't the case before the retreat weekend. And ever since then, your entire personality has changed. You're withdrawn, depressed—"

"I'm—I'm just tired, that's all," Greta protested.

"It's more than being tired, Greta," Lisa pressed. "A blind man can see it with a cane. Something happened at the retreat that upset you greatly."

"You're exaggerating. Nothing happened," Greta said, jerking her arm away.

"I think it was listening to all the women share their stories of sexual assault that upset you, wasn't it, Greta?" Kelly offered.

Greta darted an anxious look to Kelly but said nothing. Kelly took that as an opening and leaned forward a little more.

"Lisa learned about your sister's suicide," Kelly said in a gentle voice. "That was tragic and heartbreaking."

Greta's head jerked up like a puppet master had pulled her string. "How—how did you . . ."

"Your friend Mary told me," Lisa explained softly. "She's concerned about you, too."

"And I spoke with your roommate from the retreat, Edie. She told me you shared what happened to your sister Bonnie. The ugly assault that led to her death."

Greta's eyes became huge as she stared from Kelly to Lisa and back again. She said nothing.

"It must have been horrible for you to sit through all those women's stories of their assaults. Similar stories," Kelly continued softly. "Especially Jennifer's story. So like what happened to your sister. And it must have been a shock for you to learn that her attacker was none other than Cal Everett, the very man who had welcomed us all earlier."

Greta visibly paled as she stared at Kelly. She still didn't say anything, seemingly entranced by Kelly's words.

"Is that when you figured it out?" Kelly asked. "Listening to Jennifer tell us how the man followed her home, forced himself into her apartment, and attacked her. You realized Cal Everett was the same man who assaulted your sister."

Greta hastily looked away, then nodded.

Kelly caught Lisa's glance. "You wanted to confront him, didn't you, Greta? Force him to face what he'd done to Bonnie. He was the reason she took her life."

Greta glanced back to them, then clasped her hands on the table in front of her, staring down.

Kelly could feel the turmoil churning inside Greta. It was palpable. She fairly radiated conflict. "That's why you went to see Cal Everett late that night," Kelly continued.

Greta's head jerked up at that. Fear in her eyes, unmistakable. "Why—why would you say that?"

Kelly leaned forward even more and looked directly into Greta's eyes. "Greta, your roommate Edie told me you woke her up when you opened the door to the cabin. And you were dressed in your clothes, not your pajamas. That was because you'd been to see Everett."

Greta glanced away again.

"You waited until your roommate was asleep to

leave the cabin, didn't you?" Kelly continued. "Everyone would have left the campfire by then. It would just be you and Everett alone on the deck. Everett had been drinking all night, so he was probably in a pretty bad mood. What happened when you accused him of killing your sister? Did you get into a fight?"

The color remaining in Greta's face disappeared entirely. She stared first at Kelly, then darted a panicked gaze to Lisa. Lisa's face was drawn and tight, like she was controlling herself with great effort.

Greta stared at her hands again. Her fingers gripped each other so tightly they bled white. "I just wanted him to hear what he'd done to Bonnie. To know he was responsible for killing her," she said in a low voice.

"What happened, Greta?" Kelly asked softly. "Did he start a fight with you? Did he try to hit you? Is that why you pushed him?"

"I didn't push him!" Greta blurted, sending a panicked look from Kelly to Lisa. "I swear I didn't. He—he was drunk and cursing and—and he came right at me. I don't know . . . it all happened so fast . . . I went into defensive stance and bent down to block him. I didn't even think, I simply reacted. He charged into me, and when I blocked him, he went over the railing. Head over heels. It . . . it was so fast, I couldn't believe it."

Kelly and Lisa exchanged a look of amazement. Greta hadn't pushed Cal Everett off the deck. He had attacked *her*, and she defended herself. And Everett finally paid the price for his actions. Headfirst over the deck and onto the rocks below. It wasn't deliberate. It was an accident. Kelly released a huge breath that seemed to be pent up inside her.

Lisa leaned toward her friend, then placed her hand on Greta's arm. "Greta, you know you'll have to tell the police all of this. You need to get this awful burden off your chest. This was an accident. An awful, awful accident. Don't let it torture you any longer than it already has."

Kelly spied moisture glistening in the corners of Greta's eyes. She reached out and placed her hand on top of Greta's. "Let me call Detective Peterson, okay? You've met him before. He's a very compassionate, understanding man."

Greta bit her lip. "I know . . . I know . . . I've just been afraid to confess what happened. I've been afraid of what will happen to me. I couldn't even tell Dr. Norcross. I tried, but I couldn't. I was so afraid." Tears started to roll down Greta's cheeks now.

"Greta, we understand. Don't worry. I'll be there with you the entire time. You won't be alone. I won't leave you, I promise," Lisa swore.

"Don't be afraid, Greta. It was self-defense," Kelly reassured. "The first person I'm going to call is an attorney. Lisa and I can both attest that Marty Harrington is one of the best and most compassionate lawyers we've ever met. We've seen him in action. Trust me, Marty will take very good care of you. You won't be alone."

Greta's expression turned forlorn. "I—I don't have much money."

"Don't worry, Greta," Lisa said, slipping her arm around her friend's shoulders. "Marty works for certain clients pro bono."

Kelly watched Lisa comfort a distressed Greta while she dug her cell phone from her purse. Marty was about to work for free once again.

Twenty

Kelly zipped the back of her "garden of spring flowers" dress and smoothed the crisp fabric as she checked herself in the dresser mirror. Robin's egg blue, the saleswoman had called it. Kelly vaguely remembered rescuing baby robins in her childhood, but she hadn't seen a robin's egg for over twenty years. Whatever it was called, the shade was flattering. And the dress's scooped neck showed off the beginnings of her summer tan.

She readjusted the dangling ribbons in her hair. Megan had given each of them hair barrettes to match their dresses. Each one of "Mimi's flowers" as Burt called them had dangling ribbons in her hair. Kelly's barrette, of course, wasn't completely straight, hanging slightly askew. She tugged once again and decided that would have to do.

Steve's reflection appeared in the mirror then as he came up behind her. "Ummmm, you look gorgeous," he said, sliding his hands on her waist.

Kelly turned around and rested her hands on the lapels of his navy sports jacket. "Thanks. You clean up well, too. I really like that jacket."

"I can't remember the last time I saw you in a dress."

"Well, take a photo, because it's coming off right after we get back," Kelly teased.

Steve pulled her closer, his hands sliding up her back. "Why wait? We can take it off right now," he whispered beside her ear.

Kelly laughed. "Later. Our shower interlude took longer than expected. We're gonna have to race over to Mimi's now, or we'll be late. Megan will fuss."

"Let her fuss."

Kelly felt the zipper slide down her back as the crisp fabric eased over her shoulders.

"Well, *finally*!" Megan scolded as Kelly and Steve burst through Mimi's front door. "Where the heck have you guys been? You're a half hour late."

"Sorry, Imperial Commander." Kelly gave an apologetic smile to her friends, who were spread out across Mimi's living room, sitting or sprawled over sofas and chairs.

"Traffic was a bear," Steve added, with a remarkably straight face.

"On a *Sunday*?" Lisa exclaimed. "What'd you do? Come by way of Greeley?"

"Traffic, huh?" Jennifer approached Kelly with a knowing smile. "It'll get you every time. Let me straighten your barrette."

Kelly reached up to feel the ribbon-adorned barrette down behind her right ear. "Thanks, Jen. It must have gotten askew."

"In traffic, I know." Jennifer removed the barrette. "Let me fix your hair and your dress. It's not completely zipped."

"Imagine that," Marty said with a sly grin.

"Guys, we've been waiting for you so we can go over the last-minute details of the service," Megan continued, hands on hips. "We have to go over this stuff before guests arrive."

Megan was in full taskmaster mode, Kelly could tell. So, she decided to have a little fun. Since the traffic had put her in such a playful mood, she couldn't resist. "We await your commands!" Kelly declared and whipped out a *Starship Troopers* salute.

"Stand still," Jennifer chided, giving Kelly a little swat on the shoulder as she caught the barrette before it fell to the floor. "I need to fix this."

Megan eyed Kelly with a team manager's skeptical eye and continued, "As I was saying . . . we need to know what's happening and when, so we'll know what to do. Bridesmaids will enter after the minister walks to the gazebo. Once he gets there, he'll turn around and give us a nod. Then, we'll walk in. Kelly, you're first since you're tallest—"

"I hear and obey, Imperial Commander!" Kelly proclaimed, complete with another crisp salute, adding a heel click this time.

Pete turned away to hide his amusement. Marty leaned his head back on the sofa, clearly trying not to laugh. Lisa hid her smile behind her hand.

Megan was obviously trying to maintain her stern taskmaster expression but was losing fast. Cheeks flushed as pink as her dress, she gestured impatiently. "Steve, do something with her, would you?"

Greg snickered. "I think he already did."

Kelly held up two fingers behind her back so Jennifer would see. She heard Jen's soft laughter.

"Oh, so that's it," Jennifer announced as she firmly attached the barrette. "You guys had a twofer. No wonder you're so wound up."

The living room exploded with laughter then. Kelly felt a slight blush creep up her cheeks as she joined her friends. "Blabbermouth." She gave Jennifer a poke.

"Dude, better not do that again," Greg advised Steve. "She's outta control."

"No promises," Steve said with a grin.

"Control? Kelly?" Lisa scoffed. "What are you thinking?"

"Hey, mind your own business, Greg," Kelly parried as she plopped on the arm of Steve's chair.

"Okay, okay," Megan said, leaning beside Marty,

who was still cackling. "I'll make it easy. Once you hear the music, Kelly, start walking up the aisle toward the minister. Lisa, you're next, then Jennifer, and I'll go last."

"Do we have flowers?" Jennifer asked as she smoothed her lime green dress, curved beneath the bust.

"Yes, we're all carrying bouquets of spring flowers from Mimi's garden. All except Kelly. She gets a bunch of dandelions," Megan joked.

Kelly was about to protest when Mimi and Burt entered the living room.

"What's going on?" Mimi asked. "We heard all the laughter."

"Yeah, what's so funny?" Burt asked.

Mimi was gorgeous in a lemon yellow silk dress, which set off her frosted blonde hair perfectly as well as her coloring. Mimi was blushing already, her cheeks rosy. Burt was attired in a smartly tailored charcoal gray suit with a burgundy tie. His face was flushed also. They both looked really, really happy.

Kelly couldn't resist. She pointed to the handsome happy couple and declared, "Look! Mimi and Burt were stuck in traffic, too."

Once again, the room rocked with laughter.

"**Lift** up your feet," Kelly said to Jennifer. She gave a little kick and sent the canopied glider into motion again. It swung forward and back in a gentle arc.

"I can't believe it. Jayleen's not wearing denim."

Jennifer held up her wineglass, gesturing across Mimi's backyard.

Kelly searched through the clusters of friends and family that filled the yard until she found Colorado Cowgirl Jayleen Swinson, looking sharp in a beige pantsuit. Curt Stackhouse stood beside her, attired in a conservative gray suit. Kelly almost did a double take—she didn't recognize the Colorado Rancher.

"Curt's looking good, too." She moved her glass in an arc. "Everybody looks gorgeous today. Tomorrow we'll all go back to cutoffs and casual. Except for you. You've got to look good for clients."

Jennifer glanced to her. "Do you miss that, Kelly? Meeting clients, I mean."

"Ohhhh, I get to meet clients every now and then. Go over their accounts and all that. And during tax season, I help them with financial strategies."

"Is that enough? Sometimes I get the feeling that your alpaca clients aren't holding your interest like they used to." She shrugged and kicked the ground, sending the glider into another gentle rocking arc. "It's just a hunch. I may be wrong."

Kelly was no longer surprised by her friend's perceptiveness. Jennifer always seemed to pick up on things. "Boy, I hope you're the only one picking up those vibes. I've got to work on that transparency thing."

Jennifer smiled. "Don't worry. I'm just tuned in. What's happening? Tired of clients that are soft and fuzzy and stare at you with big brown eyes?"

"Kind of. It's gotten too easy. There's no challenge anymore. I'm just entering expenses and receipts now. Most of those clients don't need a CPA. A bookkeeper can take care of their businesses. I'm waaaay overqualified." She released a long sigh. "At first it was fun to learn a new business. Fun to meet the clients and have face-to-face planning sessions with them. But now . . . it's just not enough anymore."

"Did anything happen to turn you off? Was there a client-from-hell? I've had my share of those."

Kelly laughed softly and gave the glider another push. "No, the clients are great. It's not them, it's me. It's all me. And, yes, there was something that happened. I spent a week in Denver at CPA continuing education classes, and I got my fingers back into those complex accounting issues again. And I was hooked. I'd forgotten how much I enjoyed unraveling those puzzles."

Jennifer observed her for a minute. "So, what are you going to do? Drop your fuzzy clients? Join a CPA firm?"

Kelly wrinkled her nose and shook her head. "Noooo. I have no intention of joining a firm again. Been there, done that. But I like the idea of consulting. That's essentially what I'm doing with my new client. You know, the rancher/developer guy that Curt connected me with. Now, his work is much more interesting. He's got two different businesses, and there are all sorts of cross-connections going on. Now, *that's* challenging."

"Does Curt have any more friends like that? Why don't you ask him now? He looks like he's having a good time." Jennifer gestured with her wineglass again.

Kelly glanced around Mimi's shady backyard, turned into a veritable bower of flowers for the wedding. Every one of Mimi's guests appeared to be having a great time. The wine was flowing. Well, not flowing exactly. More like pouring from bottles. Pete had brought a wide selection of wines and spread them out on the tables with plenty of glasses. Real wineglasses, too. Pete had insisted. Some things taste better in glass, he'd said.

Consequently, all of the wedding guests were helping themselves, save for teetotaling Jayleen. With Pete's delicious appetizers and desserts, guests had lots of tasty food to choose from. Everywhere Kelly looked, she saw guests laughing and talking and eating all at the same time. Mimi and Burt wandered about the garden from cluster to cluster visiting with family and friends. Standing together, arms around each other's waists, they positively glowed.

Watching her dear friends standing beside each other beneath the grape arbor during the ceremony, gazing into each other's eyes as they exchanged vows, had brought tears to Kelly's own eyes. She never cried at weddings. But Burt and Mimi were special.

Their love for each other had developed so naturally, like the spring flowers pushing through the soil in Mimi's garden—bursting into bloom. Mimi and Burt had bloomed, all right. It was obvious, watching them gaze at each other beneath the arbor, the minister could have been speaking gibberish and they wouldn't have noticed. They only saw each other. If there was such a thing as "true love," surely this was it.

"If Mimi and Burt smiled any wider, they might burst," Jennifer laughed softly.

"Yeah, 'happy couple' doesn't even begin to describe it. They're going to be airborne any moment. We may have to tie ropes around their waists to keep them on the ground."

Kelly and Jennifer swung quietly for a minute. "That was such a beautiful ceremony. Quiet and simple," Jennifer said. "No big church fanfare. Just good friends surrounding you. That's the way it should be. When two people are meant to be together."

Kelly waited for Jennifer to say something else, but she didn't. Kelly was about to add a comment of her own when she noticed Jayleen heading their way.

"Looking good, Jayleen," she greeted her friend.

"You should wear a pantsuit more often," Jennifer observed. "It's really flattering."

"Thank you, gals, but right now, truth be told, it's getting kind of itchy. I can't wait until I can take it off," she said with a grin.

"Curt's looking real good, too," Kelly added. "I almost didn't recognize him."

Jayleen gave a brief glance over her shoulder and smiled. "Well, take a good look, because Curt can't wait to ditch his duds, too. Some of us just can't stay all spit 'n polished for too long."

"It's still early. You and Curt could still get a trail ride in this evening," Kelly suggested. "No need for dinner. Not after Pete's spread."

"You and Steve ought to come up to the canyon and join Curt and me for a ride again. It's been a while since you've done that."

"I'll put it on my daytimer, Jayleen. Promise. And Steve's, too."

"You do that. Sometime in July would be great. June is already booked up. I'll be busy hosting a retreat at my ranch. A psychologist friend suggested the idea. She's been counseling some teenage girls who've run into problems early on, and my friend thinks a few weeks in the mountains might help them sort things out."

"Whoa," Kelly said. "That sounds like a wonderful thing to do, Jayleen. Will the kids have work sessions or counseling or something?"

Jayleen nodded. "Both, actually. We'll get 'em working around the ranch, helping out with the livestock, and talking with their counselors. There's a lot of work to do, so they'll be busy. But outdoor work helps some folks to put things together, you know. Kind of like what Diane did when she came up to live with me, remember? That's when I got the idea of having a retreat for teenage girls. Try to make a difference in their lives before they've had a chance to screw things up to hell and gone. Like I did, for instance." She chuckled.

"That's a wonderful thing you're doing, Jayleen," Jennifer said.

Jayleen smiled at her. "I was wondering if you'd be interested in coming up to the ranch and participating, Jennifer. The girls could really get into those fiber sessions. Everyone needs some quiet time to think. You and I could teach them to knit and crochet. Hell, maybe they'd like to learn to spin, too. What do you say, girl?"

Jennifer stared at Jayleen for a few seconds. "You mean stay up there at your ranch with the kids for a week or two?"

"Or as long as you'd like. The entire session lasts four weeks. Whatever you'd like to do. Play it by ear, if you want."

Kelly observed her friend, watched her ponder Jayleen's suggestion, and wondered what she'd say. Inside, Kelly was fervently wishing Jennifer would say "yes." Jennifer could be a powerful Big Sister presence for some of the girls. Good for the girls and good for Jennifer.

Jennifer looked at the ground and sent the glider on another rocking arc. Kelly kept quiet, as did Jayleen. Finally, Jennifer spoke.

"You know, Jayleen, I think I'd like to do that. Let me check with Pete and my office and see how much time I can clear this month."

Jayleen's grin spread almost as wide as Mimi's and Burt's when the minister pronounced them wed. "Whatever you decide, Jennifer, is okay with me, girl."

"Good for you, Jen," Kelly added. "A summertime retreat in the canyon. Gotta love it."

"I just hope I can help—" Jennifer started, then glanced over Kelly's shoulder. "Oh, no . . . that photographer is waving at us again. I can't believe they want more pictures."

"C'mon, gals, the wedding party is waiting on you," Jayleen said as she beckoned them to follow as she walked away.

"Let's send the photographer home after these photos," Kelly said as she and Jennifer headed toward their friends, already gathering in an unruly cluster. "Then we can relax without having him snap any more candid shots."

"Good idea. You escort the photographer off the premises, while I grab that last piece of pecan pie."

"Too late. I saw the pie plate. It was empty."

"That's what you think," Jennifer said with a grin. "I saved a piece, then put a napkin around it and hid it under the wine table."

Kelly laughed out loud, causing their friends to turn as they approached. "Good thing we didn't bring Carl to the ceremony."

Jennifer's Afghan

GAUGE:

5 stitches = 1" and 5 rows = 1"

MATERIALS:

10 skeins Plymouth Galway pure wool knitting worsted (or similar)

40" circular knitting needle, size 8

INSTRUCTIONS:

Cast on 260 stitches very loosely.

Knit 5 rows (for border).

Row 1: Knit 5, purl 250, knit 5.

Row 2: Knit 5, K2 tog 3 times *YO, (K1, YO) 5 times, K2 tog 6 times; repeat from * 12 times; YO (K1, YO) 5 times, K2 tog 3 times, K5.

Rows 3 and 4: Knit.

Row 5: Repeat above 4 rows until afghan measures approximately 60" or to desired length, ending by working row 4.

Knit 4 rows for border. Bind off all stitches very loosely.

Pattern courtesy of Tea Time Quilting and Stitchery in Breckenridge, Colorado. Pattern designed by Judy Morseman of Tea Time Quilting and Stitchery.

Author's Note on Recipes

The recipes I've included in this book were contributed by my two oldest and dearest friends. Nancy and Diane and I grew up across the street from each other in what was then the sleepy little suburb of Arlington, Virginia—across the river from Washington, D.C. We were about five and six years old when we first met and became playmates, and we've been close friends ever since. Both Nancy and Diane continue to live in northern Virginia, while I live in northern Colorado now. I hope you enjoy the recipes.

Nancy's Butternut Squash Soup

When Nancy sent me her soup recipe and brief note, I was reminded of all the good times we shared growing up together. Nancy is now retired from a forty-year career in the federal government.

FROM NANCY

I have been Maggie's friend for sixty years. Those early years were spent in the old neighborhood. As latchkey kids (Nancy and Diane), we were at home tending to all the household chores including cleaning, ironing, and cooking. Later in life the cooking and ingredients became more sophisticated. I married and spent time around other good cooks. We all read *Gourmet* and *Bon Appetit* in the sixties. However, following directions specifically was not really necessary. We made do with whatever was left over as the beginning of a stew or soup, and then stews became soups and soups became sauces. Here is a squash soup recipe.

   1 butternut squash peeled and cut up (or bought that way)
   1 sweet potato or a large baking potato cut up
   3 large leeks cut up (white parts only)
   3 garlic cloves minced
   3 shallots minced
   1 stick butter to saute all of the above to a soft consistency
   Add salt and pepper and 1 tsp cumin
   1 tbsp curry powder

NANCY'S BUTTERNUT SQUASH SOUP

32 oz chicken broth
2 cups heavy cream (whipping cream)

Cook until all is soft in the liquid. Process in Cuisinart or blender to a smooth consistency. Heat later for dinner or luncheon soup. Add croutons and parsley for decoration.

Nancy Appler, Vienna, Virginia.

Diane's Famous Chocolate Chip Cookies

When Diane sent me her cookie recipe, it sounded so good I e-mailed her to throw some in the freezer and save them for me for my next visit. Diane's a real estate agent in northern Virginia.

DIANE'S REPLY
Yes, I have actually sold some of these recently. Everyone here at the office loves these cookies.

> 1 cup all-purpose flour
> ½ tsp baking soda
> ½ tsp salt
> 6 tbsp light brown sugar
> 6 tbsp sugar
> ½ cup (1 stick) butter
> 1 large egg
> 1 tsp vanilla
> 1 cup semisweet chocolate chips
> 1 cup oatmeal

Preheat oven to 375°.

Combine dry ingredients (flour, baking soda, salt, and sugars) into bowl and stir. Then add butter and egg and vanilla. Mix well. Add the chocolate chips and the oatmeal and stir together. Then drop by teaspoon onto cooking sheet.

DIANE'S FAMOUS CHOCOLATE CHIP COOKIES

Bake for 7–9 minutes until slightly golden brown. Remove from baking sheet to rack or aluminum foil or wax paper and cool.

Makes about 2.5 dozen cookies.

Diane Anthony, Vienna, Virginia.

Turn the page for a preview of
Maggie Sefton's
next Knitting Mystery . . .

Skein of the Crime

Available in hardcover
from Berkley Prime Crime!

Kelly Flynn navigated her car out of the shopping center parking lot and merged into Fort Connor's thinning late night traffic. Only a total lack of coffee would force her to stop by the grocery store on the way home from a post-game celebration at her softball team's favorite Old Town café. It was nearly midnight, but some things were too important to worry about inconvenience. Coffee was at the top of that short list.

Her cell phone sounded from the seat beside her where she'd tossed it. Kelly pulled to the right lane and slowed down before answering. Her friend Jennifer's voice came over the line.

"Good, you're still up. Did the game run long tonight?"

"Not really, but we went to our favorite café afterwards. I'm driving home now. What's up? Why're you calling so late?"

"I'm doing Mimi a favor. She tried calling you guys but forgot you and Megan and Lisa were all playing ball tonight, so she called me. Mimi needs help with one of those beginner knitting classes at Lambspun tomorrow morning. You know, the summer ones with guest teachers. Mimi will be out of the shop in the morning, and Rosa can't spare time away from customers to help, so Mimi asked if one of you guys might be able to. What's your schedule like? The class is at nine and runs an hour, so it doesn't take long."

Kelly ran through her mental day planner. No outside appointments tomorrow, just regular client work. A former corporate CPA, Kelly could now arrange her schedule at will. Her new consulting business was thriving. "Sure, I can manage that, as long as I'll be a helper. I'm not qualified to teach classes."

"Don't worry. Barbara Macenroe is teaching. She's really experienced, too. Have you met her? She's a nurse over at one of the doctor's clinics near the hospital. Tall, big-boned gal."

"That doesn't sound familiar, so I don't think I've met her yet. Does she come to the shop often?"

"I've only seen her late in the afternoons when I've dropped by after the office, so you may have missed her. But she's started teaching classes at the shop, helping take the load off Mimi. Anyway, she's a real 'take charge' sort, so you won't have to worry. You'll be her assistant, that's all. I'd do it, but it's a morning class and I'm working in the café, so I can't."

"Sure. Tell Mimi I'll be glad to help," Kelly said as she turned onto another large avenue. A Big Box store and its sprawling shopping center shone neon bright ahead. "How come you're still up? Don't tell me you and Pete were working a catering job this late."

"Okay, then I won't tell you," Jennifer joked. "Yeah, we were both beat by the time we finished. I just got out of relaxing in the tub. Now I'm heading to bed."

Kelly angled into the left-turn lane. "Me, too, as soon as I get home."

"Steve still in Denver?"

"Yeah. He's starting to stay down there a couple of nights a week. He's gotten some part-time work for another company."

"After working all day for the architect firm? That's rough."

"Yeah, it is. He barely has time to talk, let alone sleep," Kelly said, remembering the brief conversation she'd had with her boyfriend earlier that evening. "At least he'll avoid that morning commute from Fort Connor to Denver. It's beyond awful. I had to get into that rush-hour mess last week when I was heading out to meet my new client near Brighton. Man, it took me nearly two hours to get there."

"I know. I went to a regional real estate meeting a month ago in Denver and allowed over two hours so I wouldn't be late. But I still got there with only ten minutes to spare."

Kelly turned onto the street that bordered her favorite knitting shop, Lambspun. "I hear you. I don't know how Steve stands it." She waited for cars to pass, then turned onto the gravel driveway that ran between the shop and her cottage beside the golf course. Ablaze with lights, the little cottage was the only bright light in the dark. Kelly didn't like coming home to a dark house, especially an empty dark house.

"Steve doesn't have a choice, Kelly. He's only doing what he has to get through this terrible housing market. I hope things start to improve in a few months. It's brutal out there."

"Yeah, I know, and it doesn't look like it's getting any better."

"Listen, I'm gonna go to sleep. See you tomorrow."

"Bye, Jen." Kelly clicked off her cell phone, then nosed her car into its space in front of the cottage she had inherited three years ago after her aunt Helen's murder. The car's high beams bathed the front of the beige stucco and red-tiled roof cottage in bright light. Kelly heard her Rottweiler Carl barking his "welcome home" bark in the backyard. Carl could always tell the sound of her engine and knew when she returned.

Grabbing her bag, she exited the car and headed down the walk to the steps of her snug cottage. Once inside, Kelly opened the patio door where Carl stood, not so patiently, barking to come in and join her.

"Hey, Carl, how're you doing?" she said as Carl bounded inside, barely pausing for a head pat before heading toward the kitchen. Maybe forgotten food crumbs lingered.

Glancing outside to the concrete patio, Kelly searched for Carl's water dish. "Carl, did you drag your water dish into the bushes again? I swear, you must be dying of thirst by now."

She stepped out onto the patio and scanned the ground for the blue dish when a slight movement to the left caught the periphery of her eye. Turning quickly, Kelly was startled to see a young woman standing only six feet away from her on the patio.

Kelly instinctively jumped back, her heart racing double time. "What the hell?" she cried, staring at the young woman standing in the dark. "Who are *you*?"

The young woman didn't answer. She simply stared back at Kelly, smiling. Kelly could see her features from the lights shining inside the house.

"Who *are* you, and where did you come from?" Kelly demanded, peering at the girl. The young woman appeared college-aged and was slightly built with medium-length blonde hair, a pretty face, and snub nose. She was wearing a print dress that came to the tops of her knees, and she was barefoot.

Again, the girl made no answer, but her smile grew wider. She clasped her hands together in front of her and began to rock gently side to side.

Suddenly, Kelly knew. *Drugs*. The girl was stoned. Totally. That vacant, not-really-there look in her eyes, that big pumpkin grin, and the rocking. Gently rocking back and forth, as if to some inner music. *Ohhhh, yeah,* Kelly thought to herself.

She'd seen this before. Years ago in college at parties where drugs were freely available. Some chose to partake and temporarily "leave the planet behind" so to speak, and others stayed, feet firmly planted on terra firma. Kelly always stayed planted.

Kelly studied the girl again and lowered her voice, trying once more to get a response. "Where did you come from? What's your name?"

But there was no response. The girl continued to grin and rock back and forth. Kelly backed away toward the patio door and stepped inside the house, sliding the door shut. Then, she flipped the lock, just in case. Even though the girl appeared harmless, Kelly wasn't about to take a chance. Especially given that the girl was clearly not in possession of her faculties at the moment.

The girl needed medical help. No telling what drugs she'd taken or how many. There were several apartment complexes across the intersection with the Big Box shopping center. And there were also older neighborhoods housing students bordering the Old Town area. Maybe she wandered down the river trail from one of the parties.

Early September still brought late summer's warmth with it, so nights were extremely pleasant. Perfect for outside parties and gatherings like Kelly had enjoyed with her teammates tonight. On such a nice night, the girl could have wandered from anywhere in the vicinity.

Carl came up beside Kelly and stared through the glass but didn't make a sound. No barking, nothing. That surprised Kelly. Her extremely loving, sweet dog had always lived up to his Rottweiler reputation as a vigilant watchdog. Evildoers usually left Kelly's cottage alone. Whenever she heard his "intruder alert" bark in the middle of the night, she was glad he was on patrol.

"What's up with this, Carl?" she interrogated, as she went for her phone. "How come you weren't barking your head off when I came home? And you never even let on there was a stranger out there."

Carl looked up at Kelly, clearly perplexed by her concern.

"I'll bet you already knew she was spaced-out. Doggy sixth sense, huh?" Kelly punched in the numerals 9-1-1 and felt an anxious twist to her gut. The last time she'd called 911 was years ago when her father was dying of lung cancer and she needed an ambulance.

The police department's dispatcher came on the line and asked Kelly to give her name and her location.

"My name's Kelly Flynn, and I'm here in my home at 1111-A Lemay Avenue. I came home a few minutes ago and found a college-aged girl, a stranger, standing outside on my backyard patio. She appears to be stoned because she doesn't talk or answer questions. Clearly, she doesn't know where or who she is right now. I think she needs medical help."

"Officers will be there shortly, ma'am."

* * *

Kelly stood on her front stoop outside with Carl on his leash, watching the activity unfolding between her cottage and the knitting shop. The gravel driveway was crowded with a police car, an ambulance, and a regular-length fire engine. Kelly didn't understand why both an ambulance and a fire engine responded to the dispatcher's call, each with their own EMT or paramedic team. Maybe it was a slow night in Fort Connor. There must be ten people standing about, all surrounding one young girl.

Every now and then, Carl would emit a low bark or "ruff," as if he should be patrolling the entire situation.

"Easy, Carl. They don't need you there. It's crowded enough already."

Two police officers, a man and a woman, had first responded to her call. Their huge black flashlights sent bright arcs of light shining around her cottage as they circled it, then entered the backyard. They found the girl still standing on the edge of the patio, gazing up at the sky. Kelly watched from inside the house as they repeatedly asked her questions. The girl didn't respond to the police, either. She simply continued to smile broadly and rock back and forth as the wail of emergency sirens cut through the night air.

The police officers led the young girl from the backyard to the front of the cottage just as the fire engine had rolled down the gravel driveway, brushing the overhanging cottonwood branches as it did. Kelly grabbed a cola from the fridge and put Carl on his leash in order to watch the proceedings from her front step. Maybe the paramedics would have better luck communicating with the girl.

They didn't. Kelly had watched a team of four encircle the girl. Then one paramedic tried to elicit a response from her while the others checked her eyes, her heartbeat, her skin. All the while asking the girl her name, where she lived, and how she got to this location. To no avail. Kelly was actually surprised all that talking and probing didn't stimulate some kind of response.

Only once did the girl respond. But not to the paramedics. She raised both arms slowly skyward, gazed up into the heavens, and began to sing. Kelly couldn't understand a word and decided she was probably communicating with the "Mothership." She watched the professionals respond to the girl's song by asking more questions. No answers came.

Five minutes later, an ambulance had arrived, and Kelly watched the entire procedure repeated with another team of paramedics. This time the girl stopped singing and simply rocked back and forth the entire time the ambulance team examined her. Finally, those paramedics placed the girl onto a gurney and loaded her into the ambulance.

Kelly drained her cola as the ambulance backed up, yellow lights flashing and the insistent warning sound beeping shrilly before it headed out the driveway. She noticed the two police officers were headed her way. At last. She had a lot of questions. Carl also noticed them and had broken his "down" and was standing in front of her, on the defensive.

"Easy, Carl. It's okay, it's okay," Kelly reassured him, rubbing Carl's smooth black head as the two officers paused at the end of the sidewalk.

"He okay?" the young man asked, pointing toward Carl.

"Yeah, he'll be okay. Carl, *sit*," Kelly commanded. "It's okay." Carl needed a slight jerk of the collar to comply, but he sat. "Stay," Kelly ordered, palm up, adding the visual command. "Good boy."

"Nice dog," the female officer said as she and her colleague slowly approached.

"Thanks, he's a sweet boy, but he's also a good watchdog. Good dog, Carl," she said again and rubbed Carl's head.

"Did you check the yard as soon as you came home, Ms. Flynn?" the guy asked.

"No, sir. I came inside and did my usual routine. I let Carl in from the backyard. He came in and didn't let on there was anyone out there, so I was really surprised to see her."

"We realize this must have been pretty frightening," the guy said.

"Well, it certainly gave me a start, I'll say that. To turn around and see the girl standing there so close in the dark . . ." Kelly shook her head. "That was definitely spooky."

"And you said your dog wasn't barking or acting unusual."

"Nope. He acted normal. I have a feeling Carl had already decided she was stoned out of her head and consequently wasn't a threat. Because, believe me, Carl goes ballistic if anybody suspicious-looking shows up, any stranger at all. Even golfers who wander too close, looking for stray balls, sets him off."

"I think you may be right. Carl figured it out first, didn't you, boy?" the woman said, smiling.

"Tell me, officers, what do you think she was taking? Any idea? She was totally spaced. I watched you guys try to get something out of her, but nothing. Except the singing."

"The paramedics said she'd probably used either Ecstasy or LSD, judging from how fast her heart rate was," the man replied.

"Will they keep her overnight at the hospital?"

"They'll keep her until she sobers up and comes to her senses. When the drug wears off, they'll try to find the name and number of someone who could come pick her up. Then they'll release her."

Kelly stared off toward the golf course, shrouded in night. "I wonder where she came from? I know there are parties going on regularly in those houses bordering Old Town. Do you think she wandered from over there? I mean, that's a ways to walk, and she was barefoot."

"We figured she probably took the river trail," the man said, pointing. "That would bring her beside the golf course where she was bound to see your cottage all lit up. She must have headed straight for it."

"Heading toward the lights, that makes sense," Kelly

Maggie Sefton

mused out loud. "Once the university is back in session this fall, there'll be even more parties going on. I sure hope others don't start wandering across the golf course."

The fire truck's big engine revved up then, bright lights flashing.

"I don't think you have to worry, Ms. Flynn," the man called over the sound as he turned to leave. "Odds of something like this happening once is pretty low. The chance of it happening again would be almost impossible. Good night."

"Good night, officers, and thank you very much." Kelly called out, returning the policewoman's wave as she watched the fire engine lumber down the driveway toward the street.

Kelly had always been suspicious of statistics.

Dyer Consequences
A KNITTING MYSTERY
by Maggie Sefton

Kelly Flynn is eager to renovate the alpaca ranch she's just bought, but someone else has different ideas for keeping her busy. As disturbing incidents continue to pile up, Kelly knows she must try to pick up the stitches of these crimes before a killer strikes again.

**Praise for
the Knitting Mysteries**

"Cozy up with a great new author."
—**Laura Childs,** *New York Times* bestselling author
of *The Teaberry Strangler*

"A darn good series with vivid, breathing characters."
—*Mystery Scene*

"A terrific series with a heroine who grows more
and more likable with each investigation."
—*The Mystery Reader*

penguin.com

M231T0110

Don't miss any of the
Prime Crime mysteries featuring Kelly Flynn
and her eclectic knitting circle

FROM NATIONAL BESTSELLING AUTHOR
MAGGIE SEFTON

Knit One, Kill Two

Needled to Death

A Deadly Yarn

A Killer Stitch

Dyer Consequences

Fleece Navidad

Dropped Dead Stitch

Skein of the Crime

M395AS0110

NOW AVAILABLE IN ONE VOLUME

Sew Far, So Good

Three Needlecraft Mysteries
From *USA Today* Bestselling Author

MONICA FERRIS

Crewel World needlework shop owner and part-time sleuth Betsy Devonshire has a knack for stumbling upon dead bodies—and it's entangled her in more than one knotty situation. Here in one volume are three of Betsy's adventures as a not-so-seamless investigator.

Unraveled Sleeve
A Murderous Yarn
Hanging by a Thread

Free needlework patterns included!

penguin.com